A DUKE'S LOVE

Endless Love
Book 2

JR Salisbury

ARE YOU SIGNED UP FOR DRAGONBLADE'S BLOG?

You'll get the latest news and information on exclusive giveaways, exclusive excerpts, coming releases, sales, free books, cover reveals and more.

Check out our complete list of authors, too!

No spam, no junk. That's a promise!

Sign Up Here

www.dragonbladepublishing.com

Dearest Reader;

Thank you for your support of a small press. At Dragonblade Publishing, we strive to bring you the highest quality Historical Romance from some of the best authors in the business. Without your support, there is no 'us', so we sincerely hope you adore these stories and find some new favorite authors along the way.

Happy Reading!

CEO, Dragonblade Publishing

Additional Dragonblade books by Author JR Salisbury

Endless Love Series
Beauty and the Rake (Book 1)
A Duke's Love (Book 2)
The Forgotten Spare (Book 3)
Love At Last (Book 4)

CHAPTER ONE

AUGUST WAS THE height of summer, given England's short season, though there were a few subtle hints that autumn was not far behind. The sun was beginning to lower in the sky and wasn't the brightest shade of yellow when it did come out.

Arthur stopped the young bay gelding he was walking back to the stables. He patted the animal on his muscular neck. "If you don't mind, I'm going to remove my coat. It's gotten far too warm." The horse, in turn, shook his head. Arthur laughed as he came out of his dark brown jacket and laid it in front of the saddle, over the horse's withers. The horse having tripped and thrown a shoe, Arthur had no recourse but to lead the beast back to the stables. Of course it had to happen on the day he decided to test the youngster out. The bay was one he bred and was raising to sell as soon as his training was sufficient.

He picked up the reins again and the pair began walking again. Suddenly, he heard hooves thundering across the meadow. Looking up, Arthur saw nothing but a blurred image, unable to make out much more than the horse was a gray and the rider was unrecognizable. Was the gray the one he and his grooms had found wandering the estate? He couldn't be sure, and since he couldn't mount and ride after the interloper, he could only hope the pair came calling again. Arthur decided he'd tell his stablemaster and grooms to be on the lookout for the horse and rider. It wasn't that he minded people riding on his land; he simply had a strict rule that they ask before riding. But the more he thought about it, the angrier he got at the idea that whoever this was rode their horse as though a barn was on fire. Reckless. That's what it was, and he was determined to find out who this person was. The best way to do this would probably be to visit all the neighboring estates and see if he could find the gray. He was certain the rider and horse lived nearby.

Arthur patted the gelding and started walking towards the stables. After about ten minutes, he saw the building come into sight and let out a sigh of relief. Not that he minded the walk—he spent a good amount of time walking the estate instead of riding. He could see more at ground level and things he might have otherwise missed if on horseback.

As he entered the stable yard, his stable master, Mr. Smythe came hurrying out of the building as soon as he saw Arthur and his horse walking in.

"He threw a shoe, so I walked him back," Arthur said, handing the reins over to the man.

"I apologize, milord. Those were new shoes."

"It could happen to anyone, Smythe. I'm just thankful it hadn't started raining."

He stood and watched as Smythe handed the horse over to one of the grooms. After words were spoken, the young man led the bay into the building.

"That gray came racing by us like there was no tomorrow. So fast, I couldn't make out the rider," Arthur said.

"Again?"

"Yes. I'm sure the pair live close by, so I'm thinking of riding to the neighboring estates and seeing if I can't find out who they are and why they insist on riding on my land. I wouldn't mind, but this person is reckless, and I won't allow it."

"That might not be a bad idea, Your Grace. No good can come of this; someone is going to get hurt."

Arthur nodded. "Exactly. In the meantime, if anyone finds

that gray loose on the estate, catch it and bring it back here. Someone is bound to miss the gray and come looking for it."

"I'll make sure everyone knows. Would you like me to have Midnight saddled for you, Your Grace?"

Midnight was Arthur's latest mount. He'd found him at Tattersall's in London, quite by accident. So impressed by the animal and his lineage, Arthur purchased him on the spot. The stallion was massive in not only build but attitude. The pair quickly bonded.

"Perhaps later. I have an appointment, but I'll send word if I need him saddled."

Smythe nodded and watched as Arthur turned and walked through the open doors and towards the house.

Arthur's walk between the house and stables wasn't far, for which for once he was thankful. His mind was full of thoughts, mainly on this reckless and mysterious rider. Usually things like this wouldn't bother him, but like Smythe and he had agreed, the rider was on the path of getting hurt or hurting their horse if they continued the path they were on.

As he continued on the path towards the house, the manor came into view and about that time, a big red dog loped towards him. Roddy, an Irish Setter he'd acquired after Roxanne married. Usually, he didn't care for dogs inside, but the house was so quiet with his sister gone, he made an exception. Arthur bent down as the dog approached and petted him. One of the footmen must have taken him outside, and upon seeing Arthur, the dog fled the young man. Arthur had hunting dogs, but they were kept in the kennels. He would have Roddy trained to hunt since setters were excellent bird dogs. The only thing holding his training back was that he needed to mature more and also, Arthur wasn't sure he could bear to send the dog to the kennels during his training. He would have to focus and Casey, his dog trainer, made it clear he couldn't do his job if his charge was being coddled when he wasn't being trained. In another month, perhaps two, he'd have to let the gentle giant go. At least for the time being. For now, he'd enjoy the dog's company.

"Come on, Roddy. Let's see if Cook might have a bone for you."

The dog, tail wagging, began circling Arthur before settling into his place beside his master. Arthur knew Cook would scold him for bringing the red giant into her domain, but that's as far as it would go. She would give Arthur a slice of whatever she had baked, and Roddy would have his bone.

Arthur grabbed the setter's collar as they approached the kitchen door, which was standing open to let some of the heat of the kitchens out and hopefully cooler air in.

Cook, her arms crossed over her ample bosom, was waiting on them as Arthur led the dog through the kitchen.

"I'm afraid you'll have to do with a scone today. Marmalade cake is in the oven."

"Could you have someone bring it to my study, along with some tea and Roddy's bone?"

"Would you like a plate since you missed lunch, Your Grace?"

"You're the best, Cook. Cheese, meats, and some bread. And scones to top it all."

"Flattery will get you everywhere, as you well know, Your Grace."

Arthur smiled broadly and led Roddy up the stairs to the main level and on to his study. He'd rather be riding but had to turn it down knowing he had unopened correspondence from early this morning to read and respond to. Opening the door, he watched as the dog went straight to the fire to lie down. He shut the door and walked to his desk and sat down.

In front of him sat a small stack of correspondence. He recalled seeing one from the man he and Hawksbury had hired to look into a man named Crenshaw, who had accompanied his parents on their fatal journey to India. The two of them were convinced Crenshaw had something to do with the incident that led to his parents' murder. Arthur felt certain of it because Crenshaw sported his father's ring on his hand. One that had been in the family for generations.

Picking up that particular letter, he opened it and began reading the contents. It seemed that Crenshaw had taken his own ship headed to India, but at the first port, he disembarked, and the ship went on without him. Crenshaw now had returned, but was not staying in London; instead, he was in Liverpool. An interesting change of events. The detective seemed to think Crenshaw thought too many people wanted to keep tabs on him in London. He would keep an eye on Crenshaw and gave Arthur an address as to where he was staying and would keep Arthur updated on Crenshaw's activities for as long as he was needed.

He set the letter aside and picked up another. He needed to send word to Hawksbury to update him on Crenshaw's movement, but first he wanted to think it through, especially how long they needed their man to tail Crenshaw.

Except for a letter from his aunt, the rest of the letters were nothing more than updates from the accountants, and a couple of bills from London. It was about the time he was going to put the bills aside to pay them that a footman arrived with a tray bearing his meal and, most importantly, Roddy's bone.

He crossed the room and picked up the bone. Roddy was now sitting up and began wagging his tail. Arthur passed the bone to the dog and the animal eagerly took it from his master's hand. Arthur then turned his attention back to the cart and prepared a cup of tea and a plate of cheese, ham, and chicken. He pulled a piece of bread from the small loaf and placed it on top of the meats and cheese. The only sound besides the fire crackling was Roddy gnawing on his bone. Arthur decided to sit down in front of the hearth and eat while he tried to decide what they should do about Crenshaw.

Legally, they hadn't enough proof to involve the police. The detective they hired had been a police officer and quickly informed them they would have to find enough evidence of wrongdoing to try and have the man charged. It had been suggested they get the ring from Crenshaw, but that could only be done by force as Crenshaw must know the ring had belonged to Arthur's father. There was an inscription inside the ring from the first duke, and if Crenshaw had seen it, he wouldn't give it up without a fight.

A couple of reliable men could be hired for the task. Crenshaw would, of course, quickly figure out who was behind that. The other way would be to make it appear a robbery. He would be suspicious of them, but he would have no proof it was them behind it. Arthur was afraid if they did manage to get Crenshaw into custody, he'd be full of excuses of how he came into possession of the ring. All might be seen as plausible. The Crown prosecutor would have to be tough and show the court their evidence, though slim, that Crenshaw had indeed taken part in the deaths of his parents.

He would go over his thoughts, share them with Graham before any decisions were made. It would be worth their time to go to Liverpool and speak with their man, but if they did, they'd risk Crenshaw seeing them. After he and Graham spoke, he would write a letter and discuss his thoughts of what he viewed needed to happen.

Taking a second plate of food, he walked to his desk to begin a missive to Hawksbury. See if they couldn't meet for a ride in the morning with the purpose of getting his friend's thoughts on this. Hawksbury was married to Arthur's sister and was handling her interest in finding the killer or killers. They could also discuss this mysterious gray horse and rider and where they came from. Since his estate was next to Hawksbury's, it was always possible the horse had wandered onto his lands as well.

Before he knew it, Arthur had not only finished his letter to his friend, but he'd also taken care of anything else needing his immediate attention. He rose from his desk as he and Roddy left in search of the butler.

ARTHUR MET HAWKSBURY the following morning at a lone rowan tree the pair always used as a meeting spot on Arthur's estate. He'd ridden his favorite mount, Midnight. The horse was not only black as night with no markings, but he was also tall and muscular. Midnight was the sort of horse that had to be ridden daily or his temperament would turn. If that happened, no one was safe from his ill temper.

Upon seeing his friend sitting his horse beneath the shade of the tree, Arthur reined in the stallion, slowing him down as they approached.

"You haven't been waiting long, I hope," he said as he walked his horse under the canopy of the rowan.

"No, not at all."

"You haven't caught that gray with or without their rider, have you?"

Graham shook his head. "No. The beast has not been on my estate. Not that we know of."

"I plan to begin visiting estates on the off chance the gray lives close by."

"I'm sure the horse lives close. It obviously knows its way home," Graham said as he urged his horse to begin walking.

Arthur followed as they began to walk to the large meadow. "I've instructed everyone at my stables to be on the lookout for the gray, and if they can catch it, bring it back to the stable."

"Good idea. Lure the owner out once and for all."

"Yes. Whoever they are, they are reckless," Arthur said. "Any place in particular you should like to go?"

"No, I'll leave that to you today. And yes, this rider is reckless and needs to be stopped."

"Why don't we ride over to the lake. Men have been clearing and cleaning it up like you did at your lake."

"I wanted Roxanne and me to have a place we could go and have total privacy," Graham said with a cocky smile on his face. He grinned at his friend even wider. "It was totally worth it, too."

"I can imagine. I'm glad the two of you found each other

because I haven't seen her this happy in years."

Graham grunted his reply.

"Come on; let's stretch these two's legs," Arthur said, urging Midnight forward into a canter. He had brought Roddy along but hadn't seen him except for a tail. He was always off chasing something. The setter came bounding out of nowhere when he heard the change in the horses' gait. He stayed at a steady pace, keeping up with the two horses, and unless something caught his attention elsewhere, he didn't miss a stride.

Slowing down to a walk to allow the two horses time to rest from their run, Arthur began to tell his friend what their man had been able to find out about Crenshaw. He agreed they didn't need to make a trip to Liverpool on speculation they might run into Crenshaw.

"Let's leave it to the professionals. I think we need to see if what we have on Crenshaw is enough to at least pick him up for questioning," Hawksbury said.

"I agree. If we don't have enough, we can reevaluate what we do have."

Hawksbury stopped his horse and turned towards Arthur. "The man simply can't be allowed to get away with murder."

"Agreed, and he won't if we have anything to say about it."

"Shall I send word to our man and have him move forward?" Arthur asked.

His friend nodded. "Yes. The sooner we can put this behind us, the better. I know Roxanne will breathe easier."

The pair slowly continued their journey to Arthur's lake. Recent rains had made the meadow and surrounding land a lush green. Soon, though, autumn would set in and the transformation would begin. Everything would be rushed to get the fields picked for the last time and readied for next spring, and fruit trees would be picked to make jams and pastry filling. Buildings and cottages would be readied for winter. It was a cycle of life like it had been for generations past and would be for generations to come. Both men's estates were self-sustaining.

Finally, the lake came into view. It was a fair size, though some might think of it as a pond. There was plenty of room for small boats to take people on a leisurely ride around the perimeter. As they rode closer, Arthur could see a small group of three men cutting back some heavy growth on the other side. They were almost finished with this monumental task.

"It looks a lot nicer than mine," Graham grunted. "But then my wife wanted things a certain way since she likes spending time there."

"Painting?" Arthur asked.

"That and sketching, and sometimes she photographs flowers and trees and the occasional bird."

"I imagine Mary is one of her top subjects," Arthur said with a chuckle at the thought of his sister trying to get a squirming infant to be still. Mary was Graham's bastard who had been left at his door. Since then, he and Roxanne had been raising her, and Arthur had seen a softer side of his friend he hadn't seen in a while.

"Every month she takes a new photograph. Sometimes, if the weather is good, she photographs her outside in the garden."

Arthur whistled for Roddy. The dog came running out of whatever tall grass he'd found to Arthur's side. The dog was that loyal.

"Never thought I'd see you bonding with a dog."

"He's a good distraction," Arthur said. "I never realized how quiet the house was until Roxanne married you. He fills the silence with his antics."

"I bet he does. Enjoy the quiet while you can. Marriage makes a lot of changes in one's lifestyle."

"I'm sure it does," he replied as he urged his horse forward. "I think we need to check out the orchard. That is, if you have the time."

Graham arched a brow. "I have nothing planned today."

As soon as the words came out of his mouth, Arthur and his stallion flew by, leaving him to follow in their dust, though there wasn't any dust to be had. Racing like this made Arthur think of the gray and their mysterious rider, but he and Graham weren't reckless. They knew the land like the back of their hands since they'd been riding here and on Graham's estate since they were boys.

CHAPTER TWO

T WO DAYS LATER, Arthur sent word to the stables to have Midnight saddled. Today, once he finished the last of his correspondence, he was going to ride to nearby estates and see if he could find the owner of the gray who wandered onto his property or was ridden like there they were being chased by a gang of thieves. The recklessness needed to stop. If the rider was so determined to race their mount so fast, they could do it on their own land, not his. He intended on having the matter settled today.

He knew the gray couldn't live too far off. He would start with two estates that were close by. Perhaps he'd get lucky and find both the horse and its owner in the vicinity.

A short time later, Arthur found himself walking down his drive and onto the main road. Besides Graham's estate, there were two others whose entrances were nearby. He continued walking his horse down the road until he finally came on the country estate of Baron Heathcliff. Arthur was certain he wouldn't find the gray here. The baron kept a small stable and most of his horses were dark bay with black stockings. His carriage horses had no other markings. The man was also older and a widower whose children were grown with families of their own. They resided elsewhere.

Still, he would check with Heathcliff in case perhaps he'd seen the gray with or without its rider. He couldn't leave any stone unturned, and if the baron didn't know the gray's reputation, it would make him aware of the situation.

As Arthur began to ride down the baron's drive, he noted an older gentleman on horseback approaching him. It was Heathcliff himself. He had a stableboy with him who rode behind.

"Your Grace, this is indeed an honor," Heathcliff said, tipping his hat. "I was just finishing up my morning ride."

"I won't keep you long, milord. I'll get straight to the point. Have you either seen a gray horse wandering about or that same gray with a rider and galloping the horse as fast as they can go?"

"Can't say I have, and my stablemaster would tell me straight up if someone were riding without permission."

"Be on the lookout just in case they do wander onto your land."

"I shall, and thank you for the information, Your Grace," Heathcliff said. "Have you time for luncheon?"

Arthur scrubbed his gloved hand over his face. "Thank you for the invitation, milord. Another time? I am determined to try and find this horse and its owner today, and I have a couple more estates to call on."

"I understand. Another time."

Turning his stallion, Arthur began to walk away. He made a note to invite the baron for lunch, hating that he had to turn down his invitation. He knew if he'd stayed for a meal, he might not have continued on his mission of finding the errant horse. Too often people neglected their neighbors while in the country, and he would make a point of not being one of those. Besides, he'd heard the baron had an impressive collection of swords from all over the world from his travels.

He walked onto the main road and continued down until he came upon the estate of Harry Winterton, Viscount Andover. The viscount was known for being eccentric as his elaborate fencing and drive indicated. It reminded Arthur of Versailles. Not that he'd ever been inside the elaborate palace, but he had ridden by it once and seen its decadence.

Starting down the crushed shell drive, Arthur was soon met with a massive and over the top iron gate. The gate was closed and appeared locked and inaccessible. He peered through the gate, but neither the house nor any other structure came into view. He started to turn Midnight around and back to the main road. Obviously, the viscount was not in residence. He smiled, observing the road leading to the manor was not wide enough to turn a carriage around and with just enough space to get his stallion turned.

As he headed in the direction of his own estate, he dropped Midnight's reins to allow the horse to stretch his neck. He was disappointed about failing in his search. The two estates he'd visited were the closest, and he couldn't imagine a horse who'd escaped his pasture would wander far. That's what made this so frustrating.

No one seemed to know the viscount and his family well. While his wife preferred to spend the summer at their estate in Somerset with their children, he traveled between the two estates and their house in Mayfair. They were known among the ton and were quite social during the season.

The viscount's family owned two factories in the north which took raw cotton and, using looms, turned it into fabric. It was thankless, backbreaking work, but they had been able to turn them into the largest and most profitable factories in England.

Arthur peered up at the sky and saw storm clouds beginning to set in. Gathering up Midnight's reins, he urged the stallion into a fast trot. Turning down the drive to home, he broke the animal into a canter for fear the rain wasn't going to hold off much longer. Making it to the front of the house, he was met by a young boy who took the stallion's reins from him and began to lead him toward the stables.

The house was quiet as he entered. He placed his hat and gloves on a table and began to walk toward his study. The door was open, and he found Roddy curled up in front of the hearth waiting on his return. Lowering himself to the dog's line of sight, he patted the red setter for several minutes. Looking towards his desk, Arthur noted correspondence sitting on the desk he hadn't seen before. He rose and walked over to his desk and sat behind it while Roddy's tail thumped against a chair.

He thumbed through the four pieces of correspondence. Nothing out of the usual, but one stood out; an invitation from his sister Roxanne to a house party she and Hawksbury were hosting in a fortnight. This would be her first official social event since marrying his friend. Being that he lived so close, Arthur wouldn't have to stay the entire time. He could come and go as he pleased, though he was sure his sister would have his time monopolized. There would be single women there with their mothers on the chance he might find one to his liking. Roxanne was all about finding him an appropriate bride. He wasn't opposed to finding a wife; he simply wanted to do it on his own terms. If his sister happened to invite *the one*, he would pursue her.

Arthur set the invitation aside, knowing he'd accept, but writing his reply could wait. While Roxanne expected everyone to follow social etiquette, his not replying in a timely manner would drive her mad. He smiled as he imagined her stomping her foot at his tardiness. She would scold him for being late with his reply, but even after all these years, Arthur loved to tease her.

Returning to the small pile of unopened missives, he opened each one and read them. Fortunately, none of them were terribly urgent and could wait until the next day. He couldn't concentrate as his thoughts kept going back to earlier in the day as he tried and failed to find the gray horse who kept wandering on to his estate. He didn't mind that. It happened to them all at one time or another. What mattered most was the interloper who deliberately ran the same horse as fast as possible across his meadow.

Deciding he needed a break, he set the rest of the correspondence aside and poured himself a glass of whiskey from the decanter he kept on the left side of his desk. He sat back in his chair and swirled the golden liquid before taking a deep swallow. It went down smooth, and he took another. Maybe the best way to try and find this horse might be to continue what he'd started. He wouldn't go anywhere further, but he would try by returning to the viscount's. Perhaps this time the gates would be open, and someone would be in residence to answer his questions. There was something about the estate that made him uneasy. As though the viscount himself was eccentric. By pursuing the matter like that, he might get some answers. Even better, perhaps someone on his own staff knew someone working on the viscount's estate. He would make inquiries with the butler later. Either he or the housekeeper would be knowledgeable since they had been at his estate the longest. They might know one of the viscount's staff members or know if one of Arthur's staff knew anyone employed there.

Whoever it was knew his estate well. Well enough to know how to access his estate from another way. There was a rock wall that had been there since at least Arthur's grandfather's time, if not longer. He would see if his estate manager knew of any holes in the wall. Regardless of what he was told, Arthur decided he would ride along the wall tomorrow to see for himself.

He poured himself another whiskey and rose from his desk, heading over to a favorite dark brown leather chair. There was a dampness in the air, and sitting close to the fire helped ward off the chill. Roddy was glad for the company and thumped his tail on the floor in approval. Knowing the setter needed exercise, Arthur thought to take him along tomorrow. The dog was good about returning to him after sniffing out whatever caught his nose. Maybe he would be more successful than today in finding the owner of the elusive gray.

His thoughts were interrupted by a knock on the door. When the door opened, there stood Wilson, his butler. In the man's hands was a pineapple.

"I'm sorry to disturb you, Your Grace, but this just arrived from Baron Heathcliff."

"Is there a note attached?"

Wilson shook his head. "Just his calling card." He approached and handed Arthur the pineapple.

"That was very kind of him. He obviously has a working greenhouse and a pineapple stove."

"He does, Your Grace. He produces pineapples along with oranges, limes, and lemons among other fruits and vegetables in his greenhouse. Helps during the winter."

"My sister has been wanting a pineapple stove for some time," he said. He took the baron's calling card and handed the fruit back to Wilson.

"I imagine it's ripe and edible. See if it is, and if so, I'll have some with dinner."

"As you wish, Your Grace," Wilson said before turning to leave. The man had never been one to carry on conversations. He knew his place and unless his opinion was asked, kept to himself.

"Have Cook serve some to staff. It isn't often any of us get to delight in a fruit such as this. I'm sure she can cube part of it to share."

Wilson nodded and retreated from the room. It was a nice gesture on the baron's part. He would make a point of writing to Heathcliff, thanking him for the delicious fruit. Perhaps he should have the man for dinner one evening. They were neighbors and even with that, they hardly knew each other. It had been this way since his parents died. It was such an unexpected event that Arthur never truly knew the family's relationships within the community. With no funerals, but the house still in mourning, there was little contact with anyone. The vicar came weekly, but that was about all. It had been suggested by the vicar that they might think of having a remembrance service, but Arthur had rejected the idea. At least for the time being, as he wanted to be sure of his parents' deaths before doing anything.

Now the truth was known. His and Roxanne's parents had been murdered. By whom? Arthur had his suspicions and wouldn't stop until the killer or killers had been brought to justice.

THE NEXT MORNING, Arthur mounted his stallion and he and Roddy began their ride. The setter stayed to one side of his horse unless a rabbit or other small creature caught his attention for a short period of time. It was a perfect morning to go for a ride. The sky was a perfect shade of blue with white puffy clouds floating by.

He rode along the road, checking to see if there was anything unusual. A break through the trees or the wall which ran alongside most of the perimeter was his main focus. About a mile down the road, the wall became more visible, and from his view, he found no openings. He kept on until he came across an area where the wall had partially come down. A neat pile of stones sat to one side of the break. He whistled for Roddy while he jumped Midnight over the low wall. Arthur noticed a narrow path between the trees and urged Midnight to the area. The setter ran past him down the path. He followed, determined to find out if it was feasible for the gray to navigate himself through the narrow path to the meadow on the other side. A smaller horse would have no problem going through the trees. For Midnight, his size alone made it uncomfortable to ride it, so he slid off the saddle and led the stallion until they made it to the meadow.

As he peered back at the path, Arthur concluded a smaller horse could easily navigate through the woods with or without a rider. This was it. The spot where the gray snuck onto the estate without being seen. He remounted and began to scan the meadow for anything not intended to be there.

To his amazement, he saw a horse not too far away. The gray raised his head, looking around for any potential threats. Satisfied, he lowered his head again and began grazing the lush green grass. He was very much aware of his surroundings, his ears moving about as he listened intently for anything unusual.

Arthur walked one step and halted the stallion. If the gray

heard them, he was still acting as though he was oblivious to their presence. He walked a couple of steps toward the animal. Again, the horse made no sign he knew they were there. Again, Arthur walked closer until the gray lifted its head in order to watch them and decide how he should act. As soon as the horse began grazing again, Roddy ran toward him, barking, letting the beast know he was an intruder. The red setter circled the gray, barking all the time. This time, the horse reacted to the intruder. He bared his teeth, ears back and threatening to kick the setter if he had the chance.

Arthur urged the stallion towards the two, hoping his intrusion would be overlooked. As he came within walking distance to the gray horse, he slowly grabbed a good length of rope he'd attached to his saddle. He slowly widened the loop at the end and continued towards the gray. Stopping his mount, Arthur slid slowly off him. He approached slowly and carefully, not wanting to spook the animal.

He was able to pet the horse and slowly ease the noose over the horse's neck. The gray snorted as he realized he was now caught but never tried to run off. Arthur patted him on the neck and talked lowly to him, assuring him he wasn't in danger and that he wasn't going to hurt him. He began to walk him towards Midnight, still rubbing the horse's neck with his free hand. The animal snorted and looked wild-eyed as though he were going to run, but Arthur continued walking, not looking the gray in the eyes. The last thing he needed was the horse to bolt on him.

Arthur quickly realized they weren't going to be able to leave the way they'd all come, so he mounted the black stallion and began to walk through the meadow. There was a clearing leading to the other half of the meadow. Not knowing exactly what to do with the gray, he determined the best thing would be to ride to the stables and sort it out there. From his ride yesterday, Arthur had his own thoughts as to where the gray came from.

Viscount Andover's estate came to mind. It appeared to be well fortified, and no one could ride onto the property unless the gate was open. Yesterday it wasn't. He understood the viscount had more than one estate and the viscountess preferred their estate near the sea during the summer. The couple had children, but how many and how old they were, Arthur did not know. He doubted he'd ever seen any of them. Even if no one was at home right now, he didn't think anyone from a skeleton staff would have the nerve to ride the gray. It was an offense leading to termination of their employment.

The most likely way to end this would be to keep the gray at his stables. Sooner or later, someone from the Andover estate would come calling, looking for the horse. If he was wrong about ownership, the correct owner would come looking for their horse. He would instruct his stablemaster to make everyone who worked there know not to let the horse be given over to anyone unless he was present.

By the time the stables came into view, the gray had settled and walked quietly beside him. As soon as he stopped Midnight in front of the barn, everyone had congregated in front of them.

"See both of these animals get a good rub down and water. Put the gray in the stall next to Midnight and give him some hay until feeding time," Arthur said.

"Where did you find him?" someone asked.

"In the far side of the meadow. There is a hole in the wall there that will need to be repaired."

"What are you going to do with him?" his stablemaster inquired.

"Keep him. Someone will come looking for him. When that happens, I don't want the gray given to anyone unless I'm present and approve the transfer."

"Wonder if they are insistent on taking the horse?"

"You tell them the duke wishes to meet the owner of such a lovely animal."

Arthur hadn't even left the stable and a young boy appeared in the stable yard. By looking at the young boy, he figured he couldn't be more than twelve or so. Gangly like a young colt and obviously nervous about being there. Arthur noticed the boy inhaled deeply before coming closer.

"What can we do for you?" Arthur asked.

"I'm looking for my horse, a gray? He keeps breaking through the fence and usually comes here."

"So you're the one who has been racing the gray across my meadow?" Arthur asked. "I don't believe you."

The boy stood stiffly and looked Arthur right in the eyes. "I don't care if you do or not. He's my horse and I want him back."

Smythe, his stablemaster, grabbed the youngster by the arm. "Watch how you speak, boy. Do you know who you're talking to? The Duke of Hightower. Show some respect."

He swung his attention to Arthur, still looking defiant. "May I have my horse back, Your Grace?"

"Not just yet," Arthur replied. He kept his eyes on the boy, curious how he would respond to the news.

"You can't do that!"

Arthur arched a brow. "I can and I am."

"Why?"

"Because I don't believe you own such a fine animal, and I want to know who does."

"The gray belongs to me," he said defiantly.

"Until I get the answers to my questions, the gray remains here."

The boy stomped off towards the direction he came, talking under his breath all the way. He finally stopped and stared at Arthur and Smythe. He was backed into a corner and had no idea how to act or react to the situation. He finally began walking towards them. The look on his face showed he felt defeated. He probably never had to take on such a responsibility, and he shouldn't have. The true owner of the horse should have been the one to deal with the situation.

"Very well, I'll tell you what you want to know. The beast belongs to the daughter of Viscount Andover, Lady Daphne Waterton."

"Why didn't she come herself?"

"I don't know, Your Grace."

Arthur studied the boy for a moment. The viscount's daughter was most likely spoiled and never did anything that got her hands dirty. She'd find out the world didn't revolve around her once he met her.

"Very well. I will give the gray to you, but only under this condition. That I come with you so I may speak with the lady about how we can best resolve this situation in the future."

"Thank you, Your Grace."

"Smythe, see Midnight is saddled and ready the gray." He turned to the boy. "What's your name?"

"Rolo, Your Grace."

"Very well, Rolo. We'll leave in just a few minutes."

Rolo nodded.

"Is the viscount in residence?" Arthur inquired.

"No, he's at one of his other estates. Lady Daphne prefers to stay here without her parents or brothers and sisters."

Arthur thought it curious that the viscount would allow his daughter such unsupervised freedom, but who was he to judge? He wasn't a parent and hadn't a clue why people did what they did when it came to their children.

In a matter of moments, Midnight walked out of the barn, followed by the gray. Arthur effortlessly mounted and waited on Rolo to do the same. They began walking toward the main drive as Arthur didn't want the young man to know he was aware of the break in the wall.

"Does the gray have a name?" he asked.

"Vicki."

Arthur nodded and urged Midnight forward in a slow gallop.

It wasn't too long before they were turning down the drive leading to the viscount's estate. He thought it odd how little people knew their neighbors. He would have never imagined the viscount's daughter was the only family member in residence. She must be one of the viscount's older children to be given such a privilege of being allowed on her own. But he wasn't a parent, and it was none of his business how others raised their children.

Rolo dismounted the gray as they stood in front of the closed gate. He opened it and pushed the massive iron gate to one side before coming back for his mount.

"I'll take you to the front door and have the butler show you in and let him know you wish to speak with her ladyship."

"Thank you, Rolo. If you could see to Midnight. I doubt I'll be very long."

The pair continued until the house came into sight. An elaborate fountain sat in the front of the house, water splashing down to the main bowl. As they walked around it to the front, Arthur noted an older gentleman appeared at the top of the stairs. The viscount's butler, Arthur concluded.

Rolo swung off the gray and ran up to the man. Arthur concluded the boy was telling him who he was and who he wanted to see. Arthur dismounted and handed the stallion's reins to the boy as he finished his descent. Walking to the top of the stairs, he nodded at the butler, who turned and led the way into the house. If the entrance hall was this elegant, he had no doubt the rest of the house was the same.

"I'll see if Lady Daphne is taking visitors."

"Thank you. Tell her it won't take but a moment of her time," Arthur said.

"If you'll follow me, Your Grace, I believe you'll be more comfortable in the drawing room."

"Thank you."

The man swung the door open. "Here you are, Your Grace."

Arthur walked into the room. He heard the door shut behind him as he walked a little farther into the room. To one side of the hearth was a bird perch with the most beautiful red parrot he'd ever seen. The bird's wings had shocks of yellow-gold and blue and stood on his perch as he stared at this intruder. Arthur kept his eye on his feathered companion. He'd seen parrots similar to this one before, but always from afar. He'd never seen one kept as a pet before and didn't know what to expect.

CHAPTER THREE

"**B**LOODY HELL! A stranger!" The bird flapped its red, gold, and green wings for a second. "Stranger no good!"

Arthur tried to keep from smiling. It wasn't every day one came across a talking parrot, much less one that swore. He neared the bird slowly. "What's your name?"

"Bollocks!"

He bit back a laugh at the bird's response. "Your name is Bollocks?"

"Hell no! Me Sam! Sam."

"Nice to meet you, Sam."

Arthur didn't receive an answer this time. Instead, Sam stood on one foot and then the other. Was he agitated or was this normal behavior? He had no way of knowing, so keeping his distance might be best for both. The last thing he needed was an angry parrot.

At that moment, the door opened and Jameson, the butler, entered. "Lady Andover will see you momentarily," he said. He glanced at the bird. "I see you've met Sam. I hope he's been a gentleman."

"He has, though he's got quite the mouth on him."

"He does," Jameson replied. "Tea will be here momentarily. If you need anything further, please let me know." He gestured toward a bell pull in one corner of the room.

"I shall, thank you."

Alone again, except for his feathered companion. Curious choice of a pet. Nonetheless, he found the creature smarter than most others and wondered how he came to be. Perhaps the viscount had been to a South American country and brought him back for his family. An unusual pet, but one none of their friends could boast they owned.

Hearing the parrot's wings flap, he turned his attention in the direction of the bird. Arthur watched as the bird jumped down off the safety of the perch to the floor. Could the creature fly to get away from any sort of danger or would it be at the mercy of its predator?

He watched as Sam began flapping his wings before walking across the room as though it was an everyday occurrence.

"Mama, mama, mama!" the bird screeched as he put his wings back where they belonged. He didn't seem in distress, but Arthur decided to try something.

"Is something wrong, Sam?"

"Sam I am, Sam I am, bloody hell."

Sam was walking toward him, and he wasn't sure if it was good or not. If the bird were angry, he had no idea what to expect.

"Sam? Who's your mama?"

"Mama, Sam. Mama! Danger! Sam danger!"

Arthur wondered how many people knew of Sam outside of the immediate area. Probably few if any. The parrot wasn't like a dog who stayed close by and returned home if separated from its master. Unless its wings weren't clipped, he doubted a bird could survive.

"Sam, are you in danger?"

"Sam danger."

He stopped at Arthur's feet before flapping his wings and landing on the arm of the couch next to him. Before he knew what was happening, Sam was perched on his shoulder. He didn't dare move. Knowing nothing about birds, he wasn't sure if this was a good sign or a bad one. He didn't want to know if it were the latter. The parrot could bite his ear or face. A horrid thought.

"How are you in danger, Sam?" he asked again.

"Stranger, danger. Bollocks! Help Sam!"

Looking straight ahead, Arthur spoke again. "Sam, there's no one here but you and me. I have no desire to hurt you."

He heard the door open behind him. He didn't dare try to move as he wasn't sure how Sam would react. Flapping his wings made him even more unsure as Sam jumped off his shoulder and on to the floor once more. Arthur stood perfectly still, as though his legs were made of concrete.

"Mama! Mama! Bloody danger!"

"It's all right, Sam. The man won't hurt us."

Arthur turned to find himself looking into the eyes of an icy blonde goddess. Her pale blue eyes immediately caught his attention. Never had he been drawn to a woman like he was with this one before him. She was wearing a dark-green day dress. He could remember little else as he was struck by her beauty.

"I see you've met Sam, Your Grace."

His throat seized up and he had to force himself to speak. "Yes. He's quite colorful."

"Indeed." She thrust out a hand to him. "I am Lady Andover, but you may call me Lady Daphne as I am not my mother." She smiled as Arthur took her small hand in his. She was small in stature but had the presence of an Amazon warrior."

"I am the Duke of Hightower, as you know, but you may call me…"

"Hightower," she interjected before he had a chance to finish his sentence.

"Now that that's settled, I wanted to meet with you to discuss your horse, Vicki's continued escape from your property and onto mine. Mind you, I only want you to ensure you'll keep the mare in a fenced environment, so this does not continue."

"If you want to remedy the situation, you need to fix the holes in your walls and fences," she snapped.

Arthur swore her eyes darkened to a deeper shade of blue. Her demeanor had changed, and he wasn't sure he liked it. "Everything on my estate is repaired or in the midst of being repaired as we speak."

"Then we have nothing to worry about, do we?"

"Only that you need to also repair holes in your walls and fences so she doesn't continue to leave the grounds."

"The maintenance of my father's estate is none of your concern, Your Grace," she said.

Arthur ignored her comment. He was certain she was trying to get a rise out of him. "There's the matter of a mysterious rider racing across the meadow on a portion of the estate. The rider has no respect for horses and is going to end up getting hurt or the gray will end up hurt if this continues."

"You've made your point."

"My words fall on deaf ears, milady."

"Really, Your Grace, do you always have such a flair for the dramatic?"

The door opened and a footman rolled in a cart filled with dainty sandwiches, cakes, and tea. Once the young man left, Lady Daphne walked over to the cart. "How do you like your tea, Your Grace?" She set out two porcelain cups and saucers, waiting for his response.

"I'm sorry, milady. I won't be able to stay for tea. I am expecting a visitor, so I need to get back." It was all a lie, but he had no desire to spend one more minute with this selfish, arrogant young lady.

"Your wife can't entertain them for a while?"

"I'm not married," he replied curtly.

"Ah, that explains a lot. Another time?"

"Yes, another time."

She glided across the Persian carpet towards him. "Good day, Your Grace. I trust you can find your way out?"

Off to one side, Sam squawked. "Good day, Your Grace." That was finished with another swear word. "Bollocks."

"Yes, I can find my way. By the way, who taught Sam all those swear words?"

Lady Daphne smirked. "I have no idea. It certainly wasn't me." She fluttered her eyelashes, pretending to be oh-so-innocent.

Arthur turned and headed towards the door. He was about to open the oak door when he heard Lady Daphne's voice.

"It was a pleasure meeting you, Your Grace." Her voice was like syrup, all sweet while being condescending at the same time.

He nodded as he headed through the opening. "Indeed."

Grabbing his hat and gloves from a marble-topped table in the entry, Arthur left the house. He looked out towards the fountain where he found Rolo holding Midnight by his reins. The stallion was being quiet for once. He usually liked to paw impatiently as he had too much energy for standing and waiting.

"Thank you, Rolo," he said as he took the reins and threw them over the horse's head.

"He's really a good horse for being a stallion."

"Yes, he rarely gets mean. He has to be provoked."

Arthur was about to mount when Rolo gave him pause not to.

"I hope your visit with Lady Daphne went well, Your Grace."

"It was what I expected. Oh, and I met that delightful parrot, Sam."

"Sam swears a lot, doesn't he?" Rolo laughed.

"He does indeed. Do you see him often?"

"Every day. I clean up after him. He makes quite the mess with seeds and things. I also feed him unless Lady Daphne says otherwise."

Arthur laughed. He could imagine Lady Daphne as a cold, hard woman to work for. "Well, Master Rolo, I appreciate all your assistance today. Hopefully we'll meet again under better circumstances."

The young lad walked alongside him once he mounted. "I would like that, Your Grace. I'll walk with you as far as the gate."

"Excellent idea."

The pair walked side by side down the drive to the gate, Rolo talking all the way. He pointed out what he thought might interest Arthur.

Arthur thought him to be a bright boy, far more than his years. He knew things most boys his age might not, and Arthur was certain the boy had little to no family.

The gate came into view and the young man ran up to it and swung the gate open. Arthur walked to where Rolo stood. "Make sure Vicki behaves herself and I don't have to return her again."

"I shall, Your Grace."

"Next time she escapes, she's going to have to hunt a way to get in. My men have fixed or are fixing the wall."

Rolo nodded and glanced back toward the house, which was just beyond the rise in the road.

"Have a good day, Rolo. Call on me if you have a need."

"I shall, Your Grace."

Arthur cleared the opening and began to rein his stallion in. Midnight wanted to run, but Arthur kept him contained until they were off the viscount's property. All in all, the visit had been a success. Lady Daphne was not all sugar and spice. She had her moments, as he witnessed, but he had the feeling that was brought on because her parents spoiled her, giving in to whatever demand she threw their way. He decided he needed to find out more about the viscount and his family. It was highly unusual for a daughter so young to be left alone without a proper chaperone. He especially wanted to learn more about Lady Daphne.

As he turned onto the main road, he turned Midnight towards home and broke him into a trot, holding him back from going faster. The stallion was still young, and his training was not finished. He always wanted to run, and Arthur had to hold him back, so pacing him at a trot made the animal listen to what he was being asked to do. As a reward, Arthur would let him gallop once they hit his estate's drive.

"Lady Roxanne stopped by while you were riding, Your Grace," Wilson said solemnly as Arthur opened the door to his study.

"I'm sorry I missed her."

Wilson arched his brow, about the most expression he ever allowed himself. "She said to remind you her house party starts soon, and you're required at dinner this evening to discuss the events."

Arthur said nothing for a moment. He'd completely forgotten and that wasn't like him. "What time am I required to arrive?"

"Seven."

"Very well. I completely forgot about this."

"She said she thought you had because you hadn't replied to her invitation and said that was unlike you."

"My sister is right. I forgot to reply."

Wilson stood at the doorway. "Is there anything I can get you, Your Grace?"

"No, that'll be all, Wilson."

With that, the door shut and Arthur was alone in his study with Roddy. The setter thumped his tail on the rug in front of his desk. "You ought to consider yourself lucky. You don't have to endure social events. You can stay here, eat your dinner alone, and sleep. I, on the other hand, have to go and pretend to be interested in some house party my sister is planning."

The dog's tail continued to wag. Roddy was happy for the attention even if it was unusual. "Of course, this house party is merely an excuse to try and find me a wife. She can't fool me. She's determined to see me wed. Roxanne doesn't listen to my opinion on the matter. It hits deaf ears."

Sitting down at his desk, he picked up a pile of letters Wilson had placed there while he'd been out. He thumbed through them to see if any were priority over others. Invitations to other summer house parties. He was sure that's what they were because they were a favorite among the ton during the summer when everyone fled London for the countryside. Arthur had never cared for the parties. It was too long a time to commit to, and he disliked having his days filled with silly games. Even the hunting and fishing times were not to his liking because it was a way for the men to gossip about peers and little else got done. Showing up at his sister's house party would be the only one he would commit to this late in the summer, and he would pick and choose when he wanted to be there.

He would try and get a sense of who Roxanne had invited. The guests with marriageable daughters who had come along. It was usually obvious, daughters either with their pushy mothers or the girls in a gaggle on their own. Either way, it was something which needed to be dealt with delicately. No one could be offended if he didn't pay enough attention to their daughter, but at the same time, he wasn't going to be run over by anyone.

Arthur thought to the viscount's daughter, Lady Daphne. For some reason, despite her condescending attitude, he was fascinated by her. His body reacted in ways it shouldn't the moment he laid eyes on her. He wanted to get to know her better. He would send flowers to her. It was a start. After that he could invite her to go riding. He would wear her down.

Hearing the clock on the mantel chime brought Arthur out of his thoughts. He reached across his desk and, grabbing a whiskey decanter, poured himself a glass. He sat back in his chair and took a sip. There was time before he needed to ready himself for his evening. He took another long drink of the whiskey and closed his eyes for a moment. Before he knew it, he dozed off for a few minutes. Lady Daphne appeared, her beauty unmatched by any other young lady he knew. He would have her, and she would become his wife.

He jerked awake, looked around, and took the remaining sip of whiskey. Where had that come from? He was usually not so determined about a woman, but he was finding out Lady Daphne had gotten under his skin. Now he wondered if Roxanne had invited her to the party. If she had, he would try and participate in whatever games she chose. Riding? Dancing? Or was she more daring and liked things like shooting or card games like poker? He could see her playing and winning. She would be a worthy opponent.

Arthur poured another splash of whiskey, smiling at the thought of Lady Daphne out of her safe environment. Perhaps that was one reason he never knew she was in residence. Did she prefer her own familiar surroundings to those unknown to her? He would make it his mission to find out all he could about her.

Arthur knew he and Graham needed to talk about their mutual interest in finding his parents' murderer. Nothing much had been gained lately, but he himself felt as though Crenshaw was being elusive, knowing he didn't have long before the truth came out. Crenshaw was being watched and Arthur wondered if he knew he was. He had even thought of going on the same journey to India that Crenshaw offered. He and Graham had discussed it, but it was decided the trip might not be a good idea. Crenshaw was a complicated man and if pushed too much or if he thought he felt uneasy about a situation, he might run. He had the means, and finding him again might not be worth the expense.

Finally, he pushed himself away from his desk and rose. He needed to start getting ready for this evening's affair. "Come, Roddy, let's see about getting you outside so I can get ready for Roxanne's dinner."

The red setter jumped up and loped to the door. As soon as Arthur opened it, he charged through. The footman assigned to the dog wasn't hard to find. As he watched the dog leave with the young man, Arthur turned and headed to the stairs.

CHAPTER FOUR

A S THE BUTLER announced him, Arthur walked deeper into the drawing room. In front of the fire stood his brother-in-law Graham. Roxanne, his sister, sat on a gold wing-backed chair. The pair were in the middle of a conversation, but seeing him, whatever they had been discussing was forgotten. He was late and was sure Roxanne would let him know it. She believed in punctuality and that everyone should do their best to be on time.

"Arthur, you made it. I was sure you'd forgotten," Roxanne said with a hint of mischief in her voice.

"I'm a duke. The rules don't apply," he replied without missing a beat. He arched a brow and smiled at his sibling.

Graham, in the meantime, brought him a glass of whiskey. "We're glad to see you. Have you found who owns that gray horse that keeps showing up?"

"Yes, and I met the elusive owner," he replied, accepting the crystal glass of liquor.

"Who did it end up being?" Roxanne asked.

"It belongs to Lady Daphne Waterton, daughter of Viscount Andover."

"Did you meet Lady Waterton or was she not in residence?" Roxanne had a mischievous smile on her face. Arthur knew right then, because a young woman was involved, his sister was going to have fun.

"I did meet the lady. Her parents are not in residence," he replied.

"I hope she was grateful you returned her horse," Graham said.

"What was she like, Lady Daphne?" Roxanne asked.

Arthur thoughtfully took a sip of his whiskey before answering. "Lady Daphne is very self-centered, condescending, and rude. To make matters worse, she has a parrot named Sam who cusses like a sailor."

"Fascinating," Graham interjected.

"I saw nothing fascinating about it. The bird is just like his mistress in temperament, though I will admit I never heard the lady utter those words."

"Lady Daphne is coming to our house party, so be nice if you run into her, which I'm sure you will," Roxanne said as she watched her brother closely. Her eyes never left his face.

"I was certain she would be. Please do me a favor and don't seat us together or anything else that might force us to talk."

"You're usually not one to rush to judgment. You give people a chance. Your distaste for the lady is curious."

Taking a sip of his whiskey, Arthur turned his attention to Graham, who was trying his best not to smile. "Talk some sense into her."

Graham bit back a laugh and put both hands in the air in mock horror. "You're on your own. I've made it my mission not to get involved in these sorts of matters."

"I'll give you a schedule of the events and place a check next to the ones I'd like to have you attend," Roxanne said.

"I can't wait," Arthur said sarcastically. He finished off his whiskey and placed the glass down on a nearby table.

"What are you going to do if the gray shows up on your estate again?" Graham asked. He was trying to get the conversation on to another subject.

"I'll return the animal, but I'll also find the butler and ask if he knows how to contact the viscount. I will apprise him of the situation."

"You don't think that'll make the situation worse?" Roxanne asked.

"No, but frankly I don't care."

At that moment, the butler announced dinner was ready. "Perhaps our butler might be able to find the information you require through Lady Daphne's butler," Roxanne said as her devoted husband assisted her to her feet. Arthur had known they would be good for each other. They were sickeningly happy and deeply in love. If any one person deserved happiness, it was his sister. Their father had arranged a marriage for her, and the man chosen for her was cruel. Roxanne would stay clear of him as much as possible as the man thought of women as second-class citizens. Arthur could only wish he might one day find such happiness as she currently had.

Once they were all seated at the large mahogany dining table, Arthur realized he was hungrier than he realized. Knowing how meticulous his sister was, he concluded that this dinner would be a dry run for one she would serve during her house party.

"Which dinner are we testing this evening?" he asked as he accepted a glass of wine a footman had poured.

"This one is what will be served for the night before the ball," she replied.

"You're going to have a ball?"

She graced him with a smile. "But of course. The ball will be a masquerade. I think they're so much fun."

"Exactly how many people are you expecting to show up at this house party?" Arthur asked.

"Six couples will be staying here, then we have guests who live nearby and will travel to and from their homes. I expect approximately twenty. Just the perfect size. Not too big, not too small."

"Not to worry, Arthur. I have shooting and hunting excursions planned, along with card and billiard games," Graham said with a grin on his face. He seemed to enjoy seeing his old friend and brother-in-law uncomfortable. Arthur would never admit it, but he hated these sorts of parties. Even if it were a good place to find one's future duchess.

"We've also got plenty planned as a way for guests to mingle and get to know each other," Roxanne interjected.

"I'm sure you've thought of everything," Arthur replied with a hint of sarcasm in his voice.

The soup course was served, a cold asparagus soup which Arthur found quite refreshing. His sister was always trying something new like this soup. It had garlic and cream and was topped off with a small stalk of asparagus. He noted Graham was eating with gusto, which ended when Roxanne set her spoon down.

Soup bowls were replaced with a plate of two lamb chops accompanied by mint sauce. "The lamb is from the estate," Roxanne announced." I've done my best to use only local products. You can't get more local than one's own estate."

"It is delicious, and you know how particular I am about lamb," Arthur said as he took a second bite.

"I wanted to do something a bit different. Everyone serves roast of pork or beef or roast chicken. Ham was my second choice."

"I'm glad you decided on this," Graham said.

Roxanne smiled and took another bite of lamb. "I'm glad you both approve."

"What's next?" Arthur asked as he set down his knife and fork on an empty plate.

"Vegetables. I'm going to use whatever is available. Dessert will be strawberries or a mixture of fruit with cream on top."

"You've outdone yourself, Rox. People are going to talk about this house-party for some time," Arthur said.

Dinner continued with polite conversation, with the focus being on the meal rather than anything else. When the trio finally finished, they all returned to the drawing room where the men had their port and cigars and Roxanne partook with a small snifter of brandy.

"Arthur? You do have a mask for the ball, don't you?"

He gazed at her with interest. "I'm sure my valet can come up with one."

"I've had one made for you."

"Why would you do that?"

"Because I know how forgetful you can be, especially when it comes to things like a masquerade ball."

He nodded. "Thank you. That's quite thoughtful."

"Are you going to take your seat in Parliament?" Graham asked suddenly.

"Yes. It's time, and there's some legislation I would like to know more of." Arthur and Roxanne's late father had held the seat from the time his own father died. Now it was time for Arthur to take his place.

"I think you'll do a splendid job," Graham added.

"Thanks. I'm going to try my best."

"You've always had an interest in what goes on in Parliament. Ever since Papa took you as a young boy," Roxanne said.

"It's true. I love seeing how laws and bills are made."

Graham sat down in a dark-gold upholstered chair near his wife. "You're a great debater. I remember that from university. I have no doubt it'll come back to you effortlessly."

"Everyone will be returning to London soon. Parliament reconvenes the first of November this year," Arthur said.

The conversation continued, politics forgotten, to Mary and how she was thriving. She was a good baby and Roxanne and Graham were both enamored of her. Arthur finally saw an opportunity open for him to make his departure. He had taken his carriage only because it was a moonless night and not particularly made for riding.

Goodbyes were said and Arthur settled in for the short ride home. It had been an enjoyable evening. His sister was keeping her bride hunting to a minimum. She now, however, knew of the viscount's daughter living at the family estate alone, without chaperone. If she had one, they hadn't made their presence known. He hoped Roxanne wouldn't make a point of inviting the girl for tea or calling upon her. He was planning on contacting the viscount to let him know what had been going on. He'd have to be subtle about how he brought his daughter into the conversation. He didn't want to ruffle any feathers with his neighbor. Arthur smiled, thinking about the parrot the girl kept. He wondered if the bird had that much freedom when the viscount and his family were in residence. He couldn't imagine the viscountess allowing the parrot to have free roam of the residence.

He found his way to his rooms once he arrived back. It was fairly early by his standards but he didn't want to spend time in one of the large rooms alone. Having a good book he'd been meaning to read, his sitting room was perfect. He could sit in front of the fire with a brandy and read with no interruption.

His shoes came off first, followed by his cravat and jacket. He flung them over the back of a nearby chair before proceeding to his dressing area where he came out of all his clothes except his smalls, put on a robe to cover him, and walked back to the sitting room to pour a brandy. Grabbing the book off a table, he soon made himself comfortable. Opening the book, he immediately got lost in the story. His mind, however, didn't stay focused on the words in front of him. He found himself thinking about Lady Daphne, wondering if she always acted as she had when he visited or if it was a front. Perhaps she was really a quiet, demure young woman and not the spoiled girl with the obnoxious parrot he'd met. That version of her was more palatable but he seriously doubted she was anything but what he saw.

And why was she even crossing his mind? She was not the sort of young lady he wished to have on his arm, but damn he found he was attracted to her. His imagination went where it had no business going, bedding her. He shut the book and took a sip of brandy. He sat back, opened the book one more time, hoping he could concentrate without distraction. The words ran together, so Arthur closed the book one more time. There was to be no reading tonight. He cursed his body for misbehaving.

ARTHUR WAS AWAKENED by a slobbery tongue licking his face. Roddy. His valet, Ian Thomas, would bring the setter with him in the mornings if the dog hadn't spent the night with his master. If Arthur weren't awake when Thomas arrived, the valet would open the door to the duke's chambers, knowing the setter would eagerly wake his master.

He pushed the dog aside so that he might sit up. He had to attend to correspondence after breakfast before anything else was done. He and Graham were to ride later this morning. Sometimes being out of the house was better to discuss delicate matters. They had some decisions to make regarding the man they suspected of killing Arthur and Roxanne's parents. Graham had mentioned he'd received a letter from the detective they'd hired to track the man.

An hour later, Arthur was sitting down at the table in the breakfast room. Roddy had followed and was lying at his side, waiting for any scraps Arthur might throw his way. Arthur took a couple of bites of egg and sausage before picking up one of the newspapers neatly folded in a pile to his left.

Turning the page, an article caught his eye. The man they knew to have had his parents killed was now being held by Metropolitan Police in connection to three other murders. His parents' deaths weren't among those the man was being charged with. Instead, they were listed as deaths of interest. The list held five potential targets thought to be killed by the same person.

Immediately he knew he needed to go to London and tell police what he and Graham suspected. Crenshaw was unknowingly making it easier for police. He was wearing Arthur's father's ring, and once it was taken off his finger, Arthur would be able to prove the man had something to do with his parents' murder.

He needed to let Graham know, if he hadn't read the newspapers from London. Picking up the newspaper, he rose from his chair. He glanced at the footman standing next to the buffet.

"Have a tray brought to my study."

"Yes, Your Grace," the young man replied, still standing erect.

He strode to his study, sitting down at his desk. As he pulled a fresh sheet of paper out of the drawer, in walked Graham, followed by Roddy. "Have you read the papers?" Graham asked breathlessly. He obviously rode his horse; his hair was wind-blown, and he was out of breath.

"Yes. I was about to write you in case you hadn't seen it."

"I think we need to act on this while he's locked up."

"Agreed. Should we contact our man or simply go to London ourselves? We could meet up with him there and the three of us pay a visit to Metropolitan Police," Arthur said.

"We ought to go to London ourselves."

Arthur nodded. "I'll write a short note to our man and let him know we're on our way."

Graham stared at the newspaper sitting on Arthur's desk. "How many people has this man killed? More importantly, how has he gotten away with it all these years?"

Before Arthur could answer, the butler appeared. "I apologize for the interruption, Your Grace, but I was asked to tell you that the gray mare is back."

Arching a brow, he quickly addressed the situation. "Do you know if she's been caught?"

"She has, Your Grace. She's at the stables."

"Instruct them to leave her there. Inform Thomas to pack for London. We leave today. I'll return the mare myself as we leave for London."

"Yes, Your Grace."

After the man left the room, Graham turned to his friend, a smirk on his face. "Did I understand you correctly that you're returning the mare on our way to London?"

"You didn't mishear. And yes, you can meet the lady and her obnoxious bird. I need someone to be witness to what I tell her," Arthur replied, adding, "And wipe that smirk off your face."

"You know what I think?"

"No, but I'm sure you're going to tell me."

"I think the lady deliberately let the mare loose. Maybe even led her onto your property herself."

"That's a possibility. I don't know how the gray got onto the estate. I was assured everything had been fixed. There shouldn't have been any openings for her."

"A quandary at best."

A few minutes later, Graham was on his way back home and Arthur was shouting orders to have his coach readied and that food be packed for them in case they got hungry during the ride.

After picking up Graham, Arthur instructed his driver to make a stop at the viscount's estate. As usual, the gate was shut, but Arthur had watched how it was opened the last time he'd been here. With Graham walking beside him, and Arthur leading the gray mare, the pair made their way to the manor.

Someone must have seen them because when the pair reached the front of the house, they were greeted by the butler. A boy came to take the horse from Arthur, but Arthur kept a tight hold on the rope, insisting to see Lady Daphne before he gave up the mare. For a while it seemed like they were going to be in the middle of a big standoff. Finally, Lady Daphne walked through the door and stood at the top of the stairs.

"What are you doing with my mare, Your Grace?" She was smiling, indicating to Arthur that she was aware of the situation.

"Funny, but she showed up in my meadow again in spite of my men fixing the fence and wall."

"Sounds like they missed an opening," she said. She eyed Graham carefully. "Who's he?"

"There were no openings, of that I can assure you."

"You didn't answer my question."

Arthur bit back a laugh. "My conclusion is that someone

made a new opening and let the gray through. You wouldn't know anything about that, would you, Lady Daphne?"

"You still haven't answered my question," she ground out. "Who is he?" She pointed at Graham.

"Oh, this is my brother-in-law, the Earl of Otley. He lives nearby as well."

Graham bowed his head slightly. "An honor to meet you, Lady Daphne."

"Hmmm…is he always so demanding?" she asked Graham.

"He's a duke. The same rules we go by don't always apply to a duke."

"Duke or not, he doesn't scare me."

Precisely at that moment, a voice from just inside the open door could be heard. "Mama, mama, mama!"

"What the?" Graham bit out.

"Sam, the parrot I told you about," Arthur replied.

Lady Daphne had turned and stepped inside for a moment. As she returned, a large red macaw graced her forearm. "Bloody hell! Stranger!" the bird said.

"That's not nice, Sam," she scolded.

"Sam not nice."

"Who taught him to talk?" Graham inquired.

"No one. I guess you could say he taught himself," Lady Daphne replied.

"Amazing. I've never seen a parrot like him up close."

"My father brought him back from one of his trips to the Caribbean or South America."

Arthur was getting impatient for two reasons. Lady Daphne was not going to have a serious conversation about their ongoing problem of her mare on the loose. Next, he was more than ready to get on the road to London. He was going to have to make a move to get Graham away from here.

"Graham, we should be going."

His friend nodded. "You're right."

"Where are you off to?" Lady Daphne asked, as she stroked

Sam's feathers.

"London," Arthur said. "We'll finish this conversation when I return."

"There's nothing to discuss, Your Grace." She turned to Graham. "It was nice to meet you, milord. I'm looking forward to your house party."

"Until then," Graham replied.

The pair watched as the door closed behind Lady Daphne and Sam. They began the walk to the carriage without saying a word. Once they had settled in and the carriage began to roll, Graham, looking out the window, spoke.

"That parrot is phenomenal. I've never heard a bird talk before."

"Sam is something, I will admit," Arthur said, settling himself into the corner of the seat.

"And I think you've met your match with Lady Daphne."

Arthur shook his head slightly. "Like I said, she's arrogant, condescending, and has a mouth on her."

"Whatever you say. Methinks there's an attraction between the two of you."

"Don't be ridiculous. I'll grant you she's beautiful, but once she opens her mouth, that's all she wrote."

"Perhaps that's why her family lets her stay behind."

Graham bent over and pulled out the basket Arthur's cook had made. He pulled out a chunk of cheese, offering some to Arthur. Arthur broke off a piece and found a bottle of wine and two glasses. Arthur poured two glasses as Graham found the loaf of bread, still slightly warm.

"I hope my father's ring will be enough to charge him," Arthur said before taking a sip of wine.

"I'm speculating they must have other proof. Might not be from your parents' murders, but it sounds like the police have this wrapped up in a neat little bow."

Arthur nodded as he thoughtfully bit into a piece of cheese. "What I don't understand is how someone can murder people and then just walk through society as though nothing was wrong."

"He's not like you or me. The man has no conscience."

"It'll be interesting. Perhaps his tongue will loosen up after a few days in custody," Graham said as he ran his hand over his beard. He set his glass back in the basket and closed his eyes. Long carriage rides made him sleepy. A few minutes later, he heard Arthur's baritone rasp.

"Rather than us open both our residences, I suggest we stay at mine since I already let staff know we were coming."

Graham cracked an eye. "That's fine with me because I completely forgot about getting word to anyone."

"I also thought that rather than put my cook in distress by my lack of information, we could dine at White's and have a couple of steaks."

"That sounds good. It shouldn't be too crowded either since there are still a lot of people out of town for the summer."

"Quite true," Arthur said. "When we arrive, I'll get a message off and see where our man wants to meet in the morning."

"It would probably be best to meet at your house. It would give us more privacy, and afterward we could move on to Metropolitan Police."

"Yes, that would be the best way to be able to speak privately."

"On another matter, Roxanne has sent me a list of things she needs or things she's ordered that need to be picked up while we're here," Graham said with a smirk.

Arthur arched a brow and stretched out his legs. "Things for the house party?"

"I'm afraid so."

He bit out a laugh at his friend's answer. "I was actually surprised she didn't insist on coming along."

"She tried, but I convinced her I was perfectly capable of following her instructions," Graham said.

"You've got your hands full with her."

"I know, but I'm hoping she'll settle into her roles as wife, mother, and countess. I overlook some of what she says or does because I know what a hard, impossible life she had with Casper."

Arthur picked up a book he'd brought along with him and opened it to the spot he'd read through. "At least you realize that. A lot of husbands wouldn't and wouldn't be so understanding."

His words met dead silence. Arthur glanced over at his friend and found him asleep. He was envious of Graham being able to sleep in a carriage. Carriage rides were too jarring for sleep, though he had found himself taking naps on long-distance journeys. Now, trains were beginning to become a more efficient means of transportation. No more swapping out teams. Simply board a train and let it take you to your destination. At least there was something good coming from all these new-fangled inventions.

CHAPTER FIVE

ARTHUR AND GRAHAM met with the man they'd hired to gather information about Arthur's parents' murder. Mr. Sweeney, a former Metropolitan Police inspector, had been thorough with his investigation. Now they were at Mr. Sweeney's office inside an older office building. Originally planned to hold the meeting at Arthur's home, Sweeney changed his mind with no explanation, only that he preferred to meet at his office.

They sat across from him at his cluttered desk. Papers and files were everywhere, and for a moment, Arthur wondered how the man knew where anything was. Mr. Sweeney, however, seemed to know where everything was.

"How did we get to this point? Are they sure he's committed other heinous crimes?" Arthur asked, shaking his head. "He certainly fooled us."

"Yes. I was told by a source of mine that there was a couple who filed a complaint about a month ago after returning from a planned trip to India. The problem being they never made it to India and nearly fell into Mr. Crenshaw's trap."

"They were the lucky ones," Graham mused.

Sweeney ran a hand through a lock of thinning gray hair, pushing it back in place. "Yes, they were extremely lucky."

"So what happens now?" Arthur asked, crossing his leg and tapping his finger on his knee.

"The fact he was wearing your father's signet ring when arrested is the most damning evidence they have. He can deny it all he wants, but everyone knows a duke would not give up his ring. Not willingly."

Arthur nodded in agreement. "They are something passed to the duke's heir upon his demise."

"Precisely," Sweeney replied.

"What happens now?" Graham asked.

"He's been charged for other murders, but when you claim the ring, I'm quite sure he'll be charged for murder in your parents' deaths. From what I know, he used his father's business as a guide and used it for his own personal gain. By that I mean robbing and murdering clients."

"He'll be executed?" Arthur asked. "I think that's too easy a solution, but he won't be a burden to society if he were to be locked away for the remainder of his life."

"You and Roxanne will have closure," Graham said.

Arthur nodded. "That is true."

Sweeney rose to his full height, towering over Arthur and Graham. He was quite a tall man compared to most. "Gentlemen, shall we go? We're meeting with an Inspector Grady."

"Yes, I'm ready to get this settled," Arthur said.

It wasn't a long walk to get to the Metropolitan Police at their New Scotland Yard headquarters. Located on the Victoria Embankment, the new building made a statement for the agency. A more centralized location for all the ground they covered.

Arthur was quite impressed by what he observed. Everything seemed to be well organized. They were shown right away to Inspector Grady's office. The man sitting behind the desk was quite the opposite of Sweeney. Where Sweeney was tall, Grady was the opposite; short and squatty, a bit on the rotund side, he wore a reddish mustache and had piercing black eyes.

Everyone having greeted the other, they sat and waited for Grady to pull a file off the corner of his desk and dig something out of a drawer. Whatever it was, his fingers clutched around it so no one saw what he held.

"Your Grace, may I offer my condolences. I had met your father several times about a couple of years ago. I know he's missed."

"Thank you, Inspector Grady."

"I'll try and make this as brief as possible. Crenshaw right now is a guest of the Crown. He won't be going anywhere except to trial and its outcome. I have no doubt at all that he'll be found guilty."

Arthur sat forward in his chair. "Even with this report filed by this couple? It won't be a he said, they said situation?"

"No. Their descriptions and details were far too precise. Then, of course, when he was arrested, he was in possession of your father's ring. He couldn't explain his way out of that one."

"What can I do?"

"I will need you to make a statement verifying the ring, and if you could attend the trial or even make an appearance, it would be helpful. I understand you will be taking your father's seat in Parliament?"

"I can do all that. To answer your question, I have decided to take my father's seat and participate more than he did," Arthur replied. He sat back again and glanced at Graham. "The earl is married to my sister, so he represents her."

The inspector nodded. "I can imagine you're all relieved."

"Quite so," Graham said. "My wife will be glad to see this ended even though it can never bring her parents back."

"Any idea when this will go to trial?" Arthur inquired.

"I expect it'll take a couple of months but sooner if possible."

It wasn't the answer Arthur wanted, but he knew there was a lot of legal maneuvering to be done with attorneys and filings. Crenshaw's people would want to make a distraction for as long as possible.

"Does Crenshaw have representation?"

"He does, but I don't think they are who he wanted. From what I understand, his own family's firm wanted nothing to do with representing him. Not for the charge of murdering a duke and his wife. The man he has is competent but has very little experience in this type of law."

Arthur nodded thoughtfully. "I see."

Grady extended his closed fist to Arthur. "Your Grace, I thought you might like to have this back." He opened his hand and there sat his father's ring.

"Don't you need it for trial?" he asked as he reached for the gold ring.

"No, but if it is needed, we know where it is. I couldn't see it sitting in an evidence box when it could be returned to the rightful owner, so I made some inquiries and got the approval."

"Thank you. This means a lot," Arthur whispered.

Grady said nothing but nodded his response.

Sweeney, who had been quiet throughout the meeting and stood in a corner, made a sound in his throat. "Unless there's anything more, I guess we'll be on our way, Inspector."

"Yes, we should be on our way. Thank you for your time," Arthur said. "Please keep me updated."

"My pleasure and I shall, Your Grace."

The threesome walked silently out of his office and exited the building without a word amongst them. They crossed the street. The Thames was within view, making a walk back more pleasant.

"I feel like the weight of the world has been lifted," Arthur finally announced.

"I'm sure you do. I'm sure Roxanne will feel much the same," Graham agreed.

"I'll be sure to stay apprised of the case in case Grady gets busy and forgets to let you know," Sweeney said.

Arthur nodded and slid a hand inside his jacket and pulled out an envelope. He handed it to Sweeney. "I believe this is what I owe you. If it isn't, send me a final bill and I will have it taken care of immediately. There's also a little something extra for all your hard work."

Sweeney's eyes bulged as he looked inside the open envelope.

Arthur had given him cash as a bonus. "Your Grace, I can't accept this. It's far too much."

"You earned every pound, Sweeney. Take your wife out to dinner or take her on a holiday. You both deserve it."

"Very well. My thanks, Your Grace."

"Take the afternoon off. The earl and I are planning to!"

The men shook hands and Sweeney began to depart. "Thank you again, Your Grace. I'll be in touch if I hear anything about the progress of Crenshaw's case."

"I know you will. Take care," Arthur replied. He and Graham stood for a moment and watched Sweeney disappear into the crowd.

"Fancy a walk?" Graham asked.

"What do you have in mind?"

"Parliament is not too far off. We could go give your office a look over since you're going to be representing the people as an MP. Lunch if we find some place we like."

"I thought you had errands to do for my sister?"

"They're done. I wrote each one of them and asked them to have her order sent to your house," Graham said with a grin.

"You're a sly one. Wonder if she asks for something else from any of them?"

"Then I'll take care of it. I can't see wasting time going to all these shops when the orders already have been placed. With what Roxanne's spending on this party, the merchants can deliver."

They continued towards their destination. It wasn't a far walk and the day was incredibly nice with a slight breeze and blue skies and barely any clouds. It would be a perfect day for a ride in the park; the crowds would be sparse and the temperature comfortable, but that was for another time.

Soon, the massive neoclassical Westminster Palace, which was commonly referred to as the Parliament Building, came into sight. Arthur had only been inside once since his father's death and that was to inform the proper channels.

He turned to Graham. "There is plenty of time for that. Today is a time for celebration. Why don't we go back to White's, have lunch. If all of your wife's purchases have arrived, I suggest we head home. It'll be late when we arrive, but frankly, I'm ready to return. Before you know it, it'll be time to return."

Graham was still staring up at the Parliament Building. "I can understand your point of view and quite frankly, I concur. If we stay, we'll only get into business and find excuses for staying. Roxanne's house party begins next week. I don't want to disappoint her. Let's go get something to eat."

"I'm glad you agree. To be honest, I'm not sure I'm up to talking with colleagues about finding my father and mother's killer. You know the madness is going to begin as soon as it hits the newspapers. I haven't had time to digest what just happened."

Nodding, Graham laid his hand on his friend's shoulder. "I understand. It's a lot to digest. Going to White's may not be the best place to go."

"We'll request a table in a corner or a private room if one's available. I'll be fine."

"If you're sure, let's be on our way. After the morning we've had, I'm famished."

Arthur bit out a laugh. "You're always hungry."

The pair began walking without a word between them. It was indeed a glorious day, in more ways than one.

IT WAS INDEED late when Arthur's carriage stopped in front of his friend's front door. It had been a long but satisfying day. He was ready to soak in a tub of hot water, read, and get a much overdue night of sleep.

His sister Roxanne came rushing out the door upon learning they'd arrived. He knew there'd be a thousand questions, and for once he'd leave it to Graham to sort it out. Unloading her purchases would only take the footmen a matter of minutes, so he had the opportunity to make excuses not to leave the carriage.

Graham greeted his wife, who hurried over and opened the door. "Arthur, don't just sit there. Come in and have a brandy while you wait for them to unload my parcels. I want to hear everything."

"I'm fine where I am, and it won't take them but a minute. It's late, and I'm really quite tired. Graham can apprise you of everything."

She studied him for a moment, knowing she wasn't going to win this one. She was quite used to getting her own way, but she'd also learned when to call a truce. "Very well. Come by tomorrow and tell me everything."

"Like I said, Graham will tell you. I'll come by if there is nothing keeping me at the estate."

"Very well. Enjoy your evening, brother," she bit out.

He nodded. "You do the same." He felt a twinge of guilt for being short with her when there was so much to share, but he'd never get home before dawn if he stepped out of the carriage.

"Roxanne, I think you'll like the outcome. We can finally put this nightmare behind us."

She cocked her head but said nothing before she lifted her skirts, turned, and walked toward Graham. Arthur sat back against the squabs and closed his eyes, waiting for the men to finish. Finally, he heard the driver climbing up to his position. He tapped his walking stick on the roof as he'd done many times before. Moments later, the carriage rolled forward and headed home.

The house wasn't lit up like it regularly was. No one was expecting him for the next few days. He descended the carriage and walked to the front door. As he began to open the door, the young boy who slept in the kitchens for moments like this appeared. It was obvious by his appearance he'd been fast asleep. Behind him, Roddy came bounding out of nowhere, his tail wagging in excitement. Arthur took a moment to pay the red dog attention before he noticed Wilson arriving dressed in his robe and slippers.

"Is everything all right, Your Grace? We didn't receive word you would be arriving tonight."

"It's fine, Wilson. I didn't send word. It was a spur of the moment decision."

"I understand, Your Grace."

"Anything I should know about that might have happened while I was away?"

"Nothing that can't wait until morning, Your Grace."

"Hmmm…the gray. Any sightings, or has Lady Daphne learned from her actions?"

"Unfortunately, the horse was seen with a rider racing across the meadow on two occasions."

"That's what I wanted to know," Arthur replied. "I'm going to retire. I apologize for waking everyone."

"Good night, Your Grace."

A little bit later, Arthur lay back in the large tub his father had installed when he added running water to the manor. It was luxurious compared to before. No need for footmen to carry endless buckets of water from the kitchen. It was a luxury he looked forward to after being in the carriage for hours on end.

His mind flew to Lady Daphne. She was beautiful and yes, she was a pain in his arse. Her continued arrogance, ignoring him when it came to her mare, made him want to take her over his knee and spank her. He needed to talk with her again, but instead had an idea that might make her see the errors of her ways.

She was constantly in his dreams at night while he was away, and the dreams were not quite what he expected. He was attracted to her. There was a pull he'd never experienced with a woman before, and surprisingly, he didn't mind it. One night he'd even awoken from a dream where he'd proposed to her, but the dream ended suddenly, and he had no idea how she responded.

His idea was to give her a taste of her own medicine. He would plant a horse on her property and see how long before she realized or was told by one of her staff the animal was there. How long would it be until the horse was returned? Knowing her, she would send one of her staff with the animal rather than come in person herself. It would be beneath her to do so. He would love to be a fly on the wall when she found out she'd been played.

He shook his head and immersed his head in the bath water. No, he wouldn't do that. Playing into her game wasn't what he was about, and since he hadn't contacted her father, he needed to distance himself. He would, for now, just leave the gray to forage on its own. Someone would surely come for it sooner or later. He sloughed the excess water from his hair. No, instead, he would pretend he didn't know the horse was there. He had more important things to deal with at the moment than a spoiled young woman's games.

Arthur began to soap up his body. The water was cooling. That wasn't a problem, but it was late and tomorrow would be quite eventful getting caught up on everything that'd happened while away. He found he'd taken himself in hand, stroking his hard cock in an effort to get relief from the effect Lady Daphne had on him.

CHAPTER SIX

$\mathbf{A}$RTHUR GLANCED UP at the windows of the manor house where every window had candles glowing, greeting guests. The front was well lit as well, with lamps lining the side of the drive leading to the house. He stepped from his carriage and walked to the front door where he was greeted by the butler. He handed his hat and greatcoat to a waiting footman and proceeded to a reception line where his sister and brother-in-law were standing.

He took Roxanne's hand and bent over and kissed her cheek. "The house looks wonderful," he said.

"And you're late," she replied with a wink.

"I beg to differ. I told you I would attend the reception and dinner tonight. And I am."

"We're about to go into dinner."

"Excellent."

Graham gave him a knowing grin as he shook his hand. "A word of advice before you go in there. Lady Daphne is here."

Arthur cocked a brow. "Wonderful. I'll try to avoid her at all costs."

He moved into the drawing room, accepting a glass of champagne from a waiting footman. There was an eclectic group of people invited; most he knew. He'd also been warned by Graham that a few of the ladies brought their marriageable daughters when they heard Arthur would be there. He cringed at the thought as he noticed two older aristocratic women with their daughters by their side, smiling and whispering among themselves while throwing meaningful glances his way.

To avoid being mobbed so early in the evening, he walked over to a small group of men with their wives. He knew all of them, two of the men from university and the other two from other social situations. He approached the group and was introduced to everyone by Baron Heathcliff, a friend from university.

It was while he was standing amongst the group that a figure in pale gold silk walked by, accompanied by a young man Arthur wasn't sure he knew. The man looked fairly familiar, sporting a dark brown beard, longish hair that hung at his collar. As he began to speak, he realized who it was. Lady Daphne. They locked eyes for a moment as she and her friend continued walking past. She arched a pale brow as she smirked ever so slightly.

While returning his attention back to his colleagues, Roxanne pulled him away to remind him as he was the senior ranking peer, he would be seated at the head of the table with her and Graham. He acknowledged his sister's reminder, recalling that as Lady Daphne's father was a viscount, she would be seated farther down the table. Such was the pecking order of the ton. An exception could be made if he chose her as a dining partner. It was done all the time, but instead, Arthur decided he'd rather look at her from afar tonight. See how she interacted among the guests.

A few minutes later, after getting everyone ready and aware of who they'd be seated with, Arthur led the group into the large dining room where a long mahogany table was decorated with candles and flowers which were cleverly arranged so guests could see each other across the table. It would give him perfect sight of Lady Daphne wherever she was seated.

Dinner was amazing. Better than the test version he and

Graham had sampled. He was interrupted by the dowager countess Cornwall who raised her voice enough to make sure he heard her. Arthur inhaled deeply. The countess was known for her long-winded conversations. She spoke with great authority about anything she wished to discuss with her fellow diners.

"Your Grace, the opening of Parliament is fast approaching, a little later than usual, but that's neither here nor there. You've yet to take your seat since your father died. Are you planning to this year, and if not, why not resign so the seat may be occupied by someone who is truly interested?"

He thought a moment, more to keep her in suspense than anything else. The countess would make a damn fine journalist. She didn't hold back. "I will be attending this year and giving my full attention to the matters at hand."

Seeing her reaction, Arthur wondered if she had any comments, good or bad, regarding his decision.

"Wonderful news! I have no doubt you will make an excellent MP. You're so knowledgeable about so many things. Parliament needs more like you."

"Thank you, madam."

"Your father would be proud of you," she said.

He nodded and said nothing, looking to his sister for help. He knew the ladies would be departing the dining room so the men could partake in their customary port and cigars. But that was several courses off that he'd have to endure before he could relax.

It wasn't long before the countess's niece was introduced to him. Lady Winifred was her name, and she didn't have a lot to say because her aunt dominated most of what was being said. She was raven-haired with eyes that matched. She wore a sage-green gown which Arthur thought was far from the right color for her. With her dark hair, he thought she needed something brighter, not dour like the green. He couldn't form an opinion of her with her aunt present. He'd have to wait for another opportunity.

Gazing down the table, he noted Lady Daphne engaged with a couple seated across from her, along with the gentleman to her right. That didn't stop her from looking at what was going on in his direction. When she caught him watching her, she flashed a smile and went back to the conversation as though that hadn't just happened.

Once the ladies left, it was business and politics as usual. Arthur enjoyed a glass of port and listened to the varying opinions. He really wasn't interested in joining in. At functions such as these, conversations became almost redundant. It would be like that for the remainder of the house party. He would hear the same things more than once, so why join in so early in the party when it would come up again and again.

For once he was glad he lived close by and could pick and choose what he attended. Things wouldn't be disrupted at the estate. This was an important time of year. Harvests would begin. Apples and other fruit were being picked or about to be. A last crop of hay was ready, which was not for the faint of heart. It took a lot of back-breaking work by a crew of many men. He made a point of spending some time out in the fields helping them out. He never wanted to appear as too good to be involved in what his peers might call menial tasks. In Arthur's mind, everyone on the estate benefited when they all worked together. It was one thing his father had instilled in him.

Finally, they rejoined the ladies, and he had no more than accepted a brandy snifter from a footman than one of the other ladies whose daughter had accompanied her parents approached him. She wasn't subtle about what she wanted by any means.

"Your Grace, I understand you're on the marriage mart now. Is it true you're looking for your duchess?" Lady Margaret, Viscountess Everly, trilled.

Luckily, he hadn't taken a swallow of brandy, or he would have spewed it across the room. He saw his sister standing among a gaggle of women, trying to hide her amusement.

"I've always been on the look-out for a woman to fill the role of my wife and duchess. I wouldn't call it being on the marriage mart. I believe when the right woman comes along, I'll instinctively know it."

Lady Daphne, who had been standing nearby speaking with a couple he didn't recognize, turned in his direction discreetly and rolled her eyes. The audacity she possessed! She tried to conceal her amusement by unfurling her fan and hiding behind it. He chose to ignore her. There would be plenty of time for conversation. Tonight was the first of many and the opportunity would come to put her in her place without her even knowing he'd done it.

Arthur headed over to his sister. It was time to go, but before he made it that far, Graham and a young squire who'd purchased a small parcel of land with a house he was in the middle of redoing the outside from years of neglect cornered him. From what he knew of Peter Jenkins, the man's family was quite successful in the railroad business, and he'd moved to Kent because his sister's health was precarious, and the London air was more than she could tolerate. His father thought the doctors were full of nonsense and ignored their warnings for years. Jenkins took matters into his own hands by moving his sister to the country.

"Your Grace, have you met our new neighbor, Mr. Peter Jenkins? He purchased the old Oldham property," Graham said, beckoning him over.

"No, I haven't had the pleasure. I wasn't aware anyone was living there. I rode by one day and from what I could see, the roof was being redone." He extended his hand to Jenkins, a tall, gangly young man with ginger-red hair. His dress was of a successful businessman. He may not be of aristocratic upbringing, but it was obvious by his looks he'd been well brought up.

"It's an honor to meet you, Your Grace," Jenkins replied. The two shook hands and Graham guided the conversation.

"Jenkins is interested in finding a gentle mount for his sister. I don't have anything right now, but I mentioned you might."

Arthur swirled his brandy before he took a swallow. "How good a rider is your sister? I wouldn't want to put her on something she might not be able to handle if the situation were to arise."

"She's good, but I would prefer for now to see her on something gentle that doesn't spook so easily. You see, our father rarely allowed her to ride. I've taken her as much as possible in London, but now that she's living out here, I know it would be something she would enjoy."

"I have a striking bay gelding. He's about twelve, quite gentle. He almost has an instinct about his rider's needs. You're welcome to bring your sister and see if they'd suit."

"Thank you, Your Grace. I'll talk to Claudia about him," Jenkins said.

"Are you coming to more events my sister has planned? I could bring the horse, and if you're satisfied with him, you could take him home and let her ride him and get to know him on her terms."

Jenkins nodded. "I am. That's incredibly kind of you, Your Grace. I suppose I could bring Claudia to one of the day rides, and if she likes him, take him home for a trial."

"It's all set then," Arthur said.

"Thank you again, Your Grace."

"Think nothing of it. You don't need to purchase a horse that may not do for her," Arthur replied, continuing, "How is work progressing for you on the house?"

"The workmen should be done with all the outside work by the end of the month. The inside isn't quite so bad, so it can be done at any time. I wanted the outside done before bad weather sets in."

"If you gentlemen excuse me, I will bid you both good evening."

"But the evening is still young," Graham said with a smirk. "We've got skeet and a picnic tomorrow. Ask my wife times on your way out."

"Your Grace," Jenkins said with a bow. "Again, it was a pleasure to meet you."

Nodding, Arthur turned and quickly made his way towards the door. He'd had quite enough for one night. He needed to bid Roxanne good evening and listen to her go through the next day's activities. She had moved on to another of her guests and he was about to try and get her attention without having to be dragged into another tedious conversation. But Roxanne wasn't paying him attention.

"Your sister is quite popular," a feminine voice from behind him said. "She's so likeable. What happened to you?"

He whirled around to find Lady Daphne standing before him. He swallowed hard because he was once again swept up by her beauty. Her arrogance and condescending manner were another story. "If you're trying to get a rise out of me, Lady Daphne, it won't work. Now if you'll excuse me. I was on my way home."

"Yes, yes. I suppose it is late for someone like you."

"Good evening, Lady Daphne. I'm sure we'll see each other again during the festivities. It can't be helped, unfortunately." He had no idea of how to control his feelings. On one hand, she was annoying, and on the other, he wanted to take her in his arms and kiss her silly. Perhaps with a good kiss she would refrain from her unbecoming manner.

He turned and walked away. When he crossed the threshold of the drawing room, he heard his sister as she waltzed by him and stopped him. "Are you leaving without saying good evening?"

"If I could have gotten you away from your friends, I would have. Instead, I was assaulted by Lady Daphne."

Roxanne smiled broadly. "Really, Arthur, Lady Daphne assaulting you? It looked to me more like you two were exchanging barbs."

"That too. I don't know what I've done wrong, but she needs to move on. I can understand why her parents left her behind. I'm sure she's an embarrassment everywhere they go."

"If that's what you think," she replied smugly. "You'll be here for the afternoon activities?"

"Hmmm, I'm sure I have no choice in the matter." He leaned over and kissed her on the cheek. "Tomorrow then."

"Until tomorrow," she replied, adding, "Oh, and Arthur? Don't be so glum when you return."

He turned back to her. "You're not the one who's on display. I'm afraid to say anything to any female because it will be misconstrued."

"You knew this would happen. Arthur, you're a handsome, wealthy duke looking for a wife. Until you find one or you become a hermit, this is bound to happen."

He turned and began walking toward his carriage. He raised his hand. Too bad he couldn't become a hermit; it would solve a lot of this nonsense. Climbing into the carriage, he sat back and tapped his walking stick on the roof. The carriage started to move slowly. Arthur closed his eyes for a few moments, his thoughts at first going to what he needed to accomplish before he returned to this house party. He needed to ride the gelding he spoke to Jenkins about and make sure the animal would suit a young lady such as Jenkins's sister.

His thoughts wandered to Lady Daphne and his cock began to harden. Damn her! He didn't care to play her games and wondered if perhaps she was actually attracted to him as well. He still believed he needed to test his theory by kissing her with as much passion as he could muster. It was what she needed, and he intended to take the matter in his own hands the first time he was alone with her.

What if she rejected him after such a kiss? He wouldn't give up. He would find another tactic to turn her way of thinking around to his. She seemed to like to play games, or that's what it appeared to him, and she'd been doing plenty of game playing with him. A sign she felt an attraction to him, and she was resisting his subtle advances. He wasn't sure he should try and get her alone at his sister's party, not wanting to do anything that might end up embarrassing Roxanne. He could invite her riding one morning before either proceeded to the activities. That might be the best way.

At Roxanne and Graham's, there were too many young ladies whose mothers were trying their best to garner his attention to their marriageable daughters. He didn't want to encourage any of them, but he didn't want them to think he was ignoring them either. His sister had put him in a precarious position, and she knew it.

His carriage pulled down the driveway, a sliver of a moon peeking out between the clouds. The ancient oaks that lined the drive were visible with a gentle breeze moving through their limbs. He always felt a sense of belonging when he returned home. This is where generations of his father's family had lived, and future family would reside.

EARLY THE FOLLOWING morning, Arthur walked out to the stables with Roddy at his side, deciding that having the setter go along on his ride would be an excellent move to see how the gelding reacted to dogs and other animals.

Not finding the stable master, he asked one of the young grooms to saddle the bay gelding. Moments later, the boy brought the gelding and tied him and began grooming him. Arthur went over and stroked the bay's neck, moving his hand along the bay's side and back. The animal did not react, which was a good sign he tolerated being handled without a fuss. He was a striking bay, darker than a lot, and matched by four black, longer than most stockings. He had no white except for a patch of white between his eyes. A star.

As the groom brought him outside, Arthur walked around him one last time before mounting the gelding. He whistled for Roddy and the two walked towards the meadow. He would give the bay a good workout there before heading towards a wooded area to see how he reacted, then possibly to the lake. He wanted to be sure the animal had no quirks before handing him over to Jenkins for a trial run with his sister, Claudia.

He urged the bay on as they neared the meadow. The horse did everything he was asked without a concern. He was well trained and quiet enough for inexperienced riders. Arthur then clucked to the gelding, asking for a gallop. They moved quicker, without a fuss, even with Roddy running and jumping near them.

Slowing to a walk, Arthur looked up and saw Lady Daphne's gray grazing not too far off. Would she never learn? Having ridden by any and all holes in the walls or fences, he knew someone had to have made a new point of entry. Whatever the case, unless it was a large hole, someone had to be leading the horse through said hole.

He stood for a few minutes watching the animal before turning his mount towards the wooded area before them. He wanted to check how well the gelding acted in a semi-confined area with tree limbs and brush close to them. The setter ran in front of them, occasionally veering off to chase a rabbit or other small animal. They came out at the lake with no incidents. Yes, the bay should do Jenkins's sister just fine.

Sitting, observing a pair of birds fly near the water's edge, he urged the horse to the water's edge. He hadn't had a chance to return since the men had cleaned up brush and such. Soon it would be too cold to come for any length of time. If this winter was one of the colder ones, the lake would most likely ice over. He smiled to himself at the memory of having skated on this very spot. It was one of the few things his father took the time to do with him. He felt Arthur needed to be studying and learning what he would inherit one day rather than playing. Playing was for summer and even then, on a limited schedule. Still, he and Graham managed to find plenty of time to sneak off and enjoy their time together no matter what the time of year.

He vowed to himself more than once he would never keep any son of his, even his heir, from having a rounded childhood. Play was important to grow one's imagination.

Gathering the reins, he turned the gelding back towards the stable. Arthur was confident in the bay's ability and it would be a good, gentle, sound mount for Miss Claudia. Knowing Jenkins would be present for trap shooting this afternoon, he would wait and make arrangements to deliver the gelding tomorrow. He would, in the meantime, have one of the grooms bathe and give the bay a good, thorough brushing just like they always did. Only this time with a little extra finesse.

Retracing their steps back to the meadow, Arthur noted the gray grazing until the animal heard them and then watched them curiously from afar. Roddy, seeing the intruder, went bounding over to the gray as he circled the animal a couple of times before losing interest. Arthur whistled to the setter and urged the bay into a slow gallop. He would ignore the gray's presence but would have someone once again check for any holes in the walls or fencing.

He also decided to not mention anything to Lady Daphne if she were in attendance this afternoon. He would pretend he had no knowledge of her horse trespassing on his land because she might not be able to not say something about it. She loved thinking she had the upper hand, and he would let her think she did. It would make for an interesting time, baiting her like that.

Met by one of the grooms when he arrived back at the stable, he slid off the bay and gave the boy a set of instructions for preparing the horse for a possible new home. He turned and checked on his own mount who was pawing at the ground in a paddock he'd been placed in. He'd either take Midnight out in the morning for a ride or ride him to the house party rather than take his carriage.

He walked to the paddock, and the black lifted his neck and quickly walked to where Arthur was now standing. He stroked the stallion's neck for several minutes before turning to walk to the house.

Arthur took the stairs two at a time when he arrived in the house. Thomas, his valet, had laid out a change of clothes. His plan had been to change on his own without Thomas fussing over him, but the man was too quick and began helping Arthur ready for the afternoon's events.

"I doubt I'll be attending dinner this evening, but it wouldn't hurt to have things ready in case I find myself forced to go. You know how my sister can be. Sometimes she acts as though she hears only what she wants. Her house party is a prime example."

"No problem, Your Grace. Do you know what tomorrow's activities are?"

Arthur scrubbed his hand over his face for a moment as he thought. "I believe there's a hunting party tomorrow. Not positive though."

"I'm sure it is the hunting party tomorrow and fly fishing in the river the following day," Thomas replied.

The young man had been a footman when Arthur first became duke. His father's valet, who'd served his father for decades, decided the time was perfect for him to retire. As per his father's instructions, the man received a pension and cottage for his lifetime of service. Thomas had begun working as Arthur's valet a year before, and it only made sense for him to continue in that position despite the butler suggesting an underbutler for the position. Instead, he kept Thomas.

Arthur checked himself in the mirror one last time. "Hopefully, there won't be too many ladies interested in trap shooting this afternoon. I can't tell you how disturbing it is to be on display. It's as though I were a lap dog or something. Lady Roxanne has gone too far this time."

"It's surely not that bad, Your Grace?"

"Yes, it is, but now that the party has started, perhaps everyone will act normally. I think I'm capable of choosing a wife, though you wouldn't think so with all the young ladies attending with their parents."

"Oh my," Thomas said, brushing Arthur's shoulders one last time.

"The best way to handle the situation is to not give any one lady special attention unless I feel there might be reason to get to know her better."

The valet nodded. "Be aware, women can be quite cunning when in groups."

"You're too kind, Thomas. Ruthless was more the word I was looking for. Anyway, I suppose I best return before my sister sends a party looking for me."

Arthur turned and walked out. Since it was such a glorious autumn day, he'd decided to take his curricle and drive himself. Soon the cold weather would set in and he'd have only one option. His carriage.

He arrived at the house, greeted by the butler. "Everyone has gathered for lunch outdoors just outside the gardens, Your Grace."

Arthur nodded. "Excellent. Thank you."

The French doors were open so Arthur didn't have an opportunity to gather his thoughts before joining everyone. He walked through the doors and onto the terrace. He took a deep breath and walked down the steps and across the gardens.

Upon arrival, he noticed tables set up, along with a large tent to shade the ladies from the sun. Everyone appeared to be mingling, making him wonder if they were waiting on him. Surely not. He saw Graham approaching. He had a smirk on his face which wasn't a good sign.

"Glad you could join us."

"Surely I can't be that late, if I'm late at all," Arthur responded.

"You're fine, but the young ladies have all been asking about you."

Arthur groaned. "Of course they are."

"Go say hello to Roxanne. I need to check on the equipment for this afternoon's activities. And no, you can't go with me." He grinned and walked off laughing.

He greeted several gentlemen on his way to find his sister and made a special point of speaking with Jenkins. "Jenkins, I rode the bay gelding this morning and I think he'll suit your sister well. If you'd like, I could bring him by in the morning and leave him."

"Excellent. If you'd like, you can tell her yourself. I brought her along since the weather was so nice and I thought she could use a change of scenery. The countess was quite accommodating."

Arthur nodded. "My sister's quite gracious. Be sure to introduce your sister to me and I'll be happy to answer any questions she might have." Another young lady of marriageable age he was going to have to go through the motions with. This house party wouldn't end soon enough.

"I will, Your Grace."

Looking across the lawn, Arthur noted Lady Daphne laughing and walking with the young man he'd seen her with the night before. He'd have to ask Graham or Roxanne who he was. Lady Daphne saw him looking at them and said something to him and began laughing at something he said. Arthur returned his attention to Jenkins who was still standing in front of him.

"I don't know about you, Jenkins, but I'm famished. I learned a long time ago never to eat breakfast when attending one of my sister's affairs."

Jenkins's eyes lit up. Being included to eat with a duke was probably something that Jenkins would talk about for a long time. "Yes, of course, Your Grace. I'll have to remember that about breakfast if lunch is involved."

The pair began to walk closer. Noticing it was a buffet, Arthur scanned what was available. Normally a footman or two would scramble to his side to ask him what he'd like, but his sister had obviously told them differently. He took a plate off a stack and began to make his choices. Roast chicken and ham. A variety of cheeses and fruits were available as well. He made his choices along with a chunk of crusty bread.

A footman did show them an empty table in the shade. Two glasses, eating utensils, and a bottle of wine were set in the middle. Without asking his dining partner if he was agreeable to the location, Arthur sat. Jenkins followed. They said nothing as both were hungry and enjoying the array of food they'd chosen.

Taking a sip of the red wine, he gazed around at the other guests. Roxanne spotted him and walked over to their table. "Is everything satisfactory, Your Grace?" she asked with a demure smile. "Mr. Jenkins?"

"Very nice, countess."

Feeling his sister's eyes on him, he replied quickly. "Quite nice. A nice change." He didn't elaborate for fear of offending Roxanne.

"I'm glad you like it. You must try dessert. There are several you'll like," she said.

He spotted Lady Daphne once more. "Who is that young man with Lady Daphne? I don't believe I know him."

Roxanne turned and looked before gazing back at Arthur. "That's Lady Daphne's brother, Lord Timothy. He's on break from university. In fact he mentioned the family would be in residence in a few days. Why?"

"Like I said, I didn't recognize him."

"Now you know." She paused for a moment as though collecting her thoughts. "I'll see you gentlemen shortly for trap shooting."

As she walked on to another of her guests, Arthur sat back and picked up a piece of Stilton cheese. He took a bite before enjoying a taste of wine. Stilton was one of his weaknesses. His staff made sure to always keep a wheel in the pantry. Noticing a young woman approaching, he glanced over at his dining partner. Jenkins obviously knew her as he was bidding her to join them. She shyly approached the table.

"Your Grace, this is my sister, Miss Claudia."

Arthur was already standing and took her hand. The girl was about sixteen or thereabouts. She was simply dressed in a pale-yellow day dress, which accented her mousy brown hair. "Miss Claudia, won't you join us?"

She glanced nervously at her brother before turning her attention to Arthur. "I shouldn't, Your Grace."

"I insist," he replied. "Your brother mentioned you needed a good, dependable mount and I think I have just such a horse."

She sat down in an extra chair. "Yes, that's correct, Your Grace. I'm not an overly experienced rider so it's important the animal doesn't spook at the least little thing."

It wasn't hard to tell that she was somewhat nervous. Miss Claudia was nothing special to look at, but she had the manners some of her aristocratic counterparts didn't possess. "I believe you'll like the gelding. He's a striking dark bay with four dark black socks and a star on his forehead. He's twelve, well trained and well mannered."

"He sounds quite nice," Miss Claudia replied.

Trying to put her at ease, Arthur motioned to the cheese plate. "How rude of me. Please enjoy some cheese and fruit. The Stilton is especially nice, if you like bleu cheeses. If not, I can highly recommend the cheddar."

He watched her pick up a piece of each and set them on a plate in front of her. "If you're interested, I can have him delivered, or your brother and I can accompany you on a ride so you can be sure he'll suit. If you decide to try him, you may keep him until you've made up your mind."

"That's quite accommodating, Your Grace."

Arthur nodded slightly. "Not at all. I want you to be sure you'll be happy with him."

His eyes caught several young ladies and even some mothers looking his way, talking among themselves. This was exactly why he hated these sorts of affairs. Guests, women in particular, had more than enough time to sharpen their claws for their next victim.

"Do you shoot trap, Miss Claudia?" He gazed at Jenkins who had a faint smile on his lips.

"Yes, my brother taught me since I came to the country. I quite enjoy it, though I'm still not very good at it."

"Remember what I said, Claudia. It takes practice," Jenkins said.

"Your brother is right. It is one of those activities that you get better at through practice."

"Like everything. The more you practice, the better you become," she said.

Arthur nodded and took a bite of cheese left on his plate. He noticed the young ladies were still watching him and his guests with bated breath. He stood and extended his hand to Jenkins and then his sister. "If you will excuse me, I need to talk to the earl about this afternoon's activities. I look forward to seeing you shortly at the trap shooting."

He walked across the lawn where Graham was finishing up a conversation with a guest. A couple of young ladies approached. He hadn't been fast enough.

"Your Grace, are you going to shoot trap?" one asked excitedly.

Another was quite to the point. "Who was that mousy thing, Your Grace?"

Fortunately, Roxanne rescued him. "Ladies, the earl is in need of the duke's ideas on a few matters before we start the next activity."

He nodded before turning in Graham's direction. "Ladies."

This was what he hated about social affairs. The unmarried young women were unbearable to be around. Especially in groups. There was nothing wrong with Miss Claudia. She wasn't the sort of woman he would court, but she was well read, polite, and quiet. As he continued to walk across the lawn, he heard Roxanne answer the question he thought didn't need him to answer.

"That is Miss Claudia Jenkins. She is in need of a riding horse and the duke has one that will suit her perfectly, not that it's any of your business."

He grinned. Leave it to his sister to let that gaggle know their behavior was inappropriate. If their mothers couldn't keep them in line, Roxanne would.

Meeting with Graham, they discussed who would go when.

Graham decided that as host, he would go first, then whoever volunteered to go next. Arthur would let a few go before him before taking his turn. He noticed Lady Daphne standing to one side alone, observing the setup of the trap equipment. She saw him looking in her direction and made an exaggerated curtsey at him before gathering her skirts and walking in their direction.

"Lady Daphne," Graham said, taking her gloved hand.

Arthur nodded deeply. "Lady Daphne."

"Are we about ready to go, gentlemen?" she asked.

"We are. Are you interested in taking a turn?" Arthur inquired.

"Yes, very much so," came her reply. "Women are going to abide by the same rules as the men, aren't they?"

"Yes," Graham said.

"Perfect. I assume we're about ready to start?"

Graham nodded. "Yes."

"I look forward to the competition." She nodded and turned, walking off where she found some chairs and sat down to wait for her turn.

Picking up a rifle, Graham grinned. "This ought to prove to be interesting. The lady has no fear and seems to have quite the competitive spirit."

"Yes, and she has a foul-mouthed parrot, don't forget. Everything she does is for shock value. It'll be interesting to see if things change once her parents arrive."

"I can't imagine her parents allowing it. Perhaps some time around her family will prove to be the thing she needs."

There were guests beginning to gather, so Graham turned his attention to them. The afternoon was perfect for trap. There was not so much as a breeze, which would make things easier, especially for the ladies who would be participating. Graham explained the rules and walked over to where participants would shoot from. He loaded his rifle, got into position, and yelled at his man to pull. Fortunately, he hit the clay projectile. This was something Graham enjoyed and practiced quite a lot. It wouldn't have done any good for the host to have missed.

The men followed, with most hitting their target. Arthur was about to take his turn when Lady Daphne came forward. She was the first lady to do so and he hoped she was as good as she bragged. On the other hand, if she missed more than once, she would probably return home to pout, making some sort of silly excuse for her poor performance.

She checked out the gun handed to her before stepping forward. Taking her aim, she shouted for the target to be released. A round of applause followed as she hit her mark. She turned to the crowd and, once again smiling, she curtsied.

"Your Grace, I believe you're next," she said, handing a man her shotgun. "Good luck."

He hit his target square on and handed the shotgun back to one of Graham's men. Turning to face the large group, he bowed and walked over to the table where the men could indulge in a glass of whiskey. After which Arthur was going to find somewhere quiet to sit but noticed the usual group of young ladies watching him. He was going to turn away, but they called after him.

"Your Grace, where did you learn to shoot so well?" one of them called out.

He turned. "My father was the one who first introduced me when I was a boy."

"Of course, I should have known. You must have been a quick study."

He didn't feel a reply was needed, which just brought up something they wanted to know.

"Isn't that just so unladylike for a young woman to shoot? I don't know how they expect to land a husband acting like that."

"I'm sorry, but I don't feel the same way. I believe if a woman is comfortable shooting, she should engage in whichever activity it is. Times are changing."

A blonde whose name he couldn't recall spoke up. "You would be comfortable with your duchess participating in men's sports?"

"Yes, of course, depending on which activity it might be. I would believe the lady, whoever she might be, would choose wisely."

A small group of older women approached. Obviously, some of the young ladies' mothers. "Your Grace, I hope they aren't bothering you. I know you are needed to help out your brother-in-law."

"No, not at all, but I should greet some of the gentlemen who've just joined us. Ladies."

Thank goodness the mother had come to his rescue. If Roxanne said anything to him, he might mention his thoughts on the young ladies. He had decided not to partake in dinner this evening, promising his sister he would attend her blasted masquerade party later in the week. He dreaded it, but if he went to what she deemed more important, she wouldn't care if he skipped some of the other dinners. Playing charades or cards after dinner was not something he cared for. Not in a situation like this. He would get trapped into playing with single girls and Roxanne would do nothing to rescue him.

He looked back at the shooting match and saw that Miss Claudia and her brother were about to take their turns. He was going to get closer but thought it best if he stay where he was. He didn't want to make her nervous since she seemed shier than most of the others. Mr. Jenkins took his turn first, hitting the clay with precise accuracy.

Miss Claudia stepped forward to take her turn. He noticed that same group of girls were off to one side watching, eager, he was sure, to try and make her fail. He looked around for Roxanne but didn't see her. As Miss Claudia took her aim, Arthur neared a little closer just in time to watch her smash the target into a hundred bits. Instinct told him to clap and congratulate her, not caring how it might look to others.

CHAPTER SEVEN

Having missed the day before because of rain, Arthur was glad to see the sun peeking around a bank of clouds. He knew the moment he set foot in that house he would be back on display, and unless the gentlemen were playing billiards, he had no interest in other activities. He used this morning to deliver the bay to Miss Claudia.

Arthur was awestruck on how easily there was a bond forming between the bay and Miss Claudia. He followed as she led the horse to the stables, the bay walking by her side. Peter, who'd been standing speaking with one of his grooms, smiled and neared his sister. "What do you think?" Peter asked his sister.

"He's very well mannered."

"Quite a beauty for a bay," Peter said.

"Isn't he?" Claudia asked her brother.

"If you have any questions, don't hesitate to let me know," Arthur said.

"Does he have a name, Your Grace?" Claudia asked, stroking the bay's velvety nose.

"Walter," he replied.

"Well, Walter and I are going in the stables to find his stall and paddock. I'm sure he'd like to settle in. Thank you again, Your Grace."

He nodded. "Perhaps you and your brother will join in on the ride my sister has planned. It would be a perfect opportunity for the two of you. You and Walter, I mean."

"I believe we will. You're right—it would be an excellent opportunity for her to ride in a crowd," Jenkins said.

"I look forward to it. If you'll excuse me. I promised my sister I'd attend this afternoon's activities," Arthur replied.

Everyone said their goodbyes, and Arthur felt as if a huge weight had been lifted from his shoulders. Walter had a home where he was sure his new mistress would pop in to see him with apples and other treats.

Heading to Graham's and Roxanne's home, he looked up at the deep blue sky. Large puffy clouds lazily meandered by. He turned into their drive and walked Midnight the rest of the way. Handing the reins to a stable boy, Arthur went in search of his sister.

He found her on the terrace, after having eaten their luncheon there. It was evident by the cheese and fruit still being enjoyed. He approached slowly. As Roxanne came toward him, he couldn't help but notice a few of the women were going to great lengths not to make eye contact.

"I apologize for being late," he said.

"That's quite all right. The men went for a ride, so since you missed that, I thought you could entertain us by playing the piano. Quite a few of the women are going inside. Some will go to their rooms to rest, and some will have time on their hands."

"So you want me to play piano for them?"

"If you wouldn't mind. You are a talented pianist, and you should share that with more people."

"Thank you for the compliment. I don't see why I should be left to entertain your guests."

She smiled sweetly. "You owe me. I invited an array of young ladies and their parents in hopes of you finding someone who might catch your fancy, but you've yet to spend any extra time with any of them except for Miss Claudia and Lady Daphne."

"I beg to differ with you. I've tried, but I'm failing as some of these women need a refresher course on how to act at situations such as this."

"Then this will be a perfect chance to get to know them. Everyone loves music," Roxanne said.

"I'd rather not. If you don't mind, I'd prefer to return home and practice some more before doing it in front of an audience."

"Very well. I'll allow it this once, but you will come for dinner. It shall be a buffet style, so it's a little less formal."

"I'll return for dinner and promise to stay and find an activity to participate in. I might even play for your guests."

Roxanne gave him a curious look. "You say you refuse to play now but might during this evening's events?"

"Yes."

"Arthur, have you ever been told you're difficult?"

"No."

She stood, giving him an out to leave. "By the way, Lady Daphne's family have arrived, and they will be attending tonight."

"Interesting. I wonder what her father will think of her behavior."

"I think you'll see a side of her never before seen."

"How's that?" Arthur asked.

"She'll be quieter and more respectful. I understand her father wants to see her married."

"All fathers want to see their daughters married. Hopefully with a decent man." Arthur cut his statement short. He reminded himself he was sure his sister had never forgiven their father for forcing her to marry at a young age. It had been a marriage made in hell.

"I agree, but hopefully we've passed arranged marriages and now couples have a choice on who should be their spouse."

"Exactly."

"Go before you get entrapped by one of the younger guests. I'll see you tonight."

"Thank you." He bent down and kissed her on the cheek

before turning and walking quickly through the house and the front door.

Luckily for Arthur, he ran into no one while leaving. He'd been afraid of running into one of the young guests. That would have meant being polite and conversing with them for a few moments. That scenario could lead to more young ladies joining them.

Knowing Midnight needed a good run, he found a trail off the road. Technically on Graham's property, it was a convenient route the pair had used many a time. As grown men, they still used it. He urged the stallion to the opening until they made it through the brush and tree lined path until they came upon one of his meadows. If he'd turned left, he would have ended up deeper into Graham's land. Arthur nudged the stallion into a canter before giving him the reins and letting the animal pick up speed.

Midnight ran faster and faster as the wind swept across Arthur's face. He loved the cooling breeze on his skin. It was an escape from reality. As a young boy, Arthur had done the exact same thing, many times. As they neared the orchard, he picked up the reins and slowed the stallion down. He would let the horse rest here for a few minutes while he found some apples to give Midnight as a treat.

Pulling a knife out of his boot, Arthur began slicing up an apple he'd procured from a nearby tree. He cut the fruit into chunks to offer the stallion. Midnight greedily took each slice offered from Arthur's hand until they were all done. Slipping the knife back in its place, he continued on to the stables.

Once they arrived, he handed the stallion over to one of the stable boys and handed the boy an extra apple. "See he gets a good grooming. You can give him this apple and extra rations later when you feed. I'll be needing the carriage around seven this evening."

"Yes, Your Grace."

Arthur patted the black on his neck and walked away. He

took the path leading to the gardens and terrace. The sun was warming on his back as he continued walking. He needed to make the most of the afternoon before he had to return to Graham and Roxanne's house party.

He walked into the house, poured himself a whiskey before he found himself in the music room where the piano sat. He sat down on the bench, took a sip of whiskey before finding a sheet of music he thought he'd practice on, playing some scales and easy pieces to warm up for the difficult piece he'd chosen.

Beethoven was one of his favorite composers along with Mozart, though he found his music a little on the somber side. He began with one of Beethoven's sonatas. He played it twice, making sure it was perfect. Another of the composer's sonatas was captivating with Arthur's interpretation. Once he finished with the two, he took a long sip of the whiskey and began with one of Mozart's lesser-known pieces. After playing it through several times, he deemed himself satisfied with his playing.

He raised to his full height, whiskey in hand, and sat down on one of the musical themed chairs. His mother had redecorated the music room, making it far more inviting than the way the previous duchess had done it. Before he knew what happened, he fell asleep, waking up to the sound of his valet trying to rouse him.

"Your Grace, you must bathe and change before you return to the festivities."

"Yes, I remember. I guess I was tired and fell asleep."

"You've been quite busy. I'm surprised you haven't done it more than now."

"Me too. It's not often I have time on my hands. I'll be up in a few minutes, so go ahead and draw the hot water."

"Your Grace," he replied and left the room.

Still seated, Arthur rubbed his hands through his hair and then beard. He found himself once again thinking of Lady Daphne. He imagined she wasn't happy about her parents' visit. The visit would cramp her lifestyle severely after being allowed to stay on her own. He bit back a laugh at the sight of her, parents and brother in tow, and how she would sulk because she had grown accustomed to her own freedom.

PEOPLE WERE GATHERED in the ballroom which had been turned into a place to host the dinner buffet. Tables were placed about one end of the room with the buffet against the far wall, where staff could easily replenish dishes without disturbing the guests. At the other end of the room, there were orange and lemon trees placed like a small grove.

Looking around the room, he saw Graham speaking with Lady Daphne's father, Viscount Andover, and an older gentleman whom he did not recognize.

"Are you ready to lead us to dinner?" Roxanne said, standing next to him. "Thank you again for doing this."

"My pleasure. That's what brothers are for. Who is that older gentleman with Viscount Andover and Graham? I don't recognize him."

"Shocking. He is Cecil Black, Earl of Bath. I wonder if Daphne's father has found who he considers the perfect man to marry his rebellious daughter."

"He is about twenty years her senior by looking at him."

Roxanne stifled a giggle. "Yes, at least."

"Where is Lady Daphne? Did she accompany her parents and intended?"

"Yes, and her mother won't let her out of her sights. So wherever her mother is, you'll find Lady Daphne."

Arthur stood and looked on in disbelief as though someone had cut a knife through his heart. His eyes wandered through the room as people were beginning to gather for dinner. Lady Daphne and her mother approached the men. The earl appeared delighted with his future countess and Lady Daphne had a scowl on her face that read displeasure.

"Are you ready? Graham's on his way."

He went and picked out many choices. Roxanne had outdone herself with the variety of food. As he left in search of a table, he was held up by a couple of gentlemen wanting his opinion on an estate matter. When he excused himself, he found a table which was smaller than the others.

As he was heading in that direction, a very familiar voice called out to him. "Your Grace, would you care to dine with us?" He looked down and saw Lady Daphne sitting at a round table with her family and the earl. She was pleading with him through her eyes. She wanted to be saved, and something told him he needed to help her.

"I'm sure His Grace has other guests to see," her father said sternly.

"No, no. I'd love to join you. It's been a while since I've seen you, Andover."

"It has," the viscount replied.

Arthur sat in the spare chair while a footman poured a glass of wine. He gazed about the table and saw Lady Daphne keeping her eyes on her plate. The mood with everyone else seemed to be forced, making him wonder if he'd interrupted a private conversation that Lady Daphne wanted no part of.

"Lady Daphne, how is Sam doing these days? Still talking?"

"How do you know about that blasted parrot?" Andover asked.

Her eyes were pleading with him, and he wasn't going to embarrass her. "One of your horses seemed to prefer our meadow, and one morning I managed to catch him and take him home. I was waiting for Lady Daphne to tell her what the gray was doing, and Sam greeted me."

"That was very kind of you to do, Your Grace," the viscountess said.

"I was also able to find a hole in one of my walls I had no knowledge of, so the gray ended up being useful."

"Everything turned out for the best," Andover said.

"Indeed," Arthur replied.

Spearing a piece of Scottish salmon, Arthur was interrupted by the earl. "Your father and I went to university together. We never saw much of each other after university. He went to the continent for his grand tour and I went to America, where I stayed a good number of years."

"Your father didn't mind you staying on?"

"His brother owned a thriving import business, so my father looked at it as a good opportunity to expand my knowledge of businesses. One day I would take the earldom, and when I did, I would be more well-rounded."

"Your father seems like he was a very bright man," Andover said.

"I'd like to think so." The earl looked across the table at him. "I understand you're looking for your duchess, Your Grace? I am seeking a woman to be my new countess."

"I keep an open mind. I feel I'll know her when I meet her. You said new countess?"

"Yes, yes, my Margaret died two years ago. I met her in New York and we moved back here. Unfortunately, during the voyage she succumbed to some sort of ailment she picked up on the ship and never made it to England."

"My condolences," Arthur murmured.

Dinner conversation continued. The viscount and viscountess kept him entertained while the earl blatantly attempted to carry on a personal conversation with Lady Daphne, who looked incredibly bored. Why shouldn't she? The man was at least old enough to be her grandfather or older father, and they had little in common. The situation reminded him of what their father had done to Roxanne. Arranging a marriage for her to an older man whose only interest in her was for her to produce children for him. Lady Daphne was too good for that sort of situation.

Feeling a hand squeezing his shoulder, Arthur looked up and saw Graham standing there. He'd come to the rescue. "I hope you don't mind, but I need my brother-in-law's expertise with some of the men's games."

"Not at all," Andover replied. "I understand billiards is going to be played."

"You heard correctly."

Lady Daphne's head rose. "Billiards? How wonderful! I love billiards."

The earl placed his hand on her arm, garnering a dark look from Lady Daphne. "Billiards is not for young ladies, my dear. I imagine you'll be playing whist or some other card game."

Suddenly, she stood. "If everyone will excuse me. I find myself in need of some air."

Arthur stood. "Lady Daphne."

He watched her flee to the other side of the room where she slid through the open door and onto the terrace. Hopefully she'd get her reprieve from her overbearing family. Knowing Graham was standing there waiting for him, he left the three at the table to go help Graham with whatever he couldn't do on his own.

"Roxanne mentioned she understood Lady Daphne's parents were looking to marry her to the Earl of Bath. That he would be able to tame her. Sounds like what Roxanne went through."

"She said as much earlier. He'll ruin the girl's spirit."

Arthur and Graham were about to the ballroom door when something made Arthur look back. When he did, he saw the Earl of Bath hurrying to the door leading to the terrace. The earl was obviously going to try and engage in conversation with Lady Daphne in hopes to convince her to marry him. Something in his gut told him otherwise.

"I'll catch up with you shortly. There's something needing my attention."

He turned and headed to the terrace before Graham could utter a word. While on his way, he acknowledged people who spoke to him, but didn't stop. He had to get to her before the earl tried to do something despicable.

When he walked out on the terrace, he could see the Earl of

Bath sternly speaking to her. Lady Daphne seemed to be trying to distance herself from him, but he wasn't allowing it. His hand grabbed her upper arm and began to try and force her towards the stairs leading to the gardens. She was having none of it, and Arthur heard her tell him she did not wish to walk in the gardens with him.

Arthur approached. "I believe the lady said she didn't wish to go to the gardens."

"This is none of your affair, Your Grace. The chit is to become my wife as soon as the arrangements can be made."

Lady Daphne pulled against his arm. "There's no way in hell I'll ever marry you," she hissed.

"I think the lady has made her opinion on the matter known. I suggest you unhand her. Now."

Reluctantly, Bath let loose of his hold on her arm. Immediately, Lady Daphne headed to the stairs leading into the gardens as quickly as she could, leaving him to deal with the earl.

Black looked in the direction of the stairs. "I need to go after her."

"You'll do no such thing. She made it quite clear she didn't wish to be around you. Might I suggest you let her have some time to herself."

"Yes, of course. I can always show her the error of her ways another time. I think I'll head inside for a brandy." He gave Arthur a dark look, showing Arthur his disdain for him having interrupted his plan before he walked back to the house.

Standing and looking down into the gardens, Arthur quietly waited. He peered down at the door to see if Black was lurking, waiting for him to leave so he could come and pursue his game. Looking in the direction of the stairs, he made his decision and headed down into the gardens.

He walked the path looking for Lady Daphne. Finally, he found her sitting on a bench. She'd been crying, her eyes red, and she was sniffling. He reached into his pocket and pulled out a square and passed it to her.

"Thank you."

"You really don't wish to marry him?"

"He's an old toad. I can't believe my father would consider someone like him."

"You knew nothing about this arrangement?"

She shook her head. "No, nothing until my parents returned with the earl in tow."

"I'm afraid he's going to ruin you to ensure the marriage since you've voiced your distaste for him."

"I think the same thing," she replied.

Arthur took in a deep breath. "Is there anyone you could go stay with? Someone your parents wouldn't think to look? A girlfriend, perhaps?"

"No one comes to mind, Your Grace."

"Arthur," he said. "I think we know each other well enough you can address me by my name. May I call you Daphne?"

"Yes, I would like that, Your Grace… um, Arthur." She gave him a coy smile.

"If I go back inside, my father will be angry. When we arrive home, I'm sure he'll lock me and Sam in my room until I agree to this arranged marriage."

He glanced at her before speaking. "Lady Roxanne, my sister's first marriage was similar to what your father is wanting to do with you. She was miserable up until he died. Her husband sent her to one of his lesser estates after their son was born with problems. It's not something I wish to see you forced to endure."

"That's awful for her. I refuse to be forced, I'm just not sure what to do."

He rose and extended his hand. "Come, let's walk." She tucked her hand into the crook of his arm as they walked. He had to command his feelings to stay at bay. If he didn't, he would find himself doing things he was saving her from.

Finally, he did stop. She gazed up at him. Arthur finally lowered his head and kissed her gently. She'd been through enough; he didn't want to scare her off. She responded to his kiss which was more than he could have hoped for.

"I do have a proposal that would send the earl packing."

"What?"

"We marry. I have a cousin who is vicar of a parish. He could help me procure a special license and marry us."

"But we barely like each other," she said with an odd smile.

Arthur smiled at her. "I'm sure we'll grow to love and respect each other as time goes on."

"I'm sorry, Your Grace… Arthur, while your offer sounds tempting, I'm afraid I have to decline."

Dumbfounded, he quickly regained his senses. "Why? You seemed to enjoy our kiss."

"Yes, it was nice, but I want to marry someone on my terms. No arranged marriage, no pity marriage. I want to choose my husband."

"I see. You are aware that if you return to the house, your father will take matters in hand, and you will probably find yourself locked in your room until your marriage to the earl."

She arched her brow. "My father can try to lock me in my room, but he won't succeed."

"You're playing with fire, Daphne."

"I'll be fine. You'll see."

"Very well. In that case, I think you should return by yourself. I'll follow shortly. That way there'll be no thought that anything occurred."

She nodded and stood on her toes, kissing him on the cheek. "You're a wonderful man, Arthur. I'm sure you will find your duchess soon."

Arthur grunted and watched as she walked away from him and towards the stair leading to the terrace. He knew if he sat back and did nothing, she would be wed to the earl. He needed to come up with a plan before this happened.

CHAPTER EIGHT

TWO DAYS LATER, Arthur found himself at the viscount's front door. He hadn't returned to the festivities after his disastrous attempt at helping Lady Daphne. He made his excuses for not going yesterday, and today it was raining and he certainly wasn't into a day of parlor games.

He'd sent word ahead to the viscount that he would be coming rather than simply showing up. It was his intention to inform Andover of his feelings for his daughter and his wish to court her. His only competitor was the earl, and given he outranked the Earl of Bath, in both title and finances, Andover might be more open. His daughter marrying a wealthy duke far outdid what the earl had to offer.

The butler showed him into the drawing room, telling him the viscount would be with him shortly. The first thing Arthur noticed as he looked about the room was that Sam, the parrot, was missing. The viscount probably didn't want the bird near strangers considering Sam's colorful language.

Hearing the door open once again, Arthur turned to see Andover entering the room. "Your Grace, what can I do for you?"

"I have a matter I wish to discuss with you. It's of a rather delicate nature."

"Go on," the viscount urged. He walked over to a sideboard and poured two whiskeys. He offered one to Arthur. "Why don't we sit?"

"It's in regard to your daughter, Lady Daphne."

"I thought as much."

Taking a sip of whiskey, Arthur looked the viscount in the eyes. "I would like your permission to court Lady Daphne."

"Does my daughter know your intentions?"

"I can't be sure. I've let her know my feelings and desire to court her, but as you know, your daughter is a complicated young lady."

"She is that," Andover said with a smile. "She can be exhausting, and she's my daughter. You do know the Earl of Bath has shown an interest to marry Lady Daphne."

"I do, and I think that would be disastrous. A marriage to the earl would break Lady Daphne's spirit."

"My daughter needs a firm hand. She's been coddled far too long."

"I'm sure I'm up to the task."

Arthur watched as Andover shifted in his seat and polished off his whiskey. He set the glass on a table next to him. "The earl has left for London to secure a special license while he conducts business. He'll be gone at least a fortnight. When he returns, he'll be expecting to marry Lady Daphne."

He wasn't expecting this. He'd hoped the earl would have admitted defeat and moved on, but apparently that wasn't the case. How could he convince the viscount otherwise?

"Would you be amenable to my escorting Lady Daphne to the masquerade party? Perhaps one or two more times before the Earl of Bath returns?"

"I'm not sure that would be wise. Everyone knows the earl's interest in my daughter." Andover sat there, his eyes closed. He was realizing he had made a pact with the devil himself.

"I could pay more attention to her for the remainder of the house party. I could take her riding, have her for dinner, those sorts of things. No one would have to know of these other times spent together."

Finally, Andover nodded. "Very well. I agree. Ask her to

dance more than is customary. That should help your cause."

"Thank you," Arthur replied. There was a glimmer of hope. He would now just need to show her the error of her ways if she married the old geezer.

"Don't thank me yet. You've got a lot of work to do if you want to win her over to your side."

Arthur arched a brow. "She's not actually considering marriage to the earl?"

"Absolutely not. She has been most vocal about not wanting me to choose who she marries."

"Of course. She made it well known to me that she would choose who she married."

The rain seemed to be getting heavier because it was hitting the French doors at an angle, causing both men to look over. Arthur knew he needed to get back home. The more the rain continued, the worse the roads would become.

"By the way, where is Sam? The house is quiet without him."

"That foul mouthed parrot is with Daphne. I told her I wouldn't tolerate him being loose and walking through the house cursing."

Arthur stood and rose to his full height. "Thank you for seeing me. I'll call on Lady Daphne another time or at my sister's for sure. The weather seems to be getting worse and I should head home."

"If you'd like to see her for a moment before you leave, I'll arrange it."

He nodded. It would be nice to see her since their ill-fated night in the garden. "I'd like that."

Andover left the room for a few minutes, returning with his daughter. Daphne smiled, seeing who it was. She was dressed in a moss-green day dress with darker green piping on the hem, sleeves, and bodice. She looked every part the goddess he knew her to be.

"Lady Daphne."

"Your Grace. It's a nasty day to be calling on people."

"It's gotten worse since I left home. I came by to speak with your father. Did he tell you why?"

She glanced at her father and then him. "No."

"I thought it best coming from you, Your Grace."

Nodding, Arthur watched her to see if he could tell what she was thinking. She was too good at hiding her feelings, even from him. "I came to ask your father if I may court you."

"What about the earl?"

"The duke is going to court you until he returns," Andover said. "At that time, you must make a decision of who you want to marry."

"Don't you think people will think it odd?"

"I don't think we'll be so blatant. I'll call on you to go riding, or for dinner. At the masquerade party, the final night of the house party, I'll ask you to dance more than twice. We'll muddle through it."

"Very well. I'll agree to this, but only because I refuse to marry that old toad."

"Daphne!" her father said sternly.

"I won't apologize because that's what he is, and I can't believe you agreed to it. What are you doing? Are you having second thoughts about the earl?"

Andover nodded. "I suppose I might be."

"Well, Your Grace, I suppose I should be looking forward to our encounters."

"I thought perhaps I might call on you tomorrow?"

She looked at her father for advice. "We're not going to the house party until dinner tomorrow. Unless you'd like to go with the ladies for a trip to the village."

"No. I'll look forward to seeing you tomorrow, Your Grace," she replied with a curtsey.

That sounded like sarcasm coming from her lips, but he took it in stride. He was sure he'd get a good tongue lashing tomorrow. She didn't like feeling she wasn't in control.

"Until then. I should get going in case this storm decides to get worse."

Andover and his daughter walked him to the front door where the three said their good-byes. Not hearing the door close as he hurriedly walked down the stairs, he looked back in the direction of the door as he approached his carriage. Lady Daphne was standing there alone with her shawl pulled tightly around her. When he caught her looking at him, she retreated into the house, closing the door behind her.

A few moments later he was in his carriage, heading back to his estate. The sky was a dark gray and the rain still coming down at an angle as he watched it from the comfort of his coach. He felt as though a giant weight had been lifted from his chest. Now all he had to do was make all this work to bring Daphne over to his side. He knew she was stubborn and arrogant, thinking she was above others. If he could show her he was on her side, things would go so much easier.

He was certain it was mostly an act. She was a strong young woman with her own opinions and there were certain things about which she did not want decisions being made for her. Marriage was one of them, and he had no intention of standing aside and watching her enter a loveless, arranged marriage like his sister had.

He would start with sending her flowers and other trinkets to let her know she was on his mind. What woman didn't like to receive flowers? Other things they could do before it got too cold was riding. He had the feeling she was quite an expert when it came to horses.

A large clap of thunder made him come to his senses and back to reality as the carriage turned down the drive heading to the manor. He'd planned to go back to the party this afternoon, but with the weather, he changed his mind. Roxanne would understand. As long as he made it to the special events, she was fine, and she knew not to push him.

Moments later, he was handing his hat and greatcoat to the butler, who in turn passed it off to a waiting footman. The air, he decided, had gotten cooler, so he thought to go to his study and finish going over the estate manager's reports. His study was one room in the house he knew to be warm on days like this.

He closed the door behind him as he entered the dark paneled room. A fire was going, making things quite comfortable. He tried to concentrate on the figures before him, but the numbers kept blurring together. He couldn't get her out of his mind; she was distracting him from his work. Maybe that was a good thing. Much of his time was devoted to the estate and other business interests. He always assumed his duchess would just fall in his lap with no effort from him. Was this what was happening with Daphne?

LADY DAPHNE SAT at the table with her parents having dinner. Of course, her brother wasn't subject to the same set of rules she was. He was a man, and men could do whatever they wanted to do. She listened as her parents were having a discussion on her father's sudden change of heart regarding both the earl and the duke. Personally, she despised both men, the earl more so. He was old and looking for a woman to replace his late countess. The duke was seemingly more interested in her than the earl was. The earl was all about money and seeing that his wife would be compliant with his wishes. She kept remembering the duke, Arthur telling her about his sister's experience in such a marriage.

"Papa, why did you accept the earl's offer of marriage so quickly?"

The viscount looked at his daughter for a moment, as though trying to choose his words carefully. Her mother watched, looking at her daughter first, then her husband.

"Your mother and I agreed it was past time for you to marry. You've had two failed seasons and there's no need for another. I thought arranging a marriage for you was the best way to secure a husband for you."

Daphne speared a piece of beef from her plate as she waited for her father to continue. "By marrying me off to the highest bidder?"

"It's nothing like that, silly girl," the viscountess said.

"No? Please enlighten me."

"I've done some digging on the earl since he first approached me about marrying you. I don't like what I found."

"So you let him go to London to procure a special license?"

"No. It was all his doing. I never agreed to anything with the man. I told him I would consider his offer."

"All right, but what about the duke?"

"His Grace came to me and told me about his feelings for you and asked me if he could court you. He impressed me so much I gave him permission," the viscount said.

"Yes, the duke will do splendidly in Parliament. He's a great speaker," Daphne said. She tried not to roll her eyes at what had just come out of her mouth.

The viscountess picked up her wine glass and took a sip. "Tell her what you found out about the earl."

"I did some research into the earl. He's in dire straits for money due to his gambling and drinking habits. He's sold everything that's not entailed. That's why your dowry is so important to him."

"Let's say if you granted the earl his marriage proposal, and he got my dowry, what's to say he won't spend that as fast as he can?"

"I'm quite sure he would spend it all."

Daphne stared at her plate one last time before having a footman remove it. "What about His Grace?"

"The exact opposite of the earl. He doesn't need the money. In fact, he mentioned he would take the dowry and save it for any daughters you and he might have. That they're taken care of should they not marry."

"Impressive."

"Yes, it is," her mother said.

Daphne smiled. "There's only one thing."

"What's that?" her father asked.

"You forget that I dislike the duke."

"I think you'll change your mind as you spend more time together."

Drat! Her father knew her better than she knew herself. She already had changed her opinion of the duke to some extent, but she certainly wouldn't let anyone know. Arthur needed to work for it. He needed to do all the things a man should do when courting, and then some.

"That remains to be seen."

"You'll make a superb duchess and make the duke proud. You're beautiful, well educated, compassionate, and kind," the viscountess said proudly.

"You always see the best, never the worst."

Her mother reached out and covered her daughter's hand with her own. "Don't overthink so much. Enjoy the duke's company, and if it's meant to be, you will know."

She glanced at her father, who was enjoying a piece of lemon cake as he listened to his wife and daughter.

"What if the Earl of Bath returns early?"

"That's highly unlikely. If he does, I'll handle everything."

Daphne shook her head. "He's not going to give up easily. He's quite determined to have me as his bride."

"No, he won't. I will handle the earl, no worries from you."

She sighed. "Very well. I trust you to make the right decisions. You always do."

The viscount smiled at her as he continued to enjoy his dessert. Daphne saw her father's good spirits as a perfect time to discuss one or two things with him.

"Papa, would it be possible to move Sam back into the drawing room? Not loose, of course, not unless he's supervised. He could stay in his large cage. He just seems so lonely in my room. You know how he loves being around people."

Her father sat back in his chair and tapped the tabletop with his fingers. "I will take it under consideration. But if I decide to allow his return, he will stay caged if you're not here to properly oversee him."

"What about if I have guests? The ladies would be mortified at his language," Daphne's mother said.

"If it's a small group of ladies, you could host them in the parlor. Or the blue drawing room," Daphne said.

The viscountess nodded. Daphne knew she hadn't considered that. By doing so, she showed her mother there were other options. "Yes, either of those would work."

"See? The two of you can work things out without me," her father chuckled.

"Of course we can," her mother said. "Once this house party is done, I should like to have a small dinner for our neighbors."

The viscount grunted and reached for a glass of port sitting in front of him. "Let us recover from this first one."

"But of course," the countess replied. She glanced over in Daphne's direction with a look of triumph. Daphne, in turn, smiled knowingly at her mother.

Taking a fork, Daphne cut a piece of cake and put it in her mouth before her mother could protest. The countess was of the belief that young ladies needed to be more aware of what they ate. Daphne didn't have that problem, but her mother still watched to make sure she didn't overindulge.

Knowing her mother was watching her, she took three bites before pushing the plate back. She reached for her wine glass and finished the remaining contents. Surely her parents would be ready to move to the drawing room. Neither budged so she took her own initiative.

"If I may be excused, I would like to decide on what to wear to tomorrow evening's function."

"Of course, my dear," her mother replied. "The new apricot silk gown would be perfect."

Daphne nodded her head as she left the room, leaving her

parents to discuss whatever worldly matters interested them. She took long steps to the staircase, taking two steps at a time. As she opened the door to her chamber, Daphne was greeted by Sam, her beloved macaw.

There was no holding the parrot back. "Bloody hell! Sam good boy."

"You're sure about that, Sam?" Daphne scratched the feathers on his neck.

"Sam like."

Daphne turned and walked to the adjoining room where gowns and dresses were held. She expected her lady's maid to be there, but the room was vacant of anyone. The apricot gown was already pulled, waiting for the wrinkles to be removed. It would be a good choice, but Daphne wasn't convinced it was the right gown for the occasion.

There was a sapphire silk gown which was her initial choice. It was elegant yet daring. The color brought out her hair color. It would definitely catch the duke's attention. She couldn't believe she even cared what the duke thought, but she found herself in a precarious situation. Marry the earl or Arthur. The choice wasn't hard. The duke was right; the earl wanted a young wife to bear him more children and accompany him to social events. The thought of the toad touching her made her shiver. The duke was handsome, took very good care of himself, was educated, and was concerned about what would happen if she married the earl.

She still couldn't believe her father didn't just tell the earl no. The earl, though, wasn't one to be told no by anyone. He would return from London with a special license and demand the two would wed. That's how the toad thought. Everything revolved around him.

At least with Arthur, they had some of the same interests. He was a delight to talk with, though she would never let him know that. Dukes were notably snobbish because of their rank. They had every reason to be, but one thing she'd noticed about Arthur was that he wasn't a typical duke. Certainly, he could play the duke card when it suited him, but for the most part, he was down to earth and approachable.

She brought herself out of her thoughts and focused on the deep-blue gown. Yes, this would work. She would shine above every other young lady hoping to gain the attention of Arthur. A duke certainly would be a fine catch for any lady but he seemed to have eyes only for her.

Daphne wandered out to her bed where her night rail was laying waiting for her. A warm robe had been placed next to it. She began to take her clothes off when Lydia rushed in to help.

"I apologize, milady. I should have been here."

"Lydia, you can't be here all the time. Even you need a break."

"Thank you, milady."

"I've decided to wear the sapphire gown tomorrow evening."

Lydia cocked her head at the change. "It's certainly beautiful and eye-catching."

"It is, isn't it?"

The maid nodded and began to unlace Daphne's corset. No further words were said unless necessary. Daphne walked into the sitting area to talk with Sam before she put him in his cage for the night. The macaw knew his routine and, like most nights, he was either in his cage or sitting on top waiting for her. Tonight he was in his cage. He was so smart he'd pulled the door closed with his beak.

"Good night, Sam," she said as she bolted the door shut on the cage and covered it with a large piece of fabric to keep out the nighttime drafts.

"Sam sleep now."

She smiled as she turned away. Moments later, she climbed into bed, hoping she'd be able to sleep sooner than later. It was hard to simply turn off the thoughts in her head. There was so much going on in her life. She had one man who thought if he obtained a special license, her father would sign off on a marriage to his only daughter. Then there was the duke, a man she couldn't stand to be in the same room with. Now she found herself drawn to Arthur and wanting to spend more time with him. Her father had given them a way to do that very thing by agreeing to let the duke court her. She'd only had one man court her, and that was two years ago. His name had been John Coe and his family members of the gentry. It all ended abruptly when she and her mother ran into him at a shop in London while escorting another young woman. He had been tongue tied and embarrassed. It was the last time Daphne ever saw him.

Tomorrow evening would be a true challenge. The duke would dance with her more than what was customary. Tongues would be wagging by the time the evening was over. The masquerade would be the final social event at the house party. Two days before everyone would meet in the ballroom with masks on. Everyone trying to figure out who was who, which wasn't hard to do. Those who opted for more elegant masks were nearly impossible to figure out.

Would he kiss her again? Tomorrow evening or perhaps at the masquerade party? His previous kiss had been quite nice, leaving her wanting more, though she'd never let him know that.

She felt her eyelids become heavy as sleep crept up on her. Daphne let it take over, fighting any thoughts of the duke until the next time. It was almost impossible to close her mind off from Arthur, but she fought it until she remembered nothing except in her dreams.

CHAPTER NINE

B Y THE TIME Arthur arrived at Graham and Roxanne's, the festivities were already underway. He'd spent the majority of his day helping his estate manager and a small crew of men make repairs on tenant cottages before the cold of winter set in. His thought had always been that, regardless of his rank, he was not above helping on the estate. His own father thought it beneath him to partake in manual labor.

He entered the ballroom without fanfare, looking around not for his sister or brother-in-law, but for Lady Daphne. He wanted to be sure to sign her dance card before it was filled. He saw her to one side in a group of ladies. A couple of other older women with their daughters. He immediately knew he would have to sign their dance cards as well as a courtesy. It would be rude of him not to.

Nearing the small group, he was met with curtseys from all the women. All eyes were on him, especially Lady Daphne's. He felt her eyes boring a hole through him.

"Ladies. I hope you're enjoying yourselves." He turned to Daphne. "Lady Daphne, might I sign your dance card?"

She handed it to him, along with the pencil and watched as he studied it carefully. Finally, he scribbled his name, not once but three times, and passed it back to her.

"I hope the supper dance and a waltz meet with your approval," he said, watching her gaze at her card. A small smile formed on her lips as she saw he'd signed up for three.

Arthur turned to Lady Katherine and Lady Jane, who were watching the whole thing unfold. "Lady Jane, Lady Katherine, may I sign your dance cards as well?"

Shyly, one at a time, each handed him their dance card. There were only one or two spots taken, so it wasn't hard for him to choose. He penciled in his name and handed the cards back to them.

"If you ladies will excuse me, I see my sister beckoning me. I'm sure she's going to scold me for being late."

This, in turn, brought giggles from Lady Katherine and Lady Jane, while the older ladies merely smiled. Lady Daphne shook her head slightly. He bowed to the ladies and walked across the room to where his sister was standing, waiting on him. Daphne's mother walked up to Roxanne and said something before continuing her way toward another group of older ladies.

"I apologize for being tardy." He didn't go into details as to what caused him to be late. If his sister wanted to know, she would ask.

"I'm just curious to know if you've lost your mind. Courting Lady Daphne while the Earl of Bath has returned to London to secure a special license to marry her?"

"If you heard the whole story, you'd know Lady Daphne's father never gave his permission. The earl was told he could call on her if Lady Daphne was agreeable, that's all. The viscount gave me permission to court his daughter. When the earl returns from London, the viscount intends to have a talk with him."

"Just watch out for yourself. The earl is deeply in debt, I understand, and has been looking for a new wife with a sizeable dowry. I don't think he's going to be happy to return and find you paying attention with whom he believes is his betrothed."

"Let him."

She shook her head. "I thought you and Lady Daphne couldn't stand each other."

"We got to know each other. That's not to say she isn't condescending and arrogant."

"Just be careful. I don't want to see you hurt." She reached out and squeezed his hand before turning to attend to other guests. "Enjoy yourself."

He nodded and watched her walk away in her dark silver gown. It had the aura of shimmering due to an intricate addition of seed pearls hand-sewn into the gown. Arthur only knew that because he'd heard Roxanne talking to a friend of hers about the gown. Women's fashion was something he had no knowledge of other than he knew what he liked. He glanced at where Daphne still stood with the other two young ladies. If she were trying to impress him, she succeeded. But that was just him. He doubted she could wear anything that wouldn't catch his attention. She was the most beautiful woman he'd ever seen, and most men seemed to agree with him given how men turned their heads whenever she walked into a room.

The music was ending, and he realized it was time for his first dance of the evening. His partner was Lady Jane. She was a nice enough looking young woman but was painfully shy. He needed to remember that and try not to engage her in conversation that might prove difficult for her. Keep it simple.

He noticed Graham and a couple of other men walking his way, and there was no way to stop; the next dance would be beginning momentarily. Giving his brother-in-law a nod, he continued to gather Lady Jane for their dance. He didn't bother to look back at the men but gave Lady Jane one-hundred percent of his attention.

She shyly placed her hand on his arm as he led her to the dance floor. As the music began, Arthur noticed dancing was something she excelled at. She never missed a step; instead, she moved as though she'd been dancing for years. It was hard to have a conversation with her due to the dance, but he managed to get a few words in.

"Lady Jane, has anyone told you what a superb dancer you are?"

She smiled shyly, looking for the words. "Thank you, Your Grace. I've been fortunate to have had some excellent tutors."

"It's obvious you paid close attention to them. You seemed to have a love for dance."

"Yes, I do."

They continued until the music wound down. He thanked her again and led her back to her mother who was waiting on them at the edge of the dance floor. As he walked away, he hoped more would sign her dance card having seen him dance with her. There were advantages to being seen dancing with a duke.

Looking about the room for Lady Daphne, he finally found her at her mother's side, with another older woman whom he recognized as the Dowager Baroness Brimley. She had lost her husband last year, and now that she was out of mourning, she was slowly reentering society.

He approached, giving a slow bow to the three women. "Ladies. I hope you're enjoying yourselves this evening." He turned to Daphne. "Lady Daphne, the supper set is about to play." He extended his hand, waiting for her to place her dainty hand in his. She did so without even looking at him. Where was the agreeable Daphne?

Leading her out to the dance floor, he found a spot and gathered her in his arms. She took her one free hand and pushed against his chest. "We're not married yet, Your Grace. Please keep an acceptable distance."

"But we're courting, soon to be betrothed," he said.

"Don't forget you're saving me from a miserable life," she snapped.

They whirled around the ballroom in silence. Arthur had no desire in getting into a war of words with her. He would let her lead the conversation for now. Besides, he was enjoying all the eyes fixated on them.

"I received your flowers this morning, Your Grace. They are beautiful. You really didn't need to."

"You are most welcome. We're courting; it's acceptable. So

yes, I needed to."

He leaned closer and whispered in her ear. No one watching would know what he was saying to her. After all, most didn't know the change in their relationship. "What makes Daphne happy besides Sam?"

"I love to ride, sketch or paint, though I'm not very good at it. I like to read on a rainy day, though there are those who would say my reading choices are sometimes questionable."

"Why are your reading choices questionable?" he asked.

"Some of the subject matter I choose is not deemed something a young lady should take an interest in. I enjoy reading about architecture, history, poetry, and even sometimes the latest novel," she said breathlessly.

He smiled down at her and didn't respond.

"You don't approve?"

"I do approve. Reading helps improve the mind. You can't stick yourself in one genre. You have a nice variety of subject matter."

"Thank you," she said softly as she repositioned her hand on his shoulder.

"Who is your favorite poet?"

"I don't have a favorite of anything. I believe everyone should be given a chance. I'll try everyone at least once."

Arthur took in what she just said for a moment. This was far from just a young, well-brought-up lady. He'd suspected that from the moment he met her. Hearing her articulate it gave him a newfound respect for her. She might let the world think she was ferocious, but under all the bristling exterior lay the heart of a caring, thoughtful woman.

The music was winding down and would be followed by a procession to the dining room. He hated the idea of her being far down in the pecking order. He glanced around for his sister. He wanted Lady Daphne at his side this evening as his dining companion.

He thanked her for the dance and asked her to join him.

Luckily Roxanne did appear seemingly out of nowhere to show him where to stand while others gathered. Keeping his grip on Daphne, he spoke. "Lady Daphne will be my dining companion for this evening."

"How delightful," she replied with a grin. "I'll make the necessary adjustments."

"I don't know if this is such a good idea," she said lowly as his sister walked away.

"I am allowed to choose with whom I wish to dine. I want everyone to see I'm courting you."

She smiled wickedly. "Which is going to confuse those who think the earl is my betrothed."

He looked down at her. She was stunning, but he knew she had a wicked side. One she didn't let many people know she possessed. "Let them be confused. It's the earl's fault for this misunderstanding. He hears what he wants to hear."

"Yes, he does. I only hope he doesn't embarrass himself when he finds out he has competition."

"He was very sure of himself when he left for London," he said.

She gave him a wicked look. "I certainly hope he didn't give the bishop an exorbitant amount of money for a special license that's never to be used."

"I doubt he did. The earl is short on funds."

Putting her hand on his arm, they began the procession to the dining room. Arthur was glad his sister's house party was almost over. It had been, by all accounts, a smashing success and it would be the talk of the ton when everyone returned to London.

As they arrived in the dining room, everyone stood, waiting for Arthur to sit. There was also a buzz in the room. He noticed guests watching him and Daphne. Lady Daphne noticed it as well and decided to make the most of it. As everyone sat down, she placed her hand on his forearm and leaned into him to say something. All the while smiling lovingly at him.

"I believe there'll be no mistaking we're courting now." She removed her hand and sat back in her chair, waiting for the meal to begin.

"You're enjoying it, aren't you?"

"Oh yes. Immensely," she replied with a wicked grin.

He nodded as a footman poured a glass of wine. "I'm glad you are. You'll make a wonderful duchess, just as I imagined."

"I'll take that as a compliment."

"It was meant as one."

The soup was the first course to come out. A bowl of delicate turtle soup was placed before them. Arthur wasn't a fan of this favorite, but he forced himself to take a couple of spoonsful before putting his spoon aside. Daphne, on the other hand, seemed to be enjoying it immensely. As he waited for the bowl to be taken away, he looked around the table to see if there was any change in the seating and if people were talking as they ate. Some avoided his gaze, others acknowledged him. For once he wished he was able to hear what was being said.

Glancing at Daphne from the corner of his eye, he noticed she was engaged in conversation with his brother-in-law, Graham. She seemed to be enjoying whatever they were talking about. He turned to his left where the Countess of Brenton sat. She had lowered her spoon to the side of the plate and was reaching for her glass of wine.

"I'm sorry the earl couldn't make it. Business sometimes does that."

She took a sip of wine before she spoke. "He promised to be here tomorrow for the masquerade ball."

"I look forward to seeing him," he replied. He and Brenton had attended Oxford together. The earl hadn't been in his trusted group of colleagues, but they shared some classes together. They lost touch after graduation. Part of life's cycle.

Soup dishes were removed, and moments later, the main course was set down in front of everyone. Tonight's meat was quail cooked in a delicate white wine sauce. Small, seasoned potatoes with asparagus accompanied the quail.

Dinner continued for the next two hours. After, the ladies left the men to their port and cigars while they enjoyed tea in the drawing room. Arthur was relieved when they cut it short to begin the final sets of dancing. He had two left with Daphne, and he could feel his body give his thoughts away as his cock began to harden. He couldn't wait to hold her in his arms again.

He promised a dance to Lady Katherine before his first dance with Daphne. Lady Katherine was quite tall, unusual for a woman. She carried herself regally and didn't pay attention to any remarks made about her towering height.

Due to the lively nature of the dance, it once again kept him from frivolous conversation. Lady Katherine seemed to enjoy herself immensely. She thanked him when the music ended and placed her hand at the crook of his arm. He returned her to her waiting mother and, with a bow, thanked Lady Katherine and left.

By his second dance with Daphne, Arthur barely noticed anyone else in the room. He wasn't aware eyes were on them since it was the third dance between them. People were trained on the couple, whispering their conclusions about the couple. Arthur only had eyes for Lady Daphne, and she was just as engrossed with him.

As the final waltz was coming to an end, Arthur felt a sadness for the evening coming to a close. "Would you like to go riding in the morning?"

"Yes, that would be quite enjoyable," she replied demurely. "I know my mother; she will want me to rest and all kinds of silly things before I dress for the ball."

"Then I'll be your knight in shining armor."

"I suppose so; saving me from my mother, even if it's only for a couple of hours."

They made their plans and finally, Arthur returned her to her anxious mother who was patiently waiting for her daughter to return to her. He bowed to both women.

"I look forward to our ride in the morning, Lady Daphne."

"As do I, Your Grace."

All this time her mother was desperately trying not to smile, but her eyes were glowing at the news she just heard. The duke had asked her daughter out for a ride. It was a start.

Arthur joined the men in a card room Graham had set up. A footman brought him a glass of brandy which he immediately indulged in. He needed to find Graham before he left. His brother-in-law found him and clapped him on the shoulder.

"Another glass?"

"I don't think so. I'm going to head home."

"Why so soon?"

"I'm tired and will have a long day tomorrow. I'm taking Lady Daphne riding."

A huge grin spread over Graham's face. "Is this getting serious?"

"Too early to tell."

"Well, I expect a full report tomorrow evening." Graham snickered.

"Go ahead, have your fun. If you would let my sister know I've left, I'd appreciate it."

"She's not going to like it."

"She can scold me later," he replied. He turned to walk out of the room. Heading to the front door, he gathered his hat and greatcoat from a footman. The weather was cooling, especially at night. But he wasn't cold. Lady Daphne left his blood running hot.

CHAPTER TEN

WHEN ARTHUR RODE his black stallion to the manor house, he noted the gray being held by a groom. Dismounting, he handed the reins over to another boy and turned to the house. The door opened just as he was about to knock. The butler greeted him and let him pass. Inside he found Daphne in the drawing room with her parents.

He greeted the trio and then turned to Daphne. "Are you ready? I saw the gray waiting."

"Yes, I am." She was dressed in a navy riding ensemble with black boots. She wore no hat, which wasn't common for ladies, but then Daphne did her all not to be like others. Her pale hair was swept up in a chignon.

The viscountess was about to say something, but as she turned to her husband, she hesitated. He noticed a look passed between them. Figuring her mother was worried about having enough time to prepare for the evening's final ball, he tried to pacify the viscountess.

"Excellent. Let's get going." He turned to her parents. "I'll have her back with plenty of time to prepare for this evening's festivities."

He followed her through the house, down the stairs, and to the waiting mounts. The groom had placed the gray in front of a mounting block to make it easy for Daphne to mount. He watched for a moment as she checked everything and made sure her saddle was to her liking. Arthur wasn't surprised she didn't ride with a side saddle and turned to mount his black without her seeing the grin on his face.

Bringing her mount next to his, she began to walk away from the house. "Where would you like to go?" she asked, turning to him.

She was the most gorgeous woman he'd ever laid eyes on and he had to sometimes pinch himself that she wasn't just a dream. She seemed to be warming to him as there hadn't been much in the way of her arrogance. Instead, she seemed to be making an effort to get to know him.

"I had thought we could ride to a lake on my property."

"We can do the same here. In fact, I bet your lake doesn't have a private summer cottage."

"There's a summer cottage?"

"Yes, evidently my grandfather, the previous viscount, had it built for my grandmother. She would spend a good portion of her summer there painting and sketching."

"Lead the way," he said. The stallion was wanting to run, and Arthur was finding it hard to hold him at a walk much longer.

Clucking to her mount, Daphne broke into a gallop, heading to a meadow. He watched, letting her have a substantial lead before letting the black gallop. It wouldn't take but a few strides to catch up to her. When he did pull up to her side, she laughed heartily, leading the gray to a stone wall to jump. The pair flew over it effortlessly. He followed, pulling up at her side where she was standing.

"You're quite the rider," he said.

"Thank you, Your Grace."

"Arthur," he corrected.

She gave him a saucy grin. "Very well. Thank you, Arthur."

"Next time I'll have to remember to bring Roddy. He loves a good romp."

"Is that the Irish Setter I see with you?"

He nodded and urged the black to walk. "I'm afraid he's about to go back to the kennel so he can learn how to retrieve."

"Don't you think that'll break his spirit? He has been with you since he was a babe. No need to confuse him."

"Every dog must have a job, or so says my kennel master."

She arched a brow. "You're the duke. If you don't want him trained to retrieve birds and waterfowl, don't."

He nodded. "You have a valid point. I'm rather attached to Roddy."

"Bring him along next time we ride," she said. "We won't have many more days to leisurely ride."

"I will. How far are we from the lake?"

"Not far at all," she said, breaking her horse into a gallop once again.

He followed at a breakneck speed as she didn't let up for what seemed like forever. Arthur thought she was being a little careless galloping as hard as she was. It could prove to be dangerous, but he hoped since this was familiar ground to her, she would keep her senses about her.

Quickly, he caught up with her and pulled ahead. Once he had enough space between him, he slowed the black to a walk. The horse needed time to recuperate from such a speed. He was quite fit, but even so, Arthur kept an eye on his mount. He had seen too many a good horse ruined by the carelessness of their rider.

She pulled her horse next to his. "Why are you slowing down? We're almost there."

"I don't believe in pushing my horse, no matter how fit he may be. Besides, it wouldn't hurt to walk and get to know each other better."

"When will you return to London?" she asked, looking over at him.

"Soon, I imagine. I'll return for the holidays."

"You'll be in session with Parliament soon, and that'll take up your time."

He nodded. "True, but they break for the holidays. I have other matters needing my attention in London."

"Are you speaking about the trial for the man who murdered your parents?"

For a moment he was shocked at her question. He had no idea she even knew about the matter. "I didn't realize you knew about that."

"Yes, I heard about it."

"I haven't decided if I want to attend. As far as I'm concerned, it's behind me, though my family and legal counsel are urging me to at least attend the opening day. And no, I haven't decided."

"I see. I imagine it would bring up things you would rather keep in the past," she said solemnly.

"Yes. There has to come a time when it's put in the past. I'm not vindictive, but I do want justice for my parents."

"I would too."

He had to change the subject and move on to something more cheerful. "Did you teach Sam how to talk so naughty?"

"No, he picked it up on his own. I'm sure when he was brought from where he came from that the sailors' salty language did influence him."

Arthur chuckled at the thought. "I'm sure that's where he picked up the majority."

"You would allow me to bring Sam should we decide to wed, wouldn't you?"

He quickly turned in the saddle toward her. "Of course you can bring him."

"Thank you. A lot of people find it hard to warm to him because they've never seen a parrot up close, let alone a foul mouthed one."

"I'd never thought of it like that before, but I think you're right. I think he'll be a delightful addition."

She granted him a smile and pointed ahead. "The lake is just over that rise."

"You'd never know it's there unless you rode over the hill," he observed. "I assume the lake is man-made."

"This one is. My grandfather designed the entire area for my grandmother."

He shifted in his saddle as he watched Daphne describe what lay in front of them. "It's quite unique."

She smiled. "It is. Would you like to see the cottage he built?"

"Yes, I would."

The pair rode down a path until they were in front of the small lake. In spite of autumn nipping at summer's heels, there was still some lush grass surrounding the body of water. To the left was a wooded area. If one didn't know what they were looking for, the cottage would remain hidden.

"Come, I'll show you the cottage," she said, turning her horse towards where the structure sat.

Arthur walked next to her as she led the way. He watched his surroundings as he'd been taught to do. It was all tranquil, a perfect place if one wanted to be alone.

As they entered the path where the cottage was located, he was amazed at the care that had been given to keep the area as it'd always been. They didn't have to go far when the cottage appeared. The front was hidden by a thin row of laurel and other trees, giving whoever was at the cottage a view of the lake. Otherwise no one would know a house stood there.

Turning to a sound in front of him, he just managed to see Daphne sliding off her gray. He met up with her and dismounted. He took the reins of both his mount and hers and tied them off to a nearby tree.

"Are you ready to see the inside?" she asked, lifting her skirts to avoid a drying puddle.

Seeing her ankles gave him thoughts he shouldn't be having. Not now. "Yes."

Daphne led the way, opening the oak door and finding her way to a parlor which was connected to a conservatory overlooking the lake. Arthur imagined her grandmother sitting in there for hours.

"This is amazing. A lot of thought was put into this," Arthur said.

"It is."

"Does your family use it?"

"No. My mother thinks it's beneath her to come here when she has such magnificent gardens by the house. Father pretends to not know it exists, but has the grounds maintained knowing I like to come here."

"What about your brother?"

"I don't believe he knows a thing about it."

"Well, I for one wouldn't let anyone know it exists."

She walked to him, laying both hands on his chest. He stared down at her, wondering what she was planning. "I don't plan to. It will be our little secret hideaway."

"Daphne, I don't know if that's a good idea." It was taking every fiber in his being not to kiss her silly.

"What isn't? I thought we needed a place where we could be alone. We are courting and need to get to know each other better before the wedding."

"You've got it all thought out, don't you?"

She arched a brow. Her hands hadn't moved. "What do I have planned out?"

"Our courtship, our future."

"I've given it some thought."

"I see."

"Arthur, if we're to be married, I don't wish to be a virgin on our wedding night. I want us to enjoy the night without that coming between us."

She had a valid point. Consummating the marriage was what brought fear to brides. Their mothers tell them tall tales of what to expect. If the act was done before, it would lead to a more pleasurable night.

He felt her hands move to his shoulders. "Make love to me, Arthur."

Leaning down, he cupped her face, staring at her perfect bow lips. It was the last thing he saw as his lips met hers. She opened to him, their tongues gently probing the other's. His cock wasn't listening to him, as though it had a mind of its own. He needed to stop this now before it went further. Their first outing shouldn't include lovemaking. Not yet. He pulled away.

"We can't. Not today."

"Am I not good enough for you, Your Grace? Isn't this what courting couples do? Take liberties with their time alone?" Her voice had raised, and it was easy to see she wasn't happy about the outcome.

"Yes, but let's get to know each other better."

"You could ruin me, and we would be expected to marry," she said, pulling away from him.

He ran his hand through his hair. "Would you really want that following us throughout our marriage?"

"Isn't it better than that toad trying to force me into marrying him? I'm afraid he'll return and challenge you to a fight or something."

"Are you now suggesting we elope?"

"That idea had occurred to me." Her eyes were pleading with him. She was terrified the earl would force himself on her in order to marry her. He was that determined.

"Let me think about it. I'm not saying yes, let's elope. I want to decide if it's feasible and how to go about it."

Her bottom lip was protruding from her pink mouth, making him want to kiss her and make it better. Instead, he began to laugh. He couldn't contain himself. The entire situation was bizarre. When he first met her, she made it obvious she didn't care for him, and now she was wanting to be his lover and wife.

"What's so funny?" she demanded, her eyes shooting daggers at him.

He couldn't quell the laughter, though he made some half-hearted tries. The laughter echoed off the walls of the cottage.

"Arthur!"

He caught his breath and reached out and took her hand. "I

apologize. That was insensitive of me."

"Are you going to tell me what's so funny?"

"It's really nothing. I would never have guessed a month ago I would be plotting how to elope with a beautiful woman."

Nodding, Daphne squeezed his larger hand. "Neither would I. I have been rather mean to you, haven't I?"

"Yes, you have."

She pulled at his fingers with some force. "Arthur! You don't have to agree with everything I say."

He grinned, pulling his fingers out of her grip. "In this case, yes, I feel it's in my best interest."

"Touché," she replied.

He wrapped his arms around her one more time. This time their lips met as though they had a thousand times before. If this was a dream, he never wanted to wake up. If it was love, he never wanted it to end. "I think we should go before we throw caution to the wind."

"I know you're right," she replied. "We can ride over to the orchard. It's a fun ride with a couple of walls to jump."

"I hope you're up to a challenge."

"Always," she replied demurely.

He kissed her one more time before letting her go. "After you, milady."

Standing and watching her turn and walk toward the door with her hips swinging for dramatics, Arthur smiled and walked behind her. He untied her mare and helped her to mount before mounting Midnight. The pair walked a good distance back the way they came until Daphne led them down another path going another direction.

"Is this the way to the orchards?" Arthur asked as he pulled up beside her.

"It is. The first wall is not too far off."

"Lead on."

After both clearing the wall, they kept going at a brisk walk. The second wall was as easy, and they continued to the orchard which was pretty much empty. Except for some apples, the fruit belonged to the wildlife for the winter. Finally, they arrived at the manor house. He handed Midnight's reins off to a waiting stableboy and escorted Daphne back to the front door which the butler opened as though he'd been standing on the other side waiting.

"I had a lovely outing, Lady Daphne. I'll see you at the ball this evening."

"I thoroughly enjoyed myself, Your Grace. I look forward to this evening."

Watching her disappear into the house, he turned and, after mounting his black, Arthur started back home. The outing had proven to be more than he'd anticipated, and once he'd pierced through Daphne's defensive armor, he found her to be quite delightful. She could hold her own with any man. This evening would prove to be a memorable one, though Arthur had no idea what lay ahead.

ARTHUR CLIMBED OUT of his carriage rather than sit and wait for his turn to exit the vehicle. The drive wasn't all that long that he couldn't manage the short distance to the house. Before shutting the door, he picked up the mask which had been sitting on the seat beside him.

Masquerade parties were over the top in his opinion. Everyone wearing masks until midnight, each pretending they didn't know who they danced with or spoke with. The opposite was usually the case. It was easy to spot some of the more high-profile aristocrats because they never deviated from their usual circle of friends.

Graham pulled him aside the moment he stepped through the door. He led him to his study where he locked the door behind himself. "Sorry for the cloak and dagger show, but I thought you needed to know Black is back from London, and he was unable to secure a special license because the bishop was away."

"Bloody hell!"

"Black is determined he's going to marry Lady Daphne, no matter what her father says."

"Does he know about Lady Daphne and myself?"

"I don't know but I imagine he will before the night's out. I just wanted you to be aware he's here and not in the best of moods."

"I appreciate the warning. Has he seen Lady Daphne?"

Graham shook his head. "To my knowledge he has not, but I believe Lady Daphne's been held up in the ladies' retiring room with her mother."

"A sign she's seen him."

Graham nodded. "You might be right."

"I guess there's only one thing to do and that's join the festivities. Thanks for the warning, Graham."

The pair left Graham's study and walked to the ballroom. Inside was a wave of people in all sorts of masks. Some had been specially made, a few Venetian masks were mixed in the crowd. Unless you could pick a person out by their movements, it was nearly impossible to tell one person from another.

He left Graham and walked about the room, trying to decide who was who. A few of the men were easy to spot because of some idiosyncrasy in the way they dressed. The ladies were not too hard to know who was behind the mask. He nodded as he passed small groups of women holding court. Obviously, they were gossiping about who they thought were behind the masks.

The music began to start after a short break. For once he was glad as the music drowned out most of the conversations. He kept walking until he neared the windows. Outside on the terrace were a pair of gentlemen engaged in a lively conversation. It didn't appear to be a friendly one.

Almost immediately, Arthur recognized Black who was pointing his finger at the other man. Black wasn't hard to recognize.

His portly stature gave him away. He assumed the other man was Lady Daphne's father, which could be a powder keg. The earl was known for his angry outbursts, like the one he was having with the viscount.

He decided it wouldn't be wise to walk out to them. Whatever they were discussing would be known the moment the pair stepped back inside.

Ever since his time with Lady Daphne at the cottage, he'd been playing out what had occurred. With the earl now empty-handed of a special license, Arthur thought perhaps he should have plans to get her out of here. At least for a while. While he had wanted to do things by the book and ask her father for permission to wed his daughter, that had been ruined by Black. He wished the viscount hadn't led Black on about marrying his daughter. With the earl rushing to London, he hadn't had the opportunity to make sure Black understood he had changed his mind.

He turned, thinking he should find his sister and see if she knew how Daphne was faring. The idea of having her evening ruined by one man went against him. Daphne had been looking forward to the ball and he wanted to see she had fun. He wanted her to be able to look back and remember the evening with good memories.

In a sea of masks, one would think it would be virtually impossible to find a particular person, but Arthur knew his sister mask or no mask. When he found her, it appeared she was coming from the ladies' retiring room. He caught her attention and motioned to an alcove just off the ballroom.

"How is Lady Daphne?"

"A mix of emotions right now. She was angry, and now she just wants to enjoy her evening," Roxanne replied.

"That's a good idea."

"Graham said we'd just keep an eye on Black and see how he behaves."

"He was on the terrace with the viscount. It looked like a

heated conversation."

She arched a brow. "The earl does not want to accept that Lady Daphne's father is against the match."

"He's allowed. There were no documents signed, and no money exchanged hands."

"I'm afraid what the earl might do once he finds out you've been given permission to court her."

"Don't worry. I can't see him trying anything tonight in front of his peers," Arthur replied.

She patted his shoulder as she turned to leave. "I certainly hope you're right. Excuse me, brother, I need to mingle with my guests."

He watched her disappear inside the ballroom. He waited behind for a few minutes before doing the same. Standing on the edge of the dance floor, Arthur looked around as couples paired up for the first dance of the evening. Looking over at the French doors, he also noted that neither the viscount nor Black were standing outside.

Watching the couples whirl by, Arthur continued to look for the two gentlemen. He also kept his eye on the door to see if Daphne and her mother appeared. He finally spotted Black speaking with a couple of other gentlemen on the other side of the ballroom. At last he found Daphne with her mother and another mother and daughter sitting in the lemon grove in a corner of the room.

Arthur decided to walk over to her and ask her for the next dance before Black found her and did the same. As he made his way to the grove of trees, he greeted fellow party goers. Some he knew, a lot he did not. Her mother was the first to recognize him when he approached.

"Your Grace, good evening," she trilled.

"Ladies. I hope you're all having an enjoyable evening."

They all agreed, making his job easier. "May I introduce my good friend, Lady Rose and her mother, Dowager Baroness Sweet," Daphne offered. The baroness's husband had passed away years ago, but she had never remarried.

"Ladies."

A few moments of small talk and Arthur could tell the first dance was ending and the next would start in the next few minutes. He turned to Daphne. "Lady Daphne, may I have the honor of this next dance?"

"You may," she beamed.

He placed her smaller hand on his arm and led her to the center of the dance floor. Arthur was very much aware her mother was watching closely, as she should. He imagined she was nervous about the earl being in attendance.

"Are you enjoying yourself?" he asked as she placed her hand on his shoulder.

"Yes, I am now." She smiled. "I'm sure you heard the earl's here and won't accept what my father told him for the hundredth time."

"Yes, I heard."

The music started and he led her around the floor, past other couples swept up in the moment. They weren't five minutes into the dance and Black decided to try and cut in. Arthur glanced at Daphne and squeezed her hand.

"If you don't mind, Your Grace, I'd like to dance with my betrothed," he smirked.

Black reached for Daphne, but she pulled away. "I am not your betrothed nor are we courting," she spat.

"We are to be married. It's just a little misunderstanding between your father and me."

"Bollocks," she cried. "The only one misunderstanding the situation is you. You need to accept the fact and move on to someone else. Someone who's more gullible than I."

Arthur decided to step in. Not that Daphne needed help, but the earl was so determined, Arthur was afraid something might transpire that shouldn't. The man was known to have a temper. Especially if he didn't get his way.

"If you'll excuse us, Black…"

"I am going to have my dance with Lady Daphne, now. Unhand her."

People were beginning to turn and watch what was transpiring. He didn't want her embarrassed any more than she might be, but Daphne beat him to it. "He will do no such thing." She looked up at him. "Would you escort me, Your Grace?"

"I'd be honored."

Arthur began to lead her through the other dancers and to the side of the room when Black yelled out, "This isn't over with. You are mine, Lady Daphne. I shall teach you some manners once we've married."

"Don't be afraid," Arthur said. He kept her close. "We'll try for another dance a bit later."

"Please don't let me out of your sight, Arthur. I don't trust that toad not to do something drastic. He does not take no for an answer."

"Understood. I won't."

He needed to speak with the viscount, though he was sure he'd heard Black's outburst. The earl was becoming desperate, and that made him dangerous.

"Are you hungry? I see the buffet is open."

She shook her head. "No, not after that confrontation."

"You can't let him dictate your life."

"I'm trying not to, but he does scare me. I'm afraid he's capable of horrible things."

"You need to show him you're not afraid of him," he replied. "Come, let's go through the buffet, get something to drink. We can sit at one of the tables and talk."

Biting her lip proved to him she was scared. She nodded. "Yes, let's."

Daphne picked her way through the buffet line. Her choices were safe, making Arthur wonder if she were that picky with all foods. He certainly hadn't noticed it before now. Then again, it was probably the confrontation with Black that was to blame for the lack of food on her plate.

He found a table to sit at and hoped no one would want to join them. He wanted to see what she was thinking. She was quite headstrong, as seen by her words to Black.

"What are you thinking about? I don't think I've seen you so quiet," he said, picking up his fork.

She looked him in the eyes before speaking. "I'm not sure you'd like to hear my thoughts."

"Try me."

She speared a shrimp off her plate and thoughtfully chewed it. "I've been thinking about your unofficial proposal."

His head jerked up. "You wish to marry? Now?"

"Why not? It would solve a lot of potential problems. Black for one. Face it, he's not about to give up. At least if we were married, he might just disappear," she said.

Arthur shook his head. "I don't think it's a good idea to marry just to get rid of the man. That seems so cold. I want to marry you because I've fallen in love with you. I want to make you my duchess."

"Arthur, I may not show it but in this short time, I've grown quite fond of you. I'm afraid to call anything love for fear I'll be left with a broken heart."

"So you're saying you're fond of me?"

"It's more than that. A lot more. I am afraid I'll wake up and find it all a dream," she replied.

"It's not a dream, Daphne. Do you have any ideas on this matter?"

Taking her fork, she moved food around on her plate. "We could elope."

"I thought all young ladies wanted a formal, large wedding. You don't?" he asked.

"Under the circumstances with Black, I'm sure my parents would understand."

He set his fork down and took a sip of wine before continuing. "We could go to Gretna Green."

"Don't you have an estate in the north? We could go there.

You could get a special license and we could marry," she replied.

"There is that option. We could spend a fortnight there. If we were to go to Gretna Green, we could also stop at my estate and spend some time."

"Remember what I suggested at the cottage?"

"Yes. If we'd stayed, I wouldn't have been able to promise you the outcome," he said.

She giggled. "Let's think about which is the more viable option. That outcome could still occur before we leave on an adventure."

He ignored her comment. "Black isn't going to take no for an answer. He'll keep coming around trying to break your father down until he gets the result he wants."

"My father won't see him. He's said his peace," she said.

Arthur swirled the wine around that was still in his glass. "Are you done?" he asked as he swallowed the remainder of his wine.

She looked at her plate. "Yes, why?"

He took her hand, bent over, and whispered in her ear, "Fancy a trip to London?"

"Now?" she asked, her eyes growing large.

"Yes. Nothing like the present."

"But I need to pack."

"You can buy anything you need."

She shook her head. "No. I can manage to pack a few things quickly, and you can do the same."

"Daphne, that'll take you far too long. I want to be on the road as soon as possible."

"Then we're at an impasse, Your Grace."

Now was not the time nor place to be stubborn. "Are you serious?"

"Quite."

"Fine. We'll need to sit down and replan this in order to accommodate you. It's obvious we won't be leaving tonight." She could be so frustrating, and he, for the most part, could deal with her. This was different. He had planned it out in his head. On the other hand, it might be for the best. She'd been confronted by Black to the point she was nervous about him. He was afraid if they waited too long, Black might come up with a scheme like kidnapping her to marry her. That wasn't going to happen if he had anything to say about it.

"You're serious?"

"I'm afraid so. Perhaps we can leave in a day or two. You can pack a bag to be ready for when we do leave. I'm not changing my mind, just when and how we do it."

She said nothing for a few moments, then nodded her head in agreement. "I think that would be the better plan. How would we go?"

"To London, then take the train to our destination," he said.

"I like that."

"What is it you like?" her father said from behind her.

"Papa, do you always eavesdrop on others?"

"No. I wanted to make sure you were all right after that incident on the dance floor," he said.

"I'm fine. His Grace has been entertaining me." She smiled at both men as though she had not a care in the world.

"Is the earl still here?" Arthur inquired.

"He's in the card room enjoying the liquor a little too much."

"Be sure to have my brother-in-law know. He'll have him put in his carriage in no time."

"I think there is a line of men who'll see to it," the viscount said with a smirk.

"No doubt," Arthur replied.

"I'll let you two get back to your conversation. I just wanted to make sure the earl hadn't ruined your evening."

"Thank you, Papa."

The viscount resumed his rounds, greeting people he knew for sure behind their masks. Arthur and Daphne watched him until he stopped to greet a couple he obviously recognized, then resumed their conversation.

"It's nice to see my father is enjoying himself. He's usually not one for social events such as this, but he seems to like this one," Daphne said.

"I would say you're right. Has he always been like that?"

"No, I believe my mother dragging him from party to party might play a part as to why he's usually so solemn in situations like this."

Arthur sat straight up in his chair. "What would you like to do now? We could dance, or I could take you back to your mother if you wish."

"Could you escort me as far as the curtain over there?" she asked innocently.

He realized she was wanting to go to the ladies' retiring room. She did not wish to walk across the room alone. "Of course, though wouldn't it be better if your mother escorted you?"

"I don't wish to disturb her. And before you ask, no, I don't care what others think. They need to get used to seeing us together."

Her statement didn't surprise him. She was an independent woman and shunned some of the ton's list of things not to do, if there was such a list. He stood to his full height and offered her his hand. She put her smaller one in his as she stood.

As they approached the curtained off room, he let his grip loosen. "I'll be right over there by that statue."

"I'll try not to be too long."

He nodded and watched her disappear behind the dark-blue curtain. Sitting in a high back crème damask chair, he summoned a passing footman for a glass of brandy. Moments later, the young man reappeared, brandy in hand. He accepted the glass and began to swirl the liquid. This should help the time pass while he waited for Daphne. He watched as people walked by, and if he couldn't guess, wondered who they were behind their fancy masks.

CHAPTER ELEVEN

ARTHUR SPRANG TO his feet at the sound of Daphne's voice. At first, he wasn't sure who she was talking to in such a raised voice. Black. It had to be him. He was the only man here this evening who would anger her. He headed in the direction of her voice. She wasn't hard to find. At a built-in seat overlooking the gardens, Daphne was standing as Black had ahold of her arm with one hand; in the other he waved a pistol. He looked wild-eyed as he stood shakily on his feet. The man was drunk, making the situation more volatile.

At the sight of Arthur, he began shouting. "Get back! She is mine and no one else's."

"I belong to no one!" Daphne boldly said.

Black, in turn, let go of her arm for a second and backhanded her. "Shut up, you stupid cow. Women are to be seen and not heard. You will thank me for showing the error of your ways."

The slap only made Daphne angrier and more determined. She tried to move away from him, but he grabbed her arm once again. People were gathering, curious as to what was happening. Graham appeared at Arthur's side.

"We've got to get that pistol away from him before he hurts someone with it," Graham remarked.

Arthur watched Black's movements for a moment. "Someone needs to keep him occupied. Make him talk to keep his mind off that pistol. Someone else needs to come behind his right side and force the gun from him. I don't think he'll fire it. He's too drunk to concentrate on any one thing."

The two men studied the other for a moment. "Why don't you keep him talking and I'll grab the gun," Arthur said.

Graham shook his head. "He has a problem with you. He's more likely to engage in conversation with you. You keep him focused talking and I'll get the pistol."

"Agreed."

But before either could advance their plan, Daphne began speaking to Black. She urged him to sit down and talk with her. If he was so determined to marry her, they needed to come to some sort of understanding. To everyone's surprise, the earl nodded his head in agreement.

"I knew you would come around," he said, his words slurring as he spoke. Black turned toward the small crowd gathered in front of them. "Someone find a bishop to bring a special license and marry us here and now."

Daphne got him to sit on the upholstered bench seat next to her. His eyelids were at half-mast. He was trying to fight the inevitable. That he would soon pass out, and with any luck, not remember anything. He would only wake up with one of the worst hangovers he'd ever encountered.

"What's she doing?" Graham asked as everyone watched the scene unfold.

"She's trying to win his trust," Arthur replied.

"She's smart and knows how to read people easily enough," Roxanne said, squeezing her way between both men. "This will be a ball no one will soon forget."

"The important thing is that he does not get agitated again. If Daphne can keep him placid, I think he'll drop the gun if she asks."

"Or he blacks out," Roxanne replied. "He can barely keep his eyes open."

Graham nodded at his wife's observation. "That would be the

easiest way to put an end to the matter."

Roxanne turned to her brother. "What are your plans? Are we to expect an announcement soon?"

"You'll have to wait and see, but if that's what occurs, you will be the first to know." He scrubbed his beard with one of his hands, realizing he had failed to cover his face with his mask after they ate. Perhaps Daphne would now agree with his idea of leaving tonight for London and eloping to Scotland on the first train they could get going north. Black was too unpredictable, and he might be drunk tonight, but he was determined, and drink was not going to keep him from his mission of making Daphne his wife.

"Fair enough," she replied. She pointed towards what was playing out. It appeared the earl was nodding off and Daphne reached over and gently removed the pistol from his hand.

Arthur held his breath as he watched. He was proud of her. She'd kept her cool and focused on what was important, ignoring anything Black spewed at her.

Handing the pistol over to Graham, Daphne rose and quickly walked over to her father first, assuring him she was fine before joining Arthur.

"You're all right?" he asked lowly.

"Yes, I'm fine, though I should admit I was shaken when he first grabbed me."

"I was sick with worry. He was too unpredictable with that pistol."

"Does anyone know where he got it?" she asked.

He shook his head. "No, but I'll be sure to ask Graham if he knows. Come, let's find you somewhere to sit and a glass of brandy."

They didn't have to go far as Roxanne came to their rescue, knowing the young woman wasn't ready to meet the throng of people waiting to see her. "Come, I have just the spot. No one will disturb you."

Following his sister down a long corridor, Arthur realized

where she was taking them. There was a room next to Graham's study which his sister had turned into her own. It was set up similarly to her husband's study, but the features were all feminine.

"There's brandy and whiskey along with wine on the sideboard. Lock the door behind you to ensure no one disturbs you."

"Thank you, Lady Roxanne," Daphne said.

"There's no need to thank me. You've just been through a difficult ordeal and don't need a crowd questioning you. Stay as long as you like."

"Thank you, sister," Arthur said as they watched her walk to the door.

"If you need anything, please don't hesitate to find me."

She left the room and closed the door behind her. Arthur began to head to the door to lock it. "If you'd rather, I can leave it unlocked. We can see if anyone disturbs us."

"It won't stop the gossips, not that I care," she said.

"Would you like a glass of wine or another brandy?"

"A brandy, please. I didn't get to drink the last one."

"Brandy it is," he said with a grin, making his way to the white-colored sideboard. He mused that most of the furniture here had been imported from France, so the wood was probably fruitwood, a popular choice in French décor.

"Arthur, I've changed my mind. I want to elope. Tonight," she said breathlessly.

He turned from pouring brandy into a snifter. "Why the sudden change?"

"Black. Drunk or not, he's determined to marry me. I don't think he'll stop until he achieves what he wants. Marriage to me means money to him, and he's desperate."

Arthur passed her a brandy. "You're sure this is what you want?"

"Yes." Her voice didn't waver. It was strong and determined.

He glanced over at the clock on the mantel. It was going on ten. "We'll need to leave now. If we're lucky, we'll be able to catch the first train north to Scotland."

She drank her glass of brandy in two large swallows. "What are we waiting for?"

"Did you wear a cape? We won't be able to get it without raising suspicion. My greatcoat is in my carriage."

"So is mine. In my father's carriage. Mother didn't want me hiding behind it when we made our entrance."

"Smart woman," he replied. "I know a way out of the house that is seldom used."

She stood up and peered at him. "Let's get going."

He nodded with a grin and led her out of the room and down the hall. When they reached the end of the hall, there was a door off to the right. He knew of the door since he was a boy. It was where Graham was supposed to enter if he was dirty from his outdoor adventures. Opening the door, they both stepped outside. Arthur turned to make sure the door was secure before taking her hand and leading her to a laurel hedge.

"Where are we going?" she whispered.

"This leads to the carriages. We'll stay behind the hedge to keep out of sight."

Moments later, they were at her father's carriage. None of the men seemed to be around, so Arthur opened the door and grabbed her cape. They stealthily moved behind the carriages until they came upon his own. His coachmen were standing by the horses, talking quietly among themselves. Opening the carriage door, Arthur assisted Daphne inside. This alerted the coachman, who Arthur met halfway.

"We're off to London as planned."

"Yes, Your Grace. It's a good night to travel as well."

"Excellent. That's what I want to hear."

He climbed inside and began to sit across from his soon-to-be wife, but she shook her head.

"There's no need in you sitting there. I would like if you sat next to me."

He made his move just as the carriage groaned and the horses began to pull it onto the drive. Once he was certain they had begun, Arthur sat down next to her.

"That's better," she remarked with a smile. The moon was at a three-quarters phase, making it easy to see.

"There are some blankets if you'd like me to get them."

She nodded. "Yes, please. This cape is warm but not enough in this colder weather."

He reached across and lifted the seat cushions. Grabbing two blankets, he unfurled one and placed it over her before doing the same for himself. He watched as she drew the blanket up to her neck and sighed.

"You know, Gretna Green is not the easiest to get to. Trains from London go to Edinburgh. You'd have to hire a carriage to get us there."

He turned his head and gazed at her. "How would you even know that?" he asked.

"I looked into it," she replied.

"I was aware it wasn't accessible by train."

She snuggled close to Arthur. "Didn't you mention having a lesser estate in York?"

"Yes, I have an estate there. Why?" He suddenly realized what she was about, but rather than let her know, he questioned her.

"I think it's beneath a duke's station to elope to Gretna Green. Plus, our wedding night would be spent there, and I don't care for strangers listening to us consummate our marriage."

"I know the bishop in York so getting a special license is not a problem. The vicar of one of the churches is a cousin of mine."

"What's he doing there?"

"Second son, and York is where they sent him." He put his arm around her and pulled her close. It was colder than it had been, and he could tell she wasn't completely warm.

"Ah, yes. Gretna Green would be the first place Black goes to find me,"

"I hadn't thought of that, but you are right. When he figures out we've absconded, that'll be the first place he'll go," Arthur replied.

"What about your sister and brother-in-law? My parents will figure it out and I'm sure be thankful to you for being my protector."

Arthur closed his eyes for a second before answering. "My sister and her husband are fine. Roxanne, I'm sure, has deduced what we're up to. They'll be among our greatest allies. I'm sure your parents will be grateful Black will be out of their lives. I'm sure if he'd gotten his way, he'd go through your dowry in a matter of months and would then go to your father looking for another handout."

The entire situation was one out of a novel. First, he despised her, and the feeling was mutual. Then they began to know each other, and feelings began to turn. Now he was eloping with her in a matter of days. He was determined he would be her protector for the rest of their lives. His duchess, it seemed, would not be quiet. Marriage wouldn't change that, and he didn't want her to change. Her opinions were refreshing to him.

"Arthur?" he heard her say. "Are you falling asleep?"

He sat up a little more. "I'm sorry. I'm afraid I was. The rhythm of the carriage does that sometimes."

"We should probably get some sleep. Tomorrow, or today is going to be a busy day," she replied.

"Yes."

"If you don't mind, I'm going to lay down on the other seat. Then you can stretch out as well." She picked up her blanket and moved to the other side of the carriage. Lying down, she pulled the blanket up to her neck and closed her eyes. Before she did, Daphne noticed Arthur had already succumbed to sleep.

DAPHNE WAS AWAKENED by the carriage coming to a halt.

Opening her eyes, she saw that Arthur was looking out the window. They'd reached London and she assumed they were in front of Arthur's London home.

"Are we in London?" she asked as she gently sat up.

"We are. We'll stay here for a couple of hours. The train north to York doesn't leave until nine. We can freshen up. If I remember, Roxanne left some dresses here. You are welcome to them if they fit. I'm sure she wouldn't mind."

She gifted him with a smile. "Thank you. Given your sister's height, I don't believe they will do, but I'll see what I can find that might be usable."

The door to the carriage opened and Arthur stepped down. She heard him talking to the driver as she waited. Moments later, Arthur returned and extended his hand. She took it and stepped out of the carriage. She gazed at the stone house in front of her and walked alongside Arthur. As they reached the front door, she noted no one had come to greet him. Probably because no one was expecting him.

The door was locked, and she watched as he began to pound on the thick oak door. He kept it up until they heard the sound of someone on the other side unlocking the locks. The door opened and a befuddled butler appeared.

"Your Grace. Forgive me, I had no idea you were on your way to London."

"I didn't decide until the last minute."

They walked into the house and Daphne removed her cape, as did Arthur. She looked upwards and saw alfresco paintings on the ceiling. She would have to remember to ask Arthur if he knew who painted them and when. They were magnificent.

She heard Arthur ask the butler to see that a small hamper was fixed for their journey as well as some tea for now. "Daphne, would you like me to show you to my sister's room?"

"Yes," she replied.

Daphne felt him take her hand and lead her to the grand staircase. Once on the private family floor, Arthur led her to a closed door. Opening it, she noticed the room was furnished by a woman. Roxanne had left her mark in this room, from the figurines that dotted the room, to the delicate portraits on the wall.

"The dressing room is over there. Help yourself to whatever you need. In fact, pack a small bag to get you through until we can get your own clothes."

"Thank you."

He leaned over and kissed her softly. "I'll be back shortly. We will need to be leaving for the station soon."

She watched his back as he went out the door, closing it behind him. Daphne couldn't help but wonder what was underneath all those clothes. It was obvious he was muscular. He loved the outdoors.

Rather than focus on his physical attributes, she walked into the dressing room. Finding about ten dresses hanging, she looked at each one individually. Finally, she found two that hopefully would do. She gathered them and took them into the main salon. She laid each one down on the bed and studied them. The lavender dress caught her eye. It was made of cotton and had darker purple embellishments, making it quite stunning. The second choice was a sage green muslin day dress with black piping. It would do for traveling, and the lavender one would be stunning as a dress for her wedding.

Trying on both dresses, she found them each a little bit too long, though she imagined she could use them in spite of that. She returned to the dressing area and began looking through the drawers for undergarments. There was everything she needed and new as well. She contemplated why Lady Roxanne would have left new chemises, night rails, and other intimate items. Perhaps in all of her excitement to marry the earl, she simply forgot they were here.

She heard a door close behind her. Turning, she saw an older woman enter, holding a piece of luggage. This must be his housekeeper. Arthur's description was spot-on.

"I am Mrs. Martin, the duke's housekeeper. He mentioned you might need to pack some clothing for your journey to York."

"It is nice to meet you, Mrs. Martin. I would like to wear the sage green dress. The other, along with undergarments, should fit just fine in that bag."

"Very well. His Grace did mention the two of you had to be at the train station before nine. While you're changing, I'll pack everything." Mrs. Martin glanced at the gown she had worn. "I'll see it cleaned while you're away."

"Thank you for your help."

She smiled. "No problem, my lady."

Minutes later, Daphne found herself in the sage green dress and new undergarments. Mrs. Martin had proved herself a gem. By the time Arthur arrived to collect her, she was ready.

"You look stunning," Arthur said with a grin.

"Thank you. I'm glad you like it. Both are too long, but I can overcome that."

Daphne noted he was freshly shaved as she inhaled his wintergreen scent. His clothes were also new, and he wasn't dressed in formal evening attire. His appearance sent her body into a melange of unfamiliar feelings. The only other time she'd ever had these feelings was when he kissed her. It had been magical. She was glad that they hadn't gone any further when her body disobeyed. Their wedding night would be special and something she wouldn't soon forget. She was sure Arthur would take care of her as they consummated their marriage.

"You look beautiful. Now, come. We need to get to the train station."

The ride was easy this morning. Not a lot of people out and about other than shopkeepers and delivery men. When they reached the station, Arthur's men began scurrying. Bags were removed, along with a food hamper for later. She was surprised when a footman returned with two tickets in his hand. He handed them off to the duke, as he told them which platform the train would leave from.

By the time they reached the train, a compartment had been readied for them. Bags were placed under seats, and they barely had time to sit down when the train began to lunge forward. They were on their way. Arthur was peering out the window. She wondered what he was thinking.

"Do you visit your estate often?" she asked.

"I try to make the trip at least twice a year, and I stay until everything is in order."

"Do you like the estate?"

He turned his head from the window to face her. "Yes, I do. The house was built during the Tudor era. One of my predecessors was gifted the estate by Henry VIII."

"That's amazing. So the house is timber?"

"Yes. Very well built."

She pulled her cloak tighter. "Do you have business interests in the area?"

"The estate maintains a coal mine. It provides for a lot of jobs in the area."

"The mine is on the estate?" she asked.

He nodded. "Yes, it's in one of the far corners of the estate. You won't even know it's there when we arrive."

"You will show it to me, won't you?"

"Of course," he replied.

Daphne had found herself fascinated in Arthur's endeavors. He never really spoke of them when she was with him, making her believe he didn't wish to bore her. "How long has the mine been operating?"

"Quite a while. I believe it was opened during my father's lifetime. This particular vein is slowing down, so we're embarking on a new one almost next to the original."

"That's amazing. I understand the coal would be shipped off?"

"Yes, I have buyers that are regular. I also make sure all my tenants are provided coal during the winter months. They work hard and don't complain; some even work at the mine. I believe, as duke, it's important to take care of them."

"I knew you were thoughtful. I just didn't know how much."

He snorted. "Don't go putting me on a pedestal."

"I wouldn't think of it."

She playfully stuck her tongue out at him. Daphne knew there were some subject matters she shouldn't inquire about too much. He was opening up to her, and that was all that mattered. That would come in time. Right now, she was pleased just to watch him share.

Having heard about his parents' brutal murder, she wanted to know what he knew. She understood that he'd hired a detective and finally got the case closed and a man charged. Would he attend the trial or not? Or would he sit it out?

Daphne peered out the window, noting the landscape was beginning to change. Northern England was very much the opposite of south of London. Rather than the rolling meadows rocky terrain was more present. She remembered it from a visit her family took to Scotland to visit her mother's sister when she was a child. The countryside very much reminded her of that journey.

"I don't know about you, but I'm famished," Arthur said, reaching for the hamper.

"I am as well. We haven't really eaten since the ball."

She helped him take the covered dishes from the basket. Roast chicken, cheese, smoked meats, and fruit would take care of any hunger. Daphne squealed when she found a plate bearing seedcake. Arthur took a bottle of red wine and opened it as she began to fix them each a plate.

"Is this enough?" she asked as she passed the plate to him. He exchanged a glass of wine for the plate and sat back on the seat to eat. From the looks of it, Arthur was hungrier than he admitted.

"There's more if this doesn't suffice," he replied. "Thank you for doing that."

"You're welcome. I suppose I should get used to it, right?"

"That's going to take some getting used to," he replied.

She finished off her plate and was devouring her second piece of seedcake. It was her favorite. "How far do we have to go?"

"I believe we have about three hours until we arrive at the train station and another hour before we arrive at my estate."

Nodding, Daphne watched as Arthur fixed another plate. "Would you mind putting this up when you're finished? I believe I'm going to take a nap."

"Of course. I won't be far behind you."

"Trains make you sleepy too?"

"Yes, which can be a good thing."

Curling up on the opposite side of the compartment, Daphne never knew when she fell asleep. The train's whistle awoke her and Arthur. He peered out the window, trying to determine where they were.

"It appears we're nearing the train station in York," Arthur said.

"Wonderful. Do you have a carriage awaiting us?"

He nodded. "There should be. I sent a telegram while in London."

Moments later, the train had stopped. Arthur opened the compartment door leading to the platform. Putting their bags onto the platform, he then helped Daphne exit the car.

She looked around at all the people passing them by in a hurry. Had the telegram not gotten to his staff? Arthur was looking around and suddenly raised his hand. A man approached and the pair had a brief conversation. The footman gathered their belongings and headed to the carriage. Feeling Arthur take her hand, Daphne relaxed. He seemed to know exactly how to read her emotions and made sure she was at rights.

Settling herself next to Arthur in the carriage, she waited for the coach to get underway. "Do we go through the village?" she asked.

"No, just the outskirts. I'll be sure to bring you before we leave. I think you'll like some of the shops."

It was already the middle of the afternoon and the sun was beginning to set. She felt his arm envelop her. "You're cold?"

She nodded and watched as he removed a blanket for her. She closed her eyes as he wrapped it around her. "Thank you. That's much better."

They rode along in a peaceful silence as the carriage headed for the estate. It was so nice not to have to converse, that they got along even in silence. Some women thought they had to continually talk.

"Would you like to hear what we're going to be doing?"

"Getting married, I would guess," she said sarcastically.

"Clever woman. Yes, but I'm going to see my cousin in the morning and meet with the local bishop about securing a special license." He squeezed her hand and looked ahead.

"Does that mean we'll marry tomorrow?"

"That depends on obtaining the special license. My cousin said the bishop was visiting and would be in the area for the next fortnight. Why are you anxious to marry?"

"That is the purpose of our journey, and it appears better if we're married. You know people talk."

"Bloody hell. Let them! I didn't think you cared so much about social proprieties."

"I don't, but you're a duke with a stellar reputation. It would be a shame to put a black mark on it."

He barked out a laugh. "You let me worry about my reputation, my duchess."

"That is so foreign to me."

"You're going to make a wonderful duchess," he replied.

"I guess I'm going to have to learn on my own."

He turned toward the window before he spoke. "I know my mother would have loved you, and she would have had a marvelous time teaching you."

Daphne patted his arm, not knowing how to respond. "I'm sure she's somewhere in heaven looking down at you fondly with love."

"She's probably laughing at our antics," he replied.

"You know she is."

Daphne, not having lost a parent yet, knew nothing of what he had gone through. He probably had never let his gut feelings out to anyone. Not even his sister. He'd been keeping everything bottled up inside, which wasn't good for him. She knew she herself would be devastated when the time came for her parents to move on. Hopefully that wouldn't happen for many years.

"What happens once we've married? Will we return to Kent immediately?" she asked.

"Really?"

She felt her cheeks heat up. "You know what I mean. I'm not talking about the marriage bed."

"I thought we'd stay in my chambers for a day or two."

"A day or two?"

"Yes. You'll see. After that, I thought we could take a ride about the estate, see the mine and take you into town," he replied.

"That sounds amazing. I can't wait. You do have a riding horse I can use, don't you?"

"Yes, I think I have the perfect mount for you."

"Wonderful!" she exclaimed. "There is one thing I forgot to mention, and it's non-negotiable."

Arthur raised a brow. He knew what was coming. He'd expected it. "What's that? Sam will be coming on our journeys between estates and London?"

She looked at him in disbelief. It took a moment for it to completely sink in. "Yes. He's part of my life."

"I knew that. What will be interesting to see is how Roddy reacts to Sam."

Daphne giggled. "I imagine one good nip from Sam will put an end to the curiosity."

He smiled. "Yes, Roddy is quite curious. I'm afraid he's going to find he's met his match."

She gazed out the window. They'd been on the road quite a while and she was anxious to settle in and have a hot bath and change clothes. And dinner. She was hungry for a good hot meal.

Feeling the carriage slow, she quickly glanced at Arthur who was acting all-knowing.

"We're turning onto the drive," he said.

"Obviously, since we're now off the main road," she quipped.

She heard him chuckle deeply. His baritone made everything he said quite erotic. Erotic? Where had that come from? How would she even know if something was erotic? That was one thing he enjoyed doing. Teasing her, testing her limits. It was far better than most men. They would treat her as though she was just a simple woman who was there for his beck and call.

The carriage came to a halt moments later. She waited while Arthur climbed down and offered his hand. "Welcome to Winding Creek."

Daphne gazed about the courtyard and then at the magnificent timbered house. It was a far larger Tudor-era house, but it had been given to the family by the king. The king had never been less than extravagant. "It's amazing," she said.

"It is, isn't it. I don't come here but twice a year, sometimes three, and every time I'm more and more intrigued."

"Would you like to spend more time here?"

"Right now, I don't find it possible. Especially now, with a new marriage, my seat as an MP. Perhaps next summer we can spend more time. We'll see."

Leading her to the front door, they were met by an aging butler. His hair was snow white and he was hunched over from the many years of service.

"Carter, I thought I gave you a pension and cottage. I appreciate your loyalty, but you need to think of yourself."

"I heard you were arriving and thought I should meet you." He glanced at Daphne.

"I apologize," Arthur said. "Carter, this is my fiancée, Lady Daphne. We intend to marry in the next day or two."

"Lovely to meet you, my lady. We were all overjoyed at the news. Please do not hesitate to call on the staff should you need anything at all."

Daphne smiled at the older man. He reminded her of her grandfather, her father's sire. She didn't know him long, but the bits and pieces she remembered were his smile of adoration and his unruly white hair. "Thank you, Carter."

"Has a room been prepared for Lady Daphne?" Arthur inquired.

"Yes, Your Grace. The Elizabeth suite has been readied," he said, turning to Daphne. "I believe you'll find it to your liking. It overlooks the rose garden."

"Elizabeth suite?" Daphne said to no one in particular.

"Legend has it that Elizabeth visited and that was the suite of rooms she was given," Arthur said.

"I feel honored."

"It's only a myth, nothing more."

She looked around the main hall. "Are there books, diaries and such written in that time period?"

"Yes, my lady. You'll find everything you seek in the library," Carter replied.

"Thank you. If you gentlemen don't mind, I'd like to see my rooms. If it's no trouble, I'd like a hot bath."

Arthur put his hand on her elbow and guided her across the hall to the staircase. "I'll show you, and Carter will be sure to have a maid help you."

Entering the suite, Daphne was followed by Arthur. He hadn't been in here in ages. Nothing in the house had ever changed, and it might be time to refresh it.

"You have quite a devoted man in Carter," she said as she walked to the windows to look out at the rose garden. It was spectacular, well maintained for many years.

"Yes, though as I said before, he's supposed to be retired. The man worked here from the time he was twelve. I think he's due."

Facing the gardens, she continued. "You've never replaced him?"

"No, I haven't a reason to. I only visit a couple times a year. I've seen no need, at least while he is still alive," he replied.

Turning back around to face him, Daphne smiled. "You are a good man, Arthur."

"I've been known to have my moments," he quipped. He pointed in the direction of a separate room. "Bedroom is through there along with a dressing and bathing room."

"How delightful. Where should I meet you when I'm finished?"

"I'll come for you in two hours, if that's enough time. I'll give you the tour of the house. It can be quite a maze."

"Yes, I don't want to get lost."

He moved closer to her and wrapped his arms around her. "You're smart. I'm sure you'd figure it out," he said before lifting her face with one hand and softly kissing her on the lips. The kiss deepened. Arthur groaned at his body's traitorous behavior. He wanted her, and if he had his way, he'd make love to her right here in this room. Instead, he pulled away. "You're quite the vixen. I find it extremely hard to resist your charms."

"Soon, my love, soon," she whispered.

"And I'm going to enjoy every moment."

She wanted to reply but felt it might bring things to a head before their marriage. "I'll see you in two hours, Your Grace."

He grunted before loosening his hold on her. Turning, he walked out of the room, leaving Daphne alone.

In turn, Daphne walked into the bed chamber. In it was a large dark-stained bed frame with heavy gold curtains hung on all four sides. Hearing a noise in the bathing chamber, she turned and continued. The bathing chamber was larger than she imagined, and to one side of the room sat a large white porcelain tub. She realized the house had been plumbed for running water. Out of the corner of her eye, she saw a young girl unpacking what few clothes she had.

"I apologize if I startled you, my lady," she said nervously. "My name is Polly. I'll be your lady's maid while you're in residence."

"No need to apologize, Polly. I'm sure we'll get on famously.

I thought I'd draw a bath before I do anything else."

"I can do that. While you're bathing, I'll set out a change of clothes and take these other two dresses to be tidied up."

"His Grace and I left London in rather a hurry, which is why I have not much in the way of clothes. I'm hoping I can find a dressmaker in the village. His Grace wishes to stay for at least a fortnight, so I will need more clothes."

"Mrs. Mackenzie is a wonderful dressmaker."

"Thank you, I'll keep her in mind."

Walking over to the tub, Daphne cracked each of the taps and began filling the tub. Finally, she found the perfect combination of hot and cold and left the tub to fill. She undressed and crawled in. It was heavenly, especially after adding some orange blossom oil she found to the water. She lay back against the far end of the tub and immersed herself in the water as far as she could.

When she finally did step out of the tub, she found a robe lying on a chair along with a warm towel. There was no sign of the young maid Polly, and Daphne concluded she must have taken her other dresses to the laundry. Donning the robe, she found a fire had been lit to warm the room. It was also perfect for her to dry her hair. Polly had left her undergarments and dress on the bed. The slippers she had been wearing since the ball were cleaned and waiting on the floor.

After dressing, she sat near the fire and waited for Arthur. Closing her eyes momentarily, she was consumed by dreams, most of which she had no idea of their meaning. A knock on the door caught her attention as she rose and walked to the door. Arthur looked quite handsome, having bathed and changed his clothes.

"Are you ready for your grand tour, my lady?"

"Yes," she replied.

He led her down the room, pointing out to her his suite, which was where they would be staying after they were married. She felt her face flush and tried to turn away so Arthur wouldn't notice. They made their way to a drawing room, where a tray with tea and cakes had recently been placed.

Daphne gazed about the room. "I feel as though I'm living in the Tudor era. Has the house never been redecorated?"

"Not in my lifetime. It was one of the reasons my mother was not fond of this estate."

"Perhaps we ought to think about doing just that."

"Agreed. What if we look at beginning next summer while we're here? We can find someone who knows how to do it and bring them here to make suggestions."

"That would be perfect, Arthur. I don't want to make any major changes, just update what is already here."

She walked over to the tray and fixed a cup of tea for each of them. She passed a cup to Arthur. "Would you like something to eat?"

"I spy a couple of pieces of marmalade cake. I'll take one."

Placing the cake on the plate, she added a couple of other pieces of sweets. "Here you go."

"Thank you."

She sat down across from Arthur with her tea and a couple of small sandwiches of roast chicken and cucumber. "Tomorrow will be a busy day for you."

"Quite so, though I imagine you'll be busy yourself if we can put together a ceremony quickly."

"Is there a family chapel on the estate?"

"Yes, there is, though I can't tell you the last time it was used."

She smiled over her cup at him. "It would need cleaning up?"

"To say the least. I thought we might hold the ceremony here in the drawing room."

She glanced about the room. Perhaps some flowers from the gardens would liven it up. "Yes, I think it will do. If I can get fresh flowers in here, it should be fine. It's only you and I, the vicar, and our witnesses."

"I promise once this is all settled and we return to Kent, we'll throw a dinner party to celebrate."

She smiled demurely at him. "I'd like that. I still can't believe I'm going to be a duchess. I keep wanting to pinch myself, but if it's a dream, I don't want to wake up."

"It's not a dream, I can assure you."

"Are you going to write your sister, telling her what's transpired?"

He grinned like the naughty boy she was sure he had been years ago. "I'm sure she figured it all out, but I'll send her a letter. And you?"

"Yes, I thought we could send both out at the same time so hopefully they arrive at their destinations at the same time."

He licked his fingers as he finished his cake. "That's a great idea. How do you think they've reacted?"

"I'm sure my father will be grateful to you for eternity. He regretted his decision with Black the moment he agreed."

CHAPTER TWELVE

D APHNE FOUND NO sign of Arthur when she went downstairs the following morning. She hadn't intended to sleep so long, but her body disagreed. Finding her way to the smaller breakfast room, she told the footman what she wanted. As she waited, another poured her a glass of orange juice and a cup of tea.

Spotting the newspapers Arthur left behind, she sat where he'd sat earlier. She picked up one but quickly put it back on top of the pile. Perhaps after she ate, she'd have the stomach to read what was going on in the world.

As she sat waiting on her food, a middle-aged woman dressed in dark gray entered the room. "Milady, I don't mean to disturb you but I thought to introduce myself. I'm Miss Smith, His Grace's housekeeper."

"Yes, of course. Please come in," she replied. "His Grace seems to have left rather early."

"He mentioned he had a couple appointments first thing this morning."

She watched the woman with curiosity. "Yes, I know. I was simply surprised he left so early."

"He mentioned I should check with him once he returns. Something about flowers."

"Yes."

The housekeeper went straight into the reason for her coming to Daphne. "His Grace mentioned you will be staying a fortnight. I thought you'd like to approve a menu Cook has come up with."

"I'd love to, though I'm not sure I should."

"His Grace told me to work with you on meals during your stay."

Smiling, Daphne nodded. "Sounds just like the duke," she said.

"If I may be so bold, milady. His Grace is one of the nicest and kindest men I know. He always puts others before himself. And you'll never hear him complain."

As the housekeeper was talking, a footman brought in two steaming hot plates, setting each one in front of her. Everything smelled heavenly and she couldn't wait to dig in. "Thank you for your candid words. You've just described him as I might. I love that."

"Thank you, milady. I'll let you get back to your breakfast. If you need anything, don't hesitate to let me know."

"I shall. Has His Grace let you know the reason we're here?"

"Yes, but like I told His Grace, I won't tell anyone until I know differently."

She was happy to know someone knew or had figured out what was going on. It had been hard to keep it inside. Hopefully everything would work out as Arthur planned and they'd be married today. Her life would forever change. No longer would she be a single young lady looking for a proper husband. She would be married to a duke, and she would be a duchess. How far she and Arthur had come since their first encounter.

Digging into her eggs, she closed her eyes as she savored the bite. It was heavenly. The longer Arthur stayed away, the more nervous she would become. Not for any reason. She simply wanted to know what to expect. Nothing more. She continued to savor her breakfast until she realized her plate was almost empty. Whoever the cook was, they were skilled. Most wouldn't try anything out of the ordinary when it came to something as simple as eggs. She couldn't wait to review the menus for the time they'd be in York.

After finishing a second cup of tea, Daphne wrapped her shawl around her tighter and decided to familiarize herself with the house. She had a notebook in her dress pocket, and she could begin making notes of what she saw needing to be done in various rooms. Then, when she spoke to the decorator Arthur had in mind, she would know what she wanted done.

Deciding to begin in the drawing room, she found it easier than she thought it would be. She would look at draperies, wallcoverings, and what shape the upholstery was all in. No telling when anything had been replaced. If they intended to spend any length of time here, the house needed to come out of the past. A good deep cleaning of the entire house was also on her list. The staff kept it ready for the residents, but she'd already noticed dust on a side table that was more than a couple of weeks' worth.

Daphne had moved on to the library when she heard Arthur's deep, rich baritone resonate through the house. She thought he was looking for her, so she continued to finish her notes on the library. Moments later, he appeared at the doorway. By the look on his face, she knew the morning had been successful.

Arthur was at her side in two strides. He bent down and kissed boldly and passionately. "Come, there is someone I want you to meet."

She placed her notebook and pencil back into her pocket and he took her hand and began leading her out of the library.

"I gather you were successful in your endeavors this morning?"

"Very. Are you ready?" he asked.

"For what?" she asked him back innocently.

"To become my wife," he replied without looking at her. Daphne got enough of a glimpse to tell he was smiling.

"Yes."

He led her to the drawing room where a man and woman were seated near the blazing fire. The pair, upon seeing Arthur and Daphne enter, stood from the green upholstered chairs. They waited as they approached.

"May I present my soon to be wife, Lady Daphne Waterton." He turned to Daphne and continued the introduction. "May I present my cousin Henry Stone and his wife, Jane. Henry is going to marry us."

"It's nice to meet you both," Daphne said.

"Lady Daphne, it is an honor to meet the woman who's captured my cousin's heart."

Smiling, she glanced at Arthur to see him watching what transpired. This was the first member of Arthur's family outside of Roxanne she had met. "I can't take all the credit."

"She's going to be an extraordinary duchess, Arthur," Henry said.

"I have no doubt," Arthur replied.

Arthur motioned for everyone to take a seat. He turned to Daphne. "Henry's graciously agreed to marry us today. Jane is going to serve as one of our witnesses."

Daphne nodded. "Thank you."

"Are you ready?" Arthur asked. He was gazing at her as though he were trying to make sure she was real.

"I am, but if you don't mind, I'd like to tidy up my hair."

"Of course," Arthur replied.

She rose from her chair, turning and hurrying to the door. In her chambers, she looked at herself in the full-length glass. The dress was one of Roxanne's. It was the nicest and best made of the few she had with her. Her hair was the only thing needing to be fixed.

"Polly," she called out.

The maid came out of the dressing room. "I need to have my hair redone into something for a wedding. My wedding."

"Now?"

"Yes. Now," she replied. The maid looked stunned at what

she had just been told.

Daphne sat down at the dressing table and began to pull the pins out of her hair. She'd swept it up herself, but in a more casual style, but this needed something that showed she was becoming a duchess.

She observed how Polly was doing her hair. It was always best to have another person help with doing one's hair, and Polly seemed to make it look easy.

"How's this, milady? I can work some small flowers throughout if you'd like."

"That would be lovely. Let me change out of this dress before you do them."

In no time, Daphne was transformed. The next time she looked in a mirror, she would be a married woman and a duchess. Life was about to change forever.

"You look beautiful, milady."

"Thanks to you, Polly."

The young girl blushed at the compliment. "You best go downstairs and marry your duke."

"Yes," she replied and walked through the door and to Arthur.

Everyone stood as she entered the room. Arthur walked over to his bride. "You look stunning. Are you ready?"

"Yes, let's do this."

"Henry needs a minimum of two witnesses, so I asked Carter and Miss Smith. If that is agreeable with you."

She smiled at him. "Perfectly agreeable."

Arthur couldn't keep his eyes off Daphne as the ceremony began. He couldn't believe how, after spending years of half-hearted searching, his duchess had been right under his nose. She was more than he ever dared hope for. Not a meek, shy debutante, but a woman who knew what she wanted from life. He only wished his mother and father could have been here to meet her. They would have liked her and been welcoming.

Her voice was strong as she repeated her vows, looking Arthur straight in the eye. When it came to his, he found himself becoming emotional, which was completely unlike him. Emotions were kept to oneself, and for the most part, he did just that, but right now, at this moment, he couldn't help himself.

The moment they were pronounced man and wife, Arthur didn't wait. He leaned down and planted a kiss firmly on the lips. He wanted more, but this wasn't the place and there would be plenty of time to savor her lips.

Miss Smith and Carter came up and wished their congratulations before the group found their way to a sideboard which had been cleared for Daphne and Arthur to sign the registry Henry had brought. Once official business was finished, Carter and Miss Smith disappeared.

While they'd been busy, a footman had placed a champagne bucket near the hearth with four glasses and a just-opened bottle of champagne. Arthur poured four glasses and handed one to each, before he toasted his wife, cousin and his wife.

"You cannot know how much I appreciate this," Arthur said. "You are staying for a wedding luncheon Cook's prepared?"

"We would love to, Arthur. It's been far too long since Henry's gotten to spend time with extended family," Jane said.

They made small talk, at least to Daphne it was, but she soon realized how Arthur was using it to update his cousin. Henry was a third son and his options few, given the best went to the older siblings. Daphne felt he was comfortable in his decision to serve the church. Where he and his family lived was always wherever the church assigned him.

"We plan on spending a couple of times here beginning next year. Otherwise, we'll be in Kent or London. I'm taking on my father's seat in Parliament, so I'm sure we'll be in London when in session," Arthur said.

"You never know when I might have to be in London on church business," Henry said. He swallowed his remaining champagne and set the glass down. "How is Roxanne? I know she remarried after her husband died. Is she happy?"

"She is happier than I've seen her in years. She and her husband, Graham, have a good life," Arthur replied.

"That's good to hear. She deserves it. Tell her I said hello when you see her."

Carter entered the room and announced the luncheon was awaiting in the dining room. Daphne finished her champagne before rising from her seat. Arthur, who hadn't left her side, helped her and walked next to her into the dining room. The room was set in all the duke's finery. He had taken time in setting up the menu with Cook and Miss Smith. Daphne was impressed at his attention to details.

Shrimp on a bed of ice and lettuce were served first. Once everyone finished the first course, the main meat course was brought in. A tender beef roast had been cooked to perfection, sliced, and served to them with potatoes which had been mashed and butter and chives added. Red wine accompanied the meat. Conversation ceased during this course. It was one of Arthur's favorite meals. Once the plates were removed, a piece of Scottish salmon was presented with hollandaise and capers. The fish had been cut into the perfect portion, giving guests a perfect amount of fish.

Since the kitchen had had little time to prepare for this meal, a proper wedding cake hadn't been made. Instead, Cook used her skills and made a wonderful marmalade cake. Arthur was fine about that, because he wasn't impressed by the traditional fruitcake unless it was during the Christmas holidays. It was the perfect choice for everyone.

After feigning having appointments at his parish office, Henry and Jane departed, leaving Arthur and his new bride alone. It was the perfect storm.

Arthur knew his bride was on edge about what lay ahead. As much as he wanted to take her to his bed, he decided a long walk might do them both good. "Why don't we take a walk. Colder weather is knocking on the door, and there won't be a lot of time left for such activities."

She peered up at him, her blue eyes searching his. "Are you sure that's how you wish to spend our afternoon?"

"I didn't say we'd spend the whole afternoon on a walk. I thought it a good idea after all we consumed," he replied.

"Touché."

He offered her his arm. "Duchess?"

"I should get my shawl from the drawing room."

Arthur nodded and followed her as she found her way to the drawing room. Picking it up from a chair she'd earlier sat in, she wrapped the shawl around her shoulders before joining him.

"Now we can go for that walk," she said with a demure smile.

If he wasn't mistaken, she was attempting to flirt with him. Giving in to his lust, Arthur had his arms around her, his mouth on hers in a deep kiss. He parted her lips with his tongue and probed inside her mouth. Slowly she began to respond and the moment he felt her tongue dart into his mouth he felt himself losing control over his cock's desire. She had slowly put her arms around him, seemingly wanting more. He freed one arm and pulled up her skirts enough for him to stroke her inner thighs before he slowly began to insert one finger inside her wet, hot cunny. It was all he could do to contain himself. He happened to open his eyes to find her wild, doe eyes peering up at him. Rather than withdraw, Arthur slowly began to rub her, causing her to react. That reaction was to spread her legs farther apart. Her breathing quickened as she began moving with his hands. He felt her tensing and suddenly she hit her plateau. Daphne clung to him as she rode it out. By the end, she was a limp rag in his arms. It didn't take him but a second to lift her into his arms and carry her to his bedchamber. His bride's needs far surpassed any walk.

ARTHUR CARRIED HIS bride to the bed. She was still in euphoria when he gently placed her down on the mattress. He left her and made sure the door was locked in his dressing room and then did the same with the main door. This was their time, and he was going to be sure they wouldn't be interrupted.

On his way back to his bride, he noted a fresh bottle of champagne had been placed to chill next to a sideboard in the sitting room. He sat for a moment to remove his boots before rejoining Daphne. He removed his cravat and loosened his shirt at the neck. Finding his way back to the bed, Arthur slid up on the bed where his duchess was beginning to sit up.

"What happened?"

"You had a very intense orgasm," he said as he placed his larger body over her petite frame. He balanced himself on his forearms as he loomed over her. Running his lips over the outline of hers, he followed with feathering kisses on her cheeks and finally her mouth. He pulled up to gaze down at her. "I promise to be gentle. This is the only time it might hurt."

"That's about the only advice my mother gave me on the matter."

"Hmmm," he grunted as his lips met hers. In a matter of moments, they were both pulling off their clothes and slinging them anywhere.

Her eyes widened as she saw his stiff member. It was probably the first time she'd ever seen a man in complete undress. He gently took her hand and placed her fingers around his cock. He groaned in pleasure.

"I didn't hurt you, did I?" she asked with the innocence of a child.

He shook his head. "I'm fine. This is what you do to me."

"Oh."

"Just lay back and I promise you won't be disappointed."

He'd wanted to take his time, but his deceiving body wasn't going to allow it. She moaned as he suckled her breasts, and he felt her fingers in his hair. Continuing his feast, Arthur found his way down to her sweet spot by feathering more kisses as he moved down her body. Spreading her legs farther apart gave him better access to her cunny. As he tasted her sweet spot, he heard her somewhere in the distance groaning and her hands pushed his head closer.

Knowing he wouldn't last if he didn't get inside her, he would explode, he mounted her and quickly found what he was after. He said nothing as he guided his cock into her wet, hot body. Somewhere beneath him, he heard her saying his name over and over. He hit her barrier and whispered to her, "This might hurt, but it'll never, ever hurt again." He pushed, feeling her clinging to him tightly. It was over. They were one. He bent over her face and kissed her. She responded as he began to rock in a motion made to make it easier for her to pick up the rhythm and join him. She was a quick learner.

"Arthur, it's coming again."

"What is my love?"

"That intense feeling. I feel as though I'm beginning to fall apart."

Moments later, they were both caught up in a frenzy. Arthur exploded, spilling himself into her just as she went over the edge into her own utopia. He lay still for a moment afterwards while his body pulsed. Never had he felt such bliss and contentment. It was as though the two of them were pre-destined to be husband and wife.

Nothing was said for the longest time. They simply lay there in each other's arms, both exhausted. Arthur pulled a blanket over them to keep them warm. His finger traced her arm from shoulder to fingertips and back before laying his arm over her. At about that time, Arthur thought he heard something. Peering down at her, he noted she was asleep and quietly snoring. He spooned in behind her and closed his eyes. Now that they were married, perhaps he could relax some. She was his wife and duchess now and someday the mother of his children. A sense of calm fell over him now.

Waking up some time later, he threw his eyes open upon not feeling Daphne's body close to him. A glimpse at the place where she had lain explained it all. She had been a virgin and he had forgotten that. He should have gotten out of bed and gotten her a warm, wet cloth to clean herself up. That's probably what she was doing right now. He climbed out of bed and padded towards the dressing room. He found her brushing her hair.

"I was wondering where you were."

"Well, wonder no more," she said. Closing the distance between them, she kissed him on the cheek.

"Did you sleep well?" he asked. "In case you didn't know, you snore."

She playfully batted him on the arm. "I do not."

"Oh, but you do," he countered.

"Don't speak to me about snoring. I'm surprised you don't make windows vibrate."

"I'll have you know I do not snore."

She giggled. "Of course, you don't, and I'm still a virgin."

"Are you mocking my snoring, wife?"

"Oh, so now you admit you snore," she said triumphantly.

Realizing he'd been outmaneuvered, Arthur wrapped his arms around her. He lifted her off the ground just enough for her to lock her legs around his torso. "This is better," he said.

"It is."

He carried her back to the bed and set her down gently. "Are you thirsty? There's an unopened bottle of champagne waiting for us," he said. "Would you like a glass?"

"Please," she replied. He noted she seemed to be relaxed being nude in front of him. He understood this not to be the case with a lot of brides. He was thankful for her willingness.

Daphne accepted the glass from him, and Arthur smiled as the bubbles got to her nose. He picked up his glass and joined her. While enjoying a sip, he almost did a double take at her new-found boldness. She sat in the middle of the bed and spread her legs, leaving nothing to the imagination as she not only sprinkled some of the bubbly between the apex of her legs before taking a finger and spreading it.

He was hard and wanted her. Swallowing the remaining champagne, Arthur took one of her hands and placed it on his hard cock and encouraged her to explore.

The remainder of the day and well into the night was theirs and theirs alone. At some point, Arthur got out of bed and added fuel to the fading fire. They hadn't eaten since the wedding luncheon, and he knew she had to be hungry as well. He found his trousers and began to put them on.

"Where are you going?" a well-sated voice inquired from the middle of the bed.

"To find us something to eat. I don't know about you, but I'm famished. Aren't you?"

She giggled. "A lady never admits she's famished. Hungry, but never famished. And yes, I am. Hungry."

"I'll be back before you know it. I'm sure Cook left us something."

"Hurry back, husband."

He opened the door and found a trolley sitting in front of the doorway. On it was a covered tray. He lifted the cloth and found dried meats, cheeses, bread, enough to make a meal. Beside it were two bottles of wine, and an apple pie. Heaven.

Rolling the cart into the sitting area, he was about to call to Daphne when she strode in with a robe wrapped around her. "What's all this?"

"Our dinner. It was waiting for us outside the door."

She lifted the cloth from the tray. "This looks good. It may not be a hot meal, but it is certainly welcome."

Daphne discovered the pie and clapped her hands. "Apple pie, one of my favorites."

"Really? Mine too." He grinned, reaching for one of the bottles of wine. "Why don't you roll the cart over to that small table. We can eat there."

Watching her made him almost forget the task at hand—opening the wine. Two plates were placed on the table, and each filled with carefully chosen selections. He approached with two glasses and passed one to her before sitting across from her and placing one in front of himself.

"This is better than I first thought," he said.

"Sometimes simple is all one needs." Daphne took a sip of wine before picking up a piece of pungent Stilton.

"I imagine you did this a lot when your parents left you on your own?"

"Only when the cook had the day off. I expected a full meal the remainder of the time, even if it was just me."

He cleared his throat before grabbing a piece of crusty white bread. Spying the butter on the trolley, he picked up the dish and knife and began to cover the bread in soft creamy butter. "I stand corrected."

"My father pays them regardless of if he's in residence or not. There's no reason for them to slack just because I'm the only one in residence."

"You have a point," he replied, taking a bite of bread.

"I guess you think bad of me for being so demanding."

"No, not at all. It shows me you already have a good grasp on how households run. I have no worry you won't do a marvelous job now that you're my duchess."

"My mother's tried to prepare me."

"And I think she's done a splendid job," he replied.

They ate in silence for a few minutes. Arthur then, with wine glass in hand, sat back in his chair. "What would you like to do tomorrow? Besides the obvious." He smirked.

She smiled demurely. "First thing is a bath. I want to soak in a hot bath. After that, you could show me the mine, or we could take a nice ride."

"That sounds good. We could also go to the village. You could find a dressmaker who might have some dresses and such pre-made."

"You wouldn't mind?" she asked.

"Not at all. We could also have lunch in town before we head back."

"I'd like that, but Arthur, if you have matters needing your attention elsewhere, we don't have to spend a fortnight here. This was spur of the moment."

"You wouldn't object if we did?"

"Not at all. Besides, people wouldn't be expecting us."

It was all settled. Arthur breathed a sigh of relief that his bride was being so accommodating. She was a smart young woman who understood how the real world operated. Unlike some of her peers, Daphne wasn't selfish. He would make it up to her many times over.

CHAPTER THIRTEEN

W HEN THE CARRIAGE turned down the crushed stone drive of Arthur's family estate in Kent, the rain began coming down harder than most of the journey from London. He'd sent word ahead to his valet as he wanted everything to be perfect when Daphne stepped down from the carriage as his duchess.

"Are you scared?" he suddenly asked.

She had been peering out the window, watching as they neared the house. Unfortunately, the rain made it almost impossible. "Scared? Me? No, not at all," she replied. She cocked her head and laughed. "Well, perhaps just a little. This is all new to me."

"You'll do fine."

"Of course I will," she replied.

The carriage came to a stop and a footman opened the door with an open umbrella to keep Daphne out of the wet. Arthur followed, umbrella in hand, and together they climbed the few steps leading to the great front door. It was open, and Wilson greeted them.

"Welcome home, Your Grace."

"Thank you, Wilson. May I present my duchess, Lady Daphne?"

"Your Grace," he murmured, bowing to her.

"Where is everyone?" Arthur asked, looking around the

room.

"I thought since the rain has set in, meeting the staff could be rescheduled until it's dry."

"I agree. It's not only wet out there, the chill and the wind wouldn't help anyone."

Daphne, who had been looking about the hall, turned her attention to the men. "Was word sent to my lady's maid?"

"Yes, Your Grace. Miss Young arrived yesterday and saw all your belongings moved into the duchess's suite."

"Thank you."

Arthur placed her hand on his arm. "I'll show Her Grace to her new chambers."

They walked across the hall to the dual staircase. Once they reached her new chambers, Arthur opened the door and walked in behind her. Everything had been cleaned and refreshed. He could tell his sister had lent her touch. Roxanne would want to be sure her new sister-in-law was at home within the walls of her chamber. Fresh flowers dotted various tables, and a fire warmed the room.

Arthur explained where everything was and then showed her a door. "This leads to my suites."

"Oh," she replied.

"My wish is for you and me to sleep there every night. The duchess's chambers might be used for you to bathe and dress."

"I would like that. Open the door. I'd like to see my husband's rooms."

He did and followed her inside. The sitting room had been cleaned and polished, and he was caught off guard at the sight of fresh flowers in his rooms. But he knew it had been done in a way to make Daphne feel at home.

"What do you think?"

"I'm impressed. I expected it to be all dark and gloomy, but it's warm and welcoming. Does that make sense?"

He nodded. "Yes, it does."

"I know there are matters needing your attention. While

you're doing that, I'm going to change."

"Let me show you how to ring for staff," he said. They returned to the duchess's suites, and he walked her as far as a rope pull in the corner. "Pull it and someone will be here quickly."

"That's easy."

"I'll be off. If you need me, I'll be in my study. If not, I'll come here for you in, say, two hours?"

"That sounds wonderful," she replied. "Oh, do you know if Sam's been moved?"

"I believe they have waited until you returned so the bird isn't stressed."

"Good, because he would have been stressed coming to a new home and wondering where I was. He's truly smart, Arthur."

"You don't have to try and sell me. I know Sam, and I think this was the best choice. We'll make a point of moving him here tomorrow."

"Only if the rain has gone. Birds like Sam don't need the cold and damp. The moment the rain has moved on, I'll go and oversee his move. I'll have to find a perfect place to set his cage," Daphne said.

"The one large one?"

"That and there's another in my room," she replied.

He was at her side in one stride. He leaned down and kissed her, daring to make sure it was short, otherwise they'd end up in his bed. "I'll see you soon."

"You can count on it."

Arthur stepped inside his study and felt reality jolt him in the gut. On his desk was a large stack of unopened correspondence. He groaned at the sight. The sooner he sorted through it, the faster he'd be finished. Sitting down, he picked up three or four letters and began to sort them. Business and personal. Amazingly, most of what had arrived while they were gone was personal. People congratulating them on the marriage. Ordinarily he might wonder how word got out so quickly, but then he knew his sister had probably begun notifying friends and family as soon as he'd sent word to her. He would set it all aside so he and Daphne might go through it together.

His business correspondence was primarily monthly bills from shops the estate used. Nothing out of the ordinary. Any other business addressed to him were updates on a couple of projects he was involved in and another report from the coal mine, which he should have taken care of while in residence. However, one official looking envelope he'd overlooked caught his eye. Picking it up, he examined the outside before opening to retrieve the contents.

It was a notice from the courts informing him of the trial date for Crenshaw, the man arrested in connection with his parents' murder. The trial was scheduled to begin in London at week's end. Arthur decided when Crenshaw was arrested and charged with the crime, it would be the end of it for him. Seeing this made it real, and once again, he was split on what he wanted to do. Leave for London to sit in on the proceedings or let it go and wait from the comfort of his estate for the verdict.

His parents deserved to be represented by the family. The fact that Crenshaw had murdered a member of the peerage made the outcome more dire. He wouldn't be in his new position if that fateful day had never occurred. His father would have had many more years in life.

He would leave for London in two days. That would give him time to inform his sister of his intention and for Daphne to prepare for the journey. He couldn't just leave her in Kent. They were newlyweds and this would be perfect; all women loved to go to London. The shopping was premier, and Daphne would love spending time in the shops while he was in court.

Satisfied everything was set for London, it occurred to him that he and Daphne's father had never signed off on her dowry. Not that he intended to use it; it would be put aside for any daughters they might have. He hadn't even set it up through his solicitor to set Daphne up with an allowance for whatever fripperies she might want. He'd look into it while in London.

Fastidious as he normally was with everything he was involved in, it stressed him to see he hadn't paid attention to anything for the past couple of weeks. Pulling his cheque ledger out of a desk drawer, he began to pay the bills. This wouldn't take much of his time and it would be off his mind. If he didn't, he would be fretting over it the rest of the day.

Not paying attention to anything around him, he failed to glance up from his desk when the door opened. He still didn't look up at the sound of soft feminine feet crossing the floor.

"Did you forget about me?" Daphne asked, her bottom lip stuck out for effect.

His head jerked up and he quickly glanced at the clock on his desk. "I am so sorry, my love. I thought to take care of some of this," he said, motioning to all the paperwork littering the top of the desk. "I simply lost track of time."

"I'll forgive you… just this one time," she replied with a wink.

She sat in one of the chairs facing the desk. "Is there anything I can do to help?"

He grinned. "As a matter of fact, there is." He picked up a stack of unopened correspondence. "This is all addressed to us. Congratulating us, etc. Why don't you go ahead and go through it? Once you have, we can see to it together, and I can explain who people are that you don't know."

"I can do that," she said, taking the pile of letters from him.

Arthur nodded and returned to his work. He was almost finished, and eager to be done. Occasionally he would hear her sigh or mumble something to herself as she sifted through the letters. There was one that set her off. He caught her as she threw it down on the desk. She crossed her arms and pursed her lips. "How rude."

"What, what is it?"

"My parents, who else?"

He stopped what he was doing and looked up. "What did they do to anger you so?"

"Friends of theirs invited them to visit them at their estate on Wight. So naturally, Mother convinced my father it would be rude not to go. She couldn't even wait for us to return."

He didn't want to take sides, but in this instance, she was right. It was rude. Daphne's relationship with her mother and father was strained at times, but she had thought maybe there had been a breakthrough.

"I'm so sorry, my love."

"And don't tell me there's some logical reason as to why they had to go at this particular time. Because there isn't any, other than once again, she has to be the center of attention."

"Take a deep breath and move on to the next. Don't let her ruin your day."

Daphne grabbed her mother's letter off the desk and crumpled it into a ball and threw it straight into the fire. "There! Now I can move on to the next."

He watched her for a moment as she opened yet another and read it. She smiled so he assumed all was right. Arthur continued with his work. He was almost at the end, and unfortunately, the storm had set in for the day. There'd be no outdoor adventures today. Instead, he placed all the envelopes onto a silver tray to the left on his desk. He was done except for reading a couple of letters, but they could wait until the following morning.

The longer he watched her sitting and reading, the more he wanted her. Never had a woman affected him like this, he kept telling himself. Reminding himself how lucky he had been.

She popped her head up. "I'm finished. I have heard of or have met almost everyone who wrote."

"Good," he replied.

"Lydia has gotten me all unpacked. All we'll need to do is retrieve my horse and Sam."

"I can send a groom over for the gray. We'll see what the weather does before we get Sam."

Daphne nodded. "Excellent." She popped up out of the chair and rounded the desk, sliding onto Arthur's lap. Wrapping her arms around his neck, and before he could protest, she kissed him. Any hesitation on his part was forgotten. His hands parted her thighs, and he could feel her warmth.

"Why don't you lock the door?" Daphne suggested.

Shocked by her newfound boldness, Arthur quickly found her sweet spot which was wet for him. He ached for her, but the chair in his study wouldn't do. After minutes of arousal, he pulled her skirt back down and put her to her feet. "We can't."

"Lock the door," she replied. She pulled her skirts down and smoothed them with her hands.

"I know somewhere better. Somewhere we won't be disturbed."

"How can you be so sure we won't be disturbed?"

He grinned. "Because none of the staff know of its existence."

"I'm intrigued," she replied with a naughty grin.

Realizing he needed to inform her of their upcoming journey to London, he approached her with the matter. "There is something else I need to talk with you about."

"What is it?"

"I received notice from the courts informing me that the trial of Crenshaw, the man who murdered my parents, will begin at week's end. I plan to attend because someone needs to represent my parents. I thought you'd like to come along and do some shopping when I'm occupied elsewhere."

"Isn't it obvious what will happen to him? He'll be condemned to death. Why put yourself through that?"

"I'm sure he will be, but I want to be there when the sentence is read. I want him to see me when he's led from court."

She nodded. "I understand now. Of course I'd love to accompany you to London."

"I thought you might," he replied. "Until I got this notification, I thought I had blocked Crenshaw from my mind, but today it all came back to me."

"You're doing the right thing, Arthur. What about your sister?"

"I'm going to let her know my intentions tomorrow. We'll leave the day after."

Daphne took his larger hand in hers and looked him in the eyes. "I'll inform my maid so she can pack appropriately. How long do you think we'll be in London?"

"A fortnight. The trial, I'm sure, will be short," he replied.

Squeezing his hand, Daphne tried to pull him toward the closed door. "Would you like to show me this mysterious hidden room?"

He began walking to the door while holding her hand. "I would. You must understand that it's… well, you can decide for yourself."

"How did you find out about its existence?"

"My father showed it to me when I was old enough to understand."

They continued walking down the dark paneled hallway until they came to the main room where he led her up the stairs to the family's private chambers. Occasionally Daphne would ask if he knew who was in a portrait or where on the estate a scene was. Arthur did his best to answer her. Another thing his father had taught him. Who and where the portraits within the house were of. There were some painted by prominent artists of their time. His father had always said the family would never have to worry should times get hard, and that was part of the reason. That and good money and estate managers.

Reaching their suite, Arthur opened the door and let Daphne enter first. To his chagrin, he found his valet and a couple of footmen rolling up an older rug in order to replace it with another he'd chosen. He'd forgotten he'd charged Thomas with the task.

"Your Grace. I thought today would be perfect to change this rug out. Would you like us to return at another time?"

"No, go ahead and finish what you've started. I'm showing the duchess around the house, so she won't feel so lost."

"Thank you, Your Grace. We should be finished soon."

"Take your time. Oh, and we're going to London day after tomorrow, if you would mind getting things ready. We'll be gone about a fortnight."

"Understood, Your Grace."

Arthur peered down at his bride. "Come, my dear, let's let them finish."

She nodded and quit the room, along with Arthur. She burst out laughing when they were farther down the hall. "That's not meant to be."

"Not today," he agreed. "Why don't I show you the conservatory. It was one of my mother's favorite places."

"I'd love to see it. I understand she had quite a love of flowers."

"She did. She worked quite closely with the gardener."

Nodding, she followed Arthur through the house. "Where is Roddy? I expected to see him the moment we arrived."

"That's because, sadly, he's begun his training. I should check and see how he's progressing."

"Does this mean he won't be staying in the house?"

"I'm afraid not," Arthur replied. "He'll be living at the kennel from now on."

"That's so sad. I know how attached the dog was to you, and you seemed to enjoy his company."

"I did."

Arthur really didn't want to talk about the loss of his best friend. Roddy would make an excellent hunting dog. It was what he was bred for. It would be selfish of him to deny the setter of his heritage. Still, he missed the rambunctious Roddy.

They reached the conservatory and went in. They were hit by the warmth of the room. Orchids and other tropical flowering plants thrived in the dreary English weather.

"This is amazing," Daphne said as she turned in a circle to take in the flowers. A familiar squawk filled the room. "Sam? Is that you?" She looked at Arthur.

"Sam is bad."

"What's he doing here? Who moved him?"

Arthur shook his head. "I had no idea he was here."

A moment later, Sam appeared walking across the floor, flapping his red wings. He walked straight up to the pair as they peered down at him. Daphne extended her arm, and the macaw jumped up onto his perch. She stroked his head in reassurance.

"Pretty boy, Sam. I've missed you," Daphne told him.

"Bloody hell!"

"That's not a nice thing to say, Sam," she scolded the parrot. Turning to Arthur, she ever so slightly shook her head. "We need to find out when he arrived and who's been looking after him."

"How does he seem?"

"Okay, I think. I see his cage and things just over there."

Arthur watched as his bride, bird on her arm, walked over to where a black metal cage stood with thick branches hung around it. While she was doing that, he walked over to the bellpull to call staff. They needed to know the who and when of Sam's arrival. Not knowing anything about tropical parrots, Arthur thought whoever brought him knew enough to make sure he was somewhere warm.

He joined Daphne and Sam where Sam was walking around the top of his cage. "I just rang for staff. See if we can't get to the bottom of this."

"Good. I would be fine if I'd known he was here, but it upsets me that no one bothered to tell us he was here. I hate he's been alone in a strange place."

"I couldn't agree with you more."

A moment later, Wilson, his butler, entered. "Is there something you require, Your Grace?"

"Yes, the duchess and I were curious as to how the parrot arrived. Who brought him here and who's been looking after him?"

"And why weren't we told he was here?" Daphne demanded.

"Your father had him brought here, and MacDonald has been looking after him. It was MacDonald who suggested the conservatory."

Arthur looked over at his wife. She was still not satisfied with the explanation given them. "MacDonald is an underbutler. He looks after Roddy quite often."

"I'll have to thank him for putting Sam in here. It appears he's taken good care of him."

Turning to the older gentleman, Arthur thanked him and ordered tea for the two of them. He knew Daphne would want to spend time with Sam.

After Wilson left, Arthur sat down in a large white wicker chair. He despised these chairs, but his mother had insisted they belonged here and that had been that. "Are you satisfied Sam's been well looked after?"

"Yes, though I still am not happy we hadn't been told he was here."

"I'm sure it was just an oversight. We just arrived and all."

She flashed him a demure smile. "I'm sure you're right, and it certainly has been a whirlwind since we returned."

"It certainly has," he replied.

"I guess we'll have to wait for you to show me that room you were talking about."

"Only until tonight."

Squawking from Sam interrupted any conversation. The parrot seemed to know how to bring all conversation back to him. Until he opened his mouth. Arthur spotted him walking on the floor, coming their way.

"What are you up to, Sam?" Daphne asked. The bird was headed directly to her chair.

"Sam see. Sam see."

She bent down and scratched the bird's head. "What does Sam see?"

"Wankers. Everyone wanker."

"Sam, that's not a nice word," she scolded.

"I can imagine your mother attempting to have ladies over and Sam greets them with his colorful words," Arthur snorted.

"He holds back for no one."

"Do you wish to take him to London with us?"

"Let me think on it. I'll tell you tomorrow," she replied. "Would you like to go to London, Sam?"

Sam nodded his head and neck up and down in approval. "Sam beautiful arse."

Arthur burst out in a fit of laughter that could probably be heard throughout the house."

CHAPTER FOURTEEN

ARTHUR WAS FINISHING his correspondence at his desk in his London study when he heard the door open. He knew it was his wife. She had been very clear when they arrived a few hours ago that she would join him once she got Sam settled and changed from her traveling attire.

"Everything all right?" he asked as she came across the room. She had changed into a lavender day dress with a shawl pulled tightly around her for extra warmth. She took his breath away every time he saw her. He had plans for them as soon as he finished the missive he was writing. Arthur hoped she remembered.

"Yes, Sam is in the small parlor. It'll be easy to keep it warm enough for him."

"I was going to suggest the parlor. It should be perfect for Sam."

She smiled at him, poking her small pink tongue out to moisten her lips. It was all he could do not to groan. She knew the effect she had on him and seemed to love teasing him. "Did you lock the door when you entered?"

"Yes, but I don't understand why you want the door locked."

Clearing his throat, Arthur shut his eyes for a second. "Because I don't think you are going to want anyone walking in on us."

"Are we going to be naughty?"

"Oh, yes. Very much so," he replied.

Daphne crossed the room in quick steps and rounded the desk, placing her firm, round bottom on her husband's lap. His arm went around her waist as their lips met for a long, passionate kiss.

Arthur felt as though he'd explode if he couldn't have her. As much as he wanted to tease her and watch her face as she came to her pleasure, he knew he wouldn't last that long. Instead, he lowered her skirts he'd lifted and had begun to trail his hand to her cunny. He stood her to her feet and unfolded her long frame from his chair. He led her to the far edge of the desk and placed her facing the desk and spread her legs with his boot. Unfastening his trousers and smalls, he lifted her skirts to her waist. Taking himself in hand, he plunged into her hot, wet passage. He heard her moan as he seated her, one hand finding its way to help her. The moment he began to place his fingers on her, she began to buck, making it harder for him to contain himself as he pounded in and out. Feeling her muscles wrap around his cock, he groaned and spilled his seed within her just as she shuddered from her own orgasm. He draped himself over her as he recovered.

"I have no control when I'm making love to you," he said hoarsely. "I love you."

"I love you too, Arthur. I never thought being with a man would bring so much pleasure."

"I assume your mother and married friends don't have the same feelings as you?"

"My mother told me to just lie there and let you have your pleasure. One or two of my friends dread their husbands coming to them at night. I'm sure their mothers taught them sex is for one thing and one thing only. Producing children."

He kissed the side of her neck. "I'm so thankful we're not like them."

"As am I. I enjoyed what we just did."

"I'm glad you did," he replied.

Arthur stood behind her and fastened his clothing before taking her hand and helping her to right herself. It dawned on him she hadn't had on any undergarments. What else might she surprise him with? He took her hand and led her to a leather couch placed in front of the fire. Wrapping his arm around her, they sat there silently, enjoying the other's company.

Finally he asked, "What do you plan to do tomorrow while I'm away?"

"What are you doing tomorrow?"

He chuckled. "You're answering a question with a question?"

"I thought I might go by the dressmaker. If that's all right with you?"

"Of course it is. I'd like to have a couple of new suits made if I can find time to go to my tailor."

"Yes, you need to find time. You're going to take your father's place in Parliament, so you need to look handsome."

"And you're a duchess and need to update your wardrobe to fit your new place in the ton."

She giggled. It was something he adored hearing her do. "I promise not to go too crazy."

"Somehow, I can't see you doing that. I think you're very sensible."

"I try to be," she replied.

After a few minutes of quiet, Arthur felt himself falling asleep. He nudged Daphne. "I'm falling asleep. Why don't we go check on Sam and see how he's adapting?"

"I was falling asleep, too. Yes, let's check Sam. He makes enough noise to waken anyone."

Entering the parlor, they found the parrot on top of his cage. He appeared to be sleeping, but at the sound of Daphne's voice, the squawking began. With that, he began to use his colorful language for all to hear as he moved atop the cage.

"Why don't you order us tea?" Daphne asked.

Arthur nodded and walked to the pull. Moments later, the butler entered and listened to what Arthur wanted. When the man left, Arthur walked to the hearth to warm himself. "He's being rather quiet."

"Don't let his silence fool you. He's very much taking everything in."

"I think when you're ready to invite some of the ladies for tea, you leave Sam in the room. I think it would be quite interesting. Especially if he mimics over the course of the tea."

"That is a horrid idea, but I must admit I love the thought of Sam cussing at one or more of them."

"I'd love to be a fly on the wall when that happens."

"True, but I'd have to remove him from the room. For the ladies' sake," Daphne said.

"Of course," Arthur replied before breaking out into a fit of laughter. His action wasn't lost on the parrot, who in turn began bobbing his head.

"Shite, shite, shite," Sam chanted walking the top of his cage and bobbing his head. "Wanker head."

"He needs some new words," Arthur said.

A knock on the door and the tea tray was rolled into the room. Once the footman left, Daphne looked at the cakes and sandwiches which had been brought. She poured both herself and Arthur a cup of tea. After handing her husband the cup, she brought a plate and set it on the table. Spying a slice of seedcake, she broke off a piece and took it over to Sam.

"What do you say?" she asked, holding it just out of reach.

"Bloody hell!"

Daphne shook her head. "No, that's not the right one. You know. I taught it to you Sam."

The bird walked around the top of his cage before stopping in front of Daphne. "Thank you."

She offered the seedcake, which Sam snatched quickly. "You see, that wasn't so hard."

"Not hard, not hard. Sam know."

Turning back to Arthur, she smiled triumphantly. "He does know words that aren't bad. It's just a matter of enforcing them."

"I guess we need to be careful when talking around him."

"Yes, it can't hurt. He mimics everything he hears," Daphne said. She picked up her cup of tea and took a sip.

"He does that." Arthur picked up a piece of the seedcake and bit into it without the help of a plate or fork. Out of the corner of his eye, he could see his wife giving him a disapproving look. He decided to ignore and feign ignorance should she say something.

"If the trial doesn't start until day after tomorrow, who are you meeting with tomorrow?"

He licked his fingers clean of the seedcake stuck on them. "The crown prosecutors wish to see me and I'm going to see my solicitor to make sure what the prosecutors tell me is how he understands the trial to begin."

"Are the prosecutors going to want you to testify? Or do they wish for you to be there solely to represent the victims' family?"

"I am assuming both. I'm not sure how my testimony will help, but I'll find out tomorrow," he replied.

"I could go and sit with the other ladies up in the gallery."

Arthur smiled at her. "I appreciate you wanting to support me, but it isn't necessary."

"If you change your mind, I can always reschedule my day," she replied.

"Enjoy your day. I'm going to have the carriage take me to the crown prosecutor's office, and then have it returned so you can use it."

"You're sure? I can always take a hackney."

He shook his head. "My duchess is not using a hack to get around town."

"Very well."

Hoping she wasn't going to defy him and ignore his instructions, he tried to study her face for any significant signs of how she was truly feeling. It was no use. Daphne was far too good at masking her feelings. Hopefully that would change the more they got to know each other.

DAPHNE WAS MEETING with the housekeeper and cook regarding menus for the time they were in London when the carriage returned from taking Arthur to his meetings.

"I believe that's all," she said. "I appreciate your help in guiding me to what His Grace likes."

"You're welcome, Your Grace," the cook said.

"If you ladies will excuse me, I have an appointment to get to."

The two women left, and she quit the room as well in search of her wrap. She always loved going to a dressmaker. Being able to see what was and wasn't in style, what the ladies were wearing in Paris. It was always fascinating to her, and more so now that she'd become a duchess. It gave her an opening to things others might not be privy to.

While she needed to order an entire new wardrobe to reflect her new position, she decided it might be in her best interest not to purchase a new wardrobe all at once but order it and have it delivered in sections. That way Arthur wouldn't be overwhelmed by what she purchased. Men, even those like her husband, didn't understand what it took for a lady to look her best.

After leaving the dressmaker's, she walked down the street, looking into store windows. The carriage didn't move, but a footman followed a discreet distance behind. Needing some new gloves, she went into a shop she and her mother frequented when in London and came out with several pairs.

She climbed into the carriage and told the driver where she wanted to go a few blocks away. The sky was becoming overcast, and she knew she needed to hurry before rain started.

The shop carried canvas for embroidery and a large selection of threads. It had been ages since she'd attempted anything, but she needed something to occupy her time when Arthur was engaged elsewhere, and on days like this. She picked a large variety of the very best threads and needles along with a frame for her to keep her work taut while she worked on it.

When she finally arrived home, it was getting darker, and a light rain had started. She walked up the stairs to her rooms to inform her maid what she'd purchased and when other things would arrive. While in her dressing room, Daphne picked up a novel she'd brought along with her, knowing she would have time on her own while Arthur was busy with the trial.

She passed the butler on her way to the parlor and ordered tea. Though the rain had barely begun, the weather was leaving a chill in the air.

Opening the door to the parlor, she found Sam walking around the room on the floor. She approached him and squatted down so he could jump up on her forearm. Sam complied and Daphne slowly stood, talking to the parrot as she did. She walked to his cage and placed him on a tree branch attached to the cage top. Then she sat down on an overstuffed gold damask chair within reach of the bird cage.

Tea arrived, and she fixed herself a cup, placing it on a table in front of her chair. She opened the book she'd brought with her and tried her best to focus on the words in front of her to no avail. Closing the book, she found her teacup and took a sip. Her eyes were heavy. Maybe if she took a nap for a few minutes, she would be able to read. After all, she'd been on the go since early in the morning. She wasn't expecting anyone, and she wasn't entirely sure when Arthur would return.

Taking another sip of tea, she returned the cup to the table and closed her eyes. Sam was making bird noises from deep in his throat. It meant he was content and happy.

Her life had certainly gone full circle. From having a love-hate relationship with Arthur, to becoming his wife and duchess. It was nothing she planned, and she wouldn't trade it for the world.

CHAPTER FIFTEEN

Arthur arrived at the court early. The crown prosecutors wanted him to sit behind them, so the defendant, Crenshaw, could get a good look at one of his victim's surviving family members when he was brought into the courtroom. When he was brought in, Crenshaw stared hard at Arthur. Arthur, in turn, looked at the defendant before turning his head to what was going on in front of him.

Listening to the opening statements by the defendant's counsel and then the prosecutors was lengthy. Each trying to sway the jury early on. Crenshaw's man claimed his client was simply part of a conspiracy. That his client was a scapegoat because the prosecution couldn't pin the murders on anyone else.

The prosecution countered by stating there was plenty to prove Crenshaw guilty. They would introduce a key element that would put a nail in Crenshaw's case. Arthur's family signet ring was the key piece of evidence. The prosecutor had persuaded Arthur to let him hold the ring in safekeeping until the end of the trial. There was some worry that Crenshaw had henchmen ready to assault Arthur to steal the ring. No ring, and the case might surely go away. The ring would be kept in the prosecutor's office safe until the verdict was read.

The trial began with the defense starting out. They offered no witnesses and had advised their client not to speak on his own behalf. There was speculation they might add Arthur at the last minute but didn't.

Once the prosecution began, there was little doubt as to why the defense had no one. People had heard Crenshaw make threats against anyone who questioned him. He expected loyalty, but now, when he really needed it, people were abandoning him and helping the crown plead their case.

Arthur had been asked to take the stand on behalf of the prosecution. They wanted him to add a dose of reality to the proceedings. By using him, Arthur would make his parents human and not just words on a paper. His father had taught him how to hunt and ride a horse at an early age. He had the best tutors to complete his education before going to boarding school and later university.

Crenshaw's men never questioned what the crown presented and never cross-examined Arthur. Once the prosecution presented his family signet ring, the defense took notice, listening to Arthur's answer to every question. They thought they had the case neatly sewn up when the ring's ownership was questioned.

"Your Grace, how can you be sure this is your father's ring?"

"I would know the ring anywhere. My father never removed it, and before that, my grandfather wore it. It's been one thing the eldest son receives."

"A ring seen through the eyes of a child. How can you be so certain it is the same one?"

Arthur turned his attention to the prosecutor for a moment. What he was about to say and what the attorney was going to show was proof positive the ring's ownership was undisputable.

"On the inside of the band is an inscription which undeniably proves it belonged not only to my father, but to the very first duke."

The ring was produced and shown to the judges before the defense got their look at it. "There's no disputing who the rightful owner is," one judge said. There was a buzz heard throughout the chambers when the ring had been produced.

The judges and prosecutor thanked Arthur for his testimony. Arthur left the witness box and sat back in the chair he'd occupied earlier. He looked over at Crenshaw who was staring at him with a look of hate. Arthur wondered if the man knew his fate was sealed. It would now be in the hands of the jury and crown.

Both sides gave their closing statements before the jury retired to debate the verdict they felt Crenshaw deserved. Arthur remained seated and spoke with the prosecution when asked a question. One asked him what sort of punishment Crenshaw deserved. Arthur knew in his heart what was a fitting punishment, but he kept it to himself. The small group of men believed Crenshaw needed to be sent to Australia to a penal colony, but Arthur thought that was too easy. He would be alive and one day be allowed to live the remainder of his days free. The man had murdered his parents, and for committing such a heinous crime, he should receive what he inflicted on his parents.

It didn't take long for the jury to reach their verdict. It seemed forever before the verdict was read. Guilty on all counts which included kidnapping. It was over. Justice had prevailed. Now if the crown would deliver a fitting punishment. Arthur tried not to look or act too relieved and happy.

Crenshaw stood in the witness box as the punishment was read for each count. Death by hanging. He seemed to be dumbfounded, not believing what was happening.

Arthur took a deep breath. Not too long ago, he would have never thought he'd see this day. Still, though, he had a million questions for Crenshaw but knew it wouldn't change a thing and probably wouldn't make him feel any differently.

The guards came to take Crenshaw out. As they were walking him to the door, the man blurted out, "It's not over!" Fortunately, Arthur had his back to the man.

Arthur accepted his ring back and thanked the prosecutors for their hard work. "I hadn't thought it would be over in a day, but I'm relieved it is finished."

"The defense had no case. Any witnesses he thought they had

changed their minds, and if they'd put Crenshaw on the witness stand, he would have made it worse for himself."

"Yes, he would have. You know what's sad?" Arthur asked. "I'll never know why he did what he did."

"Sometimes, it's best if you don't know."

"You're probably right," Arthur replied. "If you gentlemen excuse me, I'm going to take my leave. Thank you once again for all you do."

He shook hands with them and turned to leave. "I look forward to seeing you in Parliament, Your Grace," Hawkins, the chief prosecutor, said. The man reached for his horsehair wig to remove it. Wigs were a long-standing tradition in British courts. While they looked historically fashionable, they actually were uncomfortable to wear.

"Thank you. I know my father didn't spend a lot of time there, but I feel it is my duty to fill my position to the best of my ability."

Hawkins nodded. "I'm sure you'll do your father proud."

"Thank you," Arthur said, adding, "When will you know when the execution will take place?"

"As soon as I know, I'll reach out to you, Your Grace."

"Thank you."

Arthur walked out of the courtroom. People were bustling to and fro. Arthur peered across the corridor where a familiar face watched him. Daphne. He hurried over to where she was standing. She beamed seeing him as he approached her. She was attired in a dark blue dress and cape, and he knew there was not a woman in London who could hold a torch to her beauty.

"How long have you been waiting?" he asked, grasping her hands in his.

"Not long. I was afraid I'd miss you, but the man standing next to the door said your case was finished."

"This is indeed a nice surprise," he replied. He put one of her hands in the crook of his arm and led her to the stairs where they would walk down to exit the building.

"I thought you might like to take me to lunch. You can tell me everything that happened."

Looking up at the sky, Arthur was pleased the midday was blue and filled with big white and gray clouds. He hoped it remained like this. "What would you like?"

"Surprise me," she replied.

"There's a shop near the entrance of the park that serves some of the best fish and chips. We could go to the park then and eat our lunch."

"That would be nice. These shops never have any room in their restaurants. The park would be a nice change."

"Yes, it would," he replied. "Let me inform my men where we're headed."

Walking to his coach, Arthur spoke with the driver. Not wanting for the carriage to be too far off in case rain began, they agreed it would be good for the coach to wait near the entrance to the park.

The restaurant was busy as ever when they approached. Surprisingly, most patrons waited for their turn without pushing or shoving to advance their way to the counter. Arthur left Daphne just outside the restaurant while he went in and ordered. It didn't take long to order their food and take it back to where she stood.

"That wasn't so bad," she said, beaming at the hot fish and chips wrapped up in newspaper.

"No, it wasn't. I've seen it a lot worse."

They began walking to the entrance of the park. It seemed they weren't the only ones who had the same idea. Nice days like this would soon be ending to give way for the colder days.

Arthur spotted a bench just outside the entrance where a couple was leaving. "Why don't we sit over there? We might not find anything farther in."

"True, and we don't want our food to get cold."

Minutes later they were sitting on the bench enjoying their meal and watching the people pass by. He glanced at her to see if she was enjoying her meal.

"Did you get everything you needed?"

She chewed her fish before answering him. "Yes. Some of it is being delivered to the house today. I have a fitting day after tomorrow for some dresses I ordered. Those will be sent to Kent when they are finished."

"It sounds as though you had a successful morning," he replied. He was almost finished with his meal, trying to slow down so he wouldn't finish too far ahead of her.

"It was." She popped a chip into her mouth. That one little gesture made him groan. He wondered if she were doing it on purpose, knowing what effect she had over him.

"Would you like to accompany me to my office at Parliament?" he asked.

"Yes, very much. I didn't know you had work there."

"I don't. I need to make it official that I intend to fill my father's seat."

She smiled demurely. "Can I do that? Accompany you?"

"You're my wife. Of course you can."

"I would love to see where you'll be helping pass laws."

He arched a brow and smiled. "Then it's settled." He glanced up at the sky. The blue skies which dominated earlier were giving way to a smattering of gray. "We'll take the carriage, just in case it decides to rain."

Daphne nodded, picking up a smaller piece of fish. "You haven't said how it went in court."

"It was a success. The judge sentenced him to death. Him having possession of my father's signet ring played a huge part. His lawyers had no witnesses and never called him."

"When will the execution take place?"

"I'm not sure. The prosecutor is to get back to me as soon as a date has been assigned."

She nodded and glanced up at him. "I know you're glad for the matter to be finally taken care of."

"Yes, it's weighed heavily on me. I'm just sorry Roxanne

couldn't have been here," he replied.

"Why don't you write her when we get home?"

He folded the empty newspaper and set it in between them. "I had already planned to do that. I don't want to leave her wondering what happened."

"She'll be much appreciative you did so," Daphne replied. She passed her newspaper to him where she'd left a smattering of chips. "I can't finish these."

Smiling, Arthur took the paper from her and quickly devoured the chips. He was glad he'd thought of this. Most women wouldn't do something like come to meet him and actually enjoy lunch on a park bench. Most women would be horrified at the thought of eating in public in such a crude fashion. After all, women of the ton preferred restaurants frequented by their own and where they could be seen by all.

"Are you ready?" He stood to his full height and offered his hand.

She took his hand and held it as he helped her stand. "Yes. We're not too far, are we?"

"No, we're not."

It took them no time to arrive at the parliament house, and soon they were standing inside Arthur's new office. He offered his wife a seat. "Do you have things you need to tend to?" she asked.

"One. If you don't mind, it'll take me a few minutes. I'll return in no time."

"I'll be right here waiting," she replied. Her sky-blue eyes watched him closely.

Leaning down, he planted a kiss on her cheek before standing. "Good."

In the short time it took Arthur to finish his business, Daphne had fallen asleep in the same chair he left her in. Stealthily, he neared her and placed a hand on her cheek. Her eyes fluttered open, taking a few minutes to remember where she was. "I must have fallen asleep. Have you been back long?"

"No, I just returned. If you're ready, we can go home."

"Yes, I'm ready."

They walked through the maze of hallways until they were at the door to the chamber. "Would you like to see inside?"

"Yes, if I may."

"Of course you may." He led her to a massive oak door which led to the place where laws were made. Hearing her gasp caused him to smile. It wasn't fancy but the room certainly had a history. Many a debate had ensued, and Arthur was sure he'd be part of many more.

She peered up at him after looking around the large room. "It's not exactly how I envisioned it."

"How's that?"

"I thought it would be more formal."

He smiled at her. "I was under that impression the first time my father brought me."

"Did you tell him?"

"No," he replied. "If you're ready, why don't we head home?"

She nodded her head, and the pair made their way to their waiting carriage. Arthur sat down next to his wife and tapped the roof with the end of his walking stick. She was so close to him, he could smell the perfume she wore. It was a flowery scent, though he didn't know what all it was made from besides gardenias. Even that was faint and not overbearing.

As the carriage pulled out into the afternoon traffic, he felt her hand wrap around his upper arm. "I've enjoyed this," she murmured.

"I have as well. We'll have to do it more often," he replied.

"I would like that. I understand there's a new exhibit of Dutch masters. Perhaps we could go tomorrow if you don't have any more pressing matters."

"Let me check my diary and make sure I'm not forgetting anything."

Daphne snuggled closer. "I know you want to leave day after tomorrow. I have a morning appointment for a dress fitting."

"That's fine. We can leave from there."

"Thank you. I thought the trial would be longer than it lasted and that we'd be here longer."

"It's fine, my love."

The carriage ride home was long and slow. There was a lot of stopping along the way, but that wasn't out of the ordinary. Finally, the carriage turned to the left. Arthur pulled back the curtains which had been closed to keep it warmer inside. The team was two streets from the house.

"Are we almost home?"

Home. Such a simple word, but hearing Daphne say it took on a whole new meaning. It meant she was settling into her new role as wife and duchess. Soon he hoped she would take on one more. Mother.

He cleared his mind. "Yes, we are."

Once inside, he handed a waiting footman his greatcoat, hat, and walking stick. He saw Daphne fussing with her cape and walked closer to help her. He slipped it off her dainty shoulders and handed it to another footman. He ordered tea to be brought to the parlor where Sam was staying, knowing she would want to see him.

"Hot tea sounds heavenly on this cold afternoon," she mused, walking across the hall with him.

"I'll meet you in the parlor. I need to put this in my study," he said, holding up a leather case he'd been carrying most of the day.

"Of course." She stood on tip toe and kissed him on the cheek.

Arthur stood for a moment watching her continue to the parlor. The gentle sway of her hips made him overcome with desire. He'd never experienced some of the emotions he felt when he was around her or even thought about her. It was all new to him, something he hoped would never end.

Did this mean he was falling in love with her? They certainly had never said the words, but the emotional connection they had seemed to make it acceptable. He needed to let her know how he felt with words, not just physical contact. They had a lifetime together and he wanted the bond they shared to grow deeper.

Perhaps he should do something like his father did with his mother. The duke wasn't a man of flowery words, so instead, at least once a week, he would leave a posy on her dressing table. It was a gesture his mother had always loved. He could leave her a stem of her favorite flower when it was in bloom. Or a book. Something that would be significant between the two of them.

He watched her until she was out of sight and turned to walk to his study. Opening the door, he felt the heat of the fire burning in the hearth. Placing the case in the chair behind the desk, he sighed. Observing a letter on the desk, he picked it up and opened it. It was from Roxanne congratulating him on the victory and inviting them to dinner the night after they returned. His first reaction was to decline. He didn't want to share time with anyone but Daphne.

Dropping the paper back on his desk, he turned and left the room. He'd first see what Daphne thought of the matter. She might feel as he did and would want to stay home. If he declined, Roxanne would understand, especially when he asked her for another date.

CHAPTER SIXTEEN

HAVING FINISHED HER dress fittings, Daphne stepped outside into the brisk but sunny day. She paused, looking around for Arthur who'd been waiting for her. Her eyes scanned up and down the sidewalk and then across the street to the bookstore. He probably was in there like he told her he would be. She was about to step down and cross the street when a hand grasped her arm roughly and pulled her back.

"Lady Daphne, what a pleasure."

She knew that voice. There was no mistaking it, nor was there any mistaking the grip he had on her. Black. She hadn't seen nor heard from him since right before her marriage to Arthur. Black had been determined to marry her, even going as far as going to a bishop.

"I wish I could say the same," she replied. "If you'll kindly let go of my arm, I am on my way to the bookstore."

He sneered, his hold on her tightening. "The bookstore can wait. I cannot. You owe me an explanation. We were to be married and the next thing I know, you've embarrassed me by marrying that duke."

"I have no intention of going anywhere with you. I owe you nothing, so I would suggest you unhand me."

Black shook his head. "I'm afraid I can't do that." He pulled her hard, so she had no choice but to return to the sidewalk.

"Sir, if you don't unhand me, I'm going to scream," Daphne said.

"Go ahead. I'll simply tell people you ran off and I'm taking you home. Who will they believe? A woman or me?"

Kicking him in the shin, Daphne used the distraction to try and free herself from his clutches. It seemed to work because the moment he let go, she scrambled away. She was about to walk across to the bookstore when a large hand had her by the shoulder and pulled her back.

"Your parents never taught you how to act like a lady," Black said. "It's time you start. By the time I'm finished with you, you'll be a proper lady."

"And didn't I tell you I was going nowhere with you?"

"That mouth. Something else needing attention."

Thrashing against his grip, Daphne tried in vain to break loose. She hoped someone would take notice and try to make sure she was fine. No one did, and she noted a few people passing them simply looked on as though she were a misbehaving wife. No one wanted to get involved. Where was Arthur? Surely someone had seen what was going on over here.

She felt him attempting to drag her toward a carriage that had just appeared. Daphne knew if she got into that carriage, she would have no control. So she began to struggle and thrash about, even screaming. She couldn't allow one of his men to assist him in getting her into the carriage.

As he began to near the glossy black carriage, she leaned in and bit his cheek as hard as she was able. Immediately, he broke his hold, his hands to his injured face, cursing her. Daphne used the time to whirl around and head across the street. She didn't dare look back, keeping her focus on the traffic and picking her way around or in front of carriages.

Then she saw her husband, and the moment his eyes met hers, he went into action. He bolted across the street, guiding her to his carriage which had just pulled up in front of the bookstore. As soon as they reached the other side of the street, Arthur spun around to see where Black was. He was standing, watching. Tipping his hat in Arthur's direction, Black turned and was hidden by his own carriage.

"Arthur?"

"Are you all right?"

"I'm fine. A bit shook up from being treated like a bag of flour. Other than that, I'm unscathed, which is more than I can say for Black."

He guided Daphne to the waiting carriage. "What did you do to him?" he asked as he assisted her up the step into the carriage.

"I kicked him in the shin, though that didn't work effectively. I then found an opportunity and bit him on the cheek. He screamed like a little girl."

"That's amazing."

She turned and sat. "Do you think he really meant to kidnap me?"

"Yes. That's what it appeared he was attempting to do."

"I should have kicked him between his legs. That would have been effective, don't you think?"

Climbing into the carriage, Arthur sat next to her, trying his best not to let her see his face. "Very effective."

"Not that it would do any good, but do you think I should file a complaint with the police?"

"It might not be a bad idea. At least there would be a record of what he attempted," he replied.

"On the other hand, they might not take me seriously."

"You're a duchess."

She graced him with a smile. "I'm still a woman, Arthur."

"That should have nothing to do with anything. If we go, I'll insist on giving them my observation of what was unfolding."

"Then let's go," she said with determination in her voice.

He patted her hand. The carriage had gone nowhere since he had not signaled them to leave. Opening the door, he stepped out to speak with his men.

It took only moments before they were on their way, making

a detour so they might make a police report over what Black had attempted. Nothing might come from it, but Daphne was aware her husband did know people there. It helped to have acquaintances in these places for times such as these. However, she worried it might provoke Black when he heard what she'd done, going to file a report about the incident.

No sooner than they walked in the door than they were greeted by a balding, dark-blond-haired man chomping the end of an unlit cigar. The pair shook hands.

"Williams, my wife needs to file an incident that just happened to her."

He nodded at Daphne. "Your Grace, I'll be happy to take your statement. If you'll come this way." He turned and began walking up a flight of stairs. Moments later, they were in his office. Daphne carefully sat in the one wooden chair available while Arthur stood behind her.

"How can I help you?" Williams inquired.

"A man was trying to kidnap me," Daphne said matter of fact.

"Do you know the man and what makes you think he was trying to kidnap you?"

Daphne began to tell Williams everything, every detail of what had happened earlier. As she spoke, Williams was furiously writing away. Arthur even added what he'd seen transpire between his wife and Black. There was no doubt in his mind if he'd gotten Daphne in his carriage, there would be nothing good to come from it. He went on to tell Williams about Black and how he wanted to force his wife into marrying him, and mentioned Black was short on funds, thus needing a dowry to help him pay some if not all of his debt. Williams said little, just kept writing.

"Do you wish to file charges for attempted kidnapping?" Williams finally asked.

Daphne turned to glance up at Arthur for assistance. "Right now, I think just a report of what transpired is all that is needed. Unless you feel filing charges the better option," Arthur replied.

"Filing charges is far more serious. I agree with you simply wanting to file a report. I might be able to see that Black gets a talking to and knows we're watching him."

"I can live with that, if my wife can," Arthur replied.

Daphne nodded. "Yes, I can live with that."

"Very well. I will have this put in an official form. I'll sign off on it and have a copy delivered to you," Williams said.

"Thank you, Inspector," Daphne said quietly.

"Yes, thank you for your help," Arthur agreed.

"Are you going to be in town a few days or should I have it sent to your home in Kent?"

"Send it to my country home. We're heading back in a day or two."

"Excellent," Williams replied. "If anything happens or you need me for anything, please don't hesitate to contact me."

The pair left feeling much better even though they'd only filed a complaint against Black. At least there would be a record of what he attempted in case he tried to approach her again. In spite of loving London, Daphne was ready to return to Kent. She was excited at the thought of her and Arthur beginning their life together. They had, but it had come with all sorts of interruptions.

Arthur stayed close to her as they made their way down the stairs and to their waiting carriage. He helped her step into the carriage and followed. Sitting next to her, he tapped the roof to let his men know he was ready to leave. Moments later, he glanced at his bride and saw she had fallen asleep. It had been a busy day for both, especially with the ordeal with Black. He was ready to return to the country.

ARTHUR ACCOMPANIED DAPHNE to the milliner, staying outside with the carriage in front of the shop. He pulled out a new book and tried to begin but Sam was making his dislikes known. His cage was across from him, covered to keep him warm from the cold. As usual, he was cursing.

"Sam! If you don't have something nice to say, please shut it!" What was he doing? He was talking to a parrot as though the bird could understand him. As smart as Sam seemed to be, it wouldn't surprise him. Take now; Sam had quieted.

"Sam pretty boy," the bird said from behind the drape.

"Yes, you are pretty."

Hearing nothing but a quiet tapping in the cage, Arthur sat back and opened his book once again. His eyes were getting heavy, so putting the book aside, he decided to stretch his legs while he waited on his wife.

He didn't have to wait long. As he stood against the side of the carriage, the milliner's door opened and out walked Daphne. That was quick. He would have thought she'd be at least an hour. Or he had a lot to learn about women now that he was married.

"Are you ready?" she asked.

"Yes, but I would have thought it would have been a lengthy process."

"She's running behind. One of her girls ran off with her beau so she's short staffed. She'll bring everything to Kent."

He nodded to a footman to open the door and turned his attention back on Daphne. "We should arrive home sooner than planned."

"I can't wait. I am growing quite fond of my new home," she replied.

"I'm glad to hear that. We could leave in the morning if you like."

Daphne arched a brow. "You don't have any more business meetings?"

"No, I'm through," he replied. He took her gloved hand in his and raised it to his mouth for a kiss.

"It's still early in the day. Could we leave today?"

Barking out a laugh, Arthur squeezed the hand he still held.

"Today? You certainly are in a hurry."

"Yes, I am. I want to go home and spend time without interruption with my husband."

"You do?"

"Yes. In fact, I thought we could be naughty on the ride home."

Arthur snorted. "My wife seems to have turned into a wanton woman since we married."

Sam flapped his wings from behind the drape. "Wanton. Wanton," the bird mimicked.

"I really don't know how we can make love with Sam present. I'm afraid he's going to learn inappropriate words and sounds," Arthur said.

"You are right. He picks up on everything. He has enough of a bad vocabulary without us teaching him more."

Arthur pulled out a book he'd purchased in London and made himself comfortable in the corner. "Why don't we see how he acts once we're out of London?"

"That sounds like a good idea. Perhaps he'll get bored and fall asleep," Daphne replied.

"We can always wish," Arthur said with an arched brow. "Would you like to lie down? You can put your head in my lap."

"Yes, but not until we're out of London."

"Very well."

He opened his book and began to read. The book was about the newly rich Americans who'd made their fortune in things like railroads, banking, land, steam ships. There were quite a few of them. Arthur had always wanted to visit America. See places like New York City and Boston. Maybe Daphne might be interested and would agree to taking their wedding trip there. It would be a trip of a lifetime, something they'd always remember and talk fondly about in years to come.

Glancing over at his bride, he was surprised to find her asleep. He pulled out a blanket to cover her. She didn't move or make a sound as he made sure she was covered from the cold. The sun had been out all day, but it hadn't warmed up. Warmer days such as that were going to be few and far between for the next few months. Arthur liked the brisk days. His horses were frisky from the cold, and before long it would be time to visit the tenants. It had been a long-standing tradition to give them a Christmas fowl and other needed items to help them get through the winter.

But they still had plenty of time to plan everything. Feeling his eyes grow heavy, Arthur closed the book and leaned back against the squabs and closed his eyes. His mind slipped to riding across the estate with Roddy, exploring every square inch of the land. The next thing he knew, he was being tossed around. Immediately, he knew it was a broken wheel. Daphne was awakened suddenly. Arthur kept a grip on her arm. Sam's cage hadn't moved, but it was heavy and sturdy.

The carriage came to a halt. Arthur jumped out to assess the damage. A back wheel had broken, most likely from a hole in the road. The spokes had come apart as well, rendering the wheel even more useless. They weren't far from a coaching inn. He could send a couple of the men to see if there was a wheelwright close by, and if not, if there was a carriage he could hire to take them the rest of the way. His men could stay with the carriage and see about having the wheel replaced. He didn't want to have them staying at an inn this close to home, and moving Sam around in the cooler weather would not be the best for him.

Sticking his head back into the carriage, he saw Daphne sitting on the other seat next to Sam's cage, speaking lowly to him. "Is he all right?"

"Yes, just a little shook up at the abruptness of the wheel coming off."

"I've sent a couple of men to the coaching inn to see if there isn't a carriage we can hire and to see if there's a wheelwright close by."

"I guess if there's no carriage, we'll have to stay at the inn."

Arthur shook his head. "No. If there's no carriage available, I'll send someone to the estate to bring another carriage."

"Good, because Sam doesn't need to be out in this cold. The cover is thick, but he needs to get in somewhere warm."

Daphne wrapped her cape around her tighter. He felt bad, but the broken wheel had been unavoidable. His carriages were all carefully maintained. But even with all that care, things were bound to happen.

"If there's no carriage for hire, perhaps we can use a wagon and move you and Sam inside the inn until one of my spare carriages arrives."

She nodded. "That would be acceptable, wouldn't it, Sam?"

"Yes, Sam likes."

"He didn't really understand what you said to him, did he?"

"Of course he does. Sam's very smart for a parrot. You've even said as much."

He grinned. "I suppose I have. We'll get you somewhere warm as soon as possible, Sam."

There he was, talking to a parrot again. Marrying Daphne had him doing all sorts of things he never thought he'd do. She had made him into a lovesick puppy. He imagined she knew it too. Life with her was never going to be dull. She was adventurous where the majority of women simply wanted to live a quieter life.

Daphne wanted to discover what life had to offer. She didn't want to hide behind other matrons, spending her time going to have tea and listening to all the gossip. That wasn't her and might explain why she had few close friends. The ones who were married were having children and making their husbands look good. She wanted all that, but on her terms. Together they wanted to get to know each other. Too few couples actually knew their spouses' idiosyncrasies because no matter how things were changing in the world, men still thought women, even their wives, were not their equal. Fortunately for Daphne, Arthur was not like that.

After what seemed like an eternity, a shiny black carriage appeared. By the coat of arms on the door, it belonged to his brother-in-law, Graham. As soon as it came to a halt, Graham jumped out.

"I heard the Duke of Hightower's carriage had a broken wheel," he said, walking over to assess the wheel. "Roxanne and I were enjoying a meal at the coaching inn before heading home."

"You couldn't have come at a better time," Arthur replied.

"Let's get you both to the inn. You can get warm, have a meal before we all leave. Your man can take care of your carriage."

Arthur patted his friend on the shoulder. "That's the best thing I've heard all day. By the way, we have Sam with us, and Daphne's not going to let him out of her sight."

"The more the merrier!"

"Graham, you're a lifesaver," Daphne exclaimed, looking out the open door.

He smiled warmly. "Happy to help."

Moments later, the four were in Graham's carriage and headed to the coaching inn. Daphne sat next to Sam, lifting the cover to check on him.

Upon seeing Daphne's face, Sam squawked. "My pretty!"

"Sam, behave. We'll be home soon."

"Sam good."

"That's good to know. We'll get you to a warm spot and get you some fruit."

"Sam love."

Graham chuckled. Not having spent any time with Sam, it hit him as funny that Daphne and the parrot could seem to have a conversation between themselves. "He certainly is opinionated."

"He is that, and he's on his best behavior."

"I don't even want to know when he's not."

"That's easy. He swears a lot," Daphne replied.

Graham barked out a laugh as the four of them started back to the coaching inn. The ride wasn't that long. It was where Arthur had wanted to take a break even without the wheel incident. Two of Graham's men carried Sam's covered cage into the inn. Aside from squawking from under the cloth, Sam managed to stay calm.

They found Roxanne seated at a table near the fire, drinking a hot cup of tea. She peered up from the table and broke into a smile at the sight of her brother and his bride. Looking like a cat that had just licked a bowl of cream, she put her hands around the hot tea. "Hello, brother, Daphne. I take it that's the notorious Sam under that cover," she said, cupping her hands around the warm cup.

"Yes," Daphne replied.

"Come, sit down," Roxanne said, pointing to a chair next to her. "We'll get you something to eat before we head home."

"I'm so grateful," Daphne said. "If you hadn't been here, I'm afraid we would have been spending the night here."

Roxanne nodded, looking at her brother with a grin. "Everything turned out for the best."

A young girl placed a bowl of stew in front of both Daphne and Arthur, returning with a basket of warm bread. Arthur began to eat, realizing he was hungrier than he thought to be. He normally abhorred stew of any sort, but this had extra seasonings that brought out the flavor of the beef. He picked up a loaf of the bread and tore a piece, then slathered it with butter. Sometimes, simple food beat anything to be found. Looking at his wife, he noted that instead of taking care of herself first, she was feeding apple slices to Sam. People were watching Sam with amazement. It was the first time anyone had seen such an animal. And a bird that talked no less!

"Daphne, put some slices in his cage and eat. He can eat them on his own."

In turn, she stuck her tongue out at him but did as he requested. He heard Roxanne launch into a fit of laughter. "She knows you well, Arthur. I can see this marriage is going to be a fun one."

"What took you to London?" Graham asked, trying to get his wife in line and not have so much fun teasing her brother. "Besides the trial."

"Parliament and a few other meetings," he replied.

"At least one of us represented the family," Roxanne said, shaking her head. "Crenshaw being in possession of Father's ring is what did him in?"

"Yes, it was probably the one thing that sealed his fate," Arthur replied. He took a bite of bread and with the next, he dipped it in his bowl to sop up any remaining stew.

"What did you do while Arthur was out and about?" Roxanne asked Daphne.

"I went to my dressmaker and did other shopping. Met with the housekeeper. Just stepping into my role."

Arthur noted she hadn't mentioned Black. Probably because there was no reason and he knew his sister well enough to know that it would anger her. She could be quite opinionated.

"Sam want more!"

"He certainly can talk," Roxanne commented.

"It comes naturally to the larger parrots," Daphne replied. She turned to Sam. "You've had enough. You can have more later."

"Sam sad."

Arthur stood, unfolding his tall frame from the chair. "We need to get on the road, I suppose."

"Yes, it'll be dark before you know it," Graham agreed.

After getting Sam's cage settled on the back-looking seat, Arthur and Graham settled on either side of the parrot while the ladies enjoyed the main seat. Except for Sam making sounds from behind his cover, the carriage was quiet. Roxanne had picked up a book she'd been reading earlier while the men fell fast asleep. Daphne peered out the window at the passing landscape until she could no longer keep her eyes open.

Arthur found himself in the middle of dreams that made no sense to him. It was a mismatched bits and pieces of him and Daphne. Nothing bad, always loving and constant. Still, he wished he understood more of their meaning if there was one. He cracked his eyes to see her asleep. She looked as though she were almost smiling. He wondered what sort of naughtiness she was thinking about. He'd be sure to find out tonight. The trip to London had been so busy, it left little time for spending days in bed with her. That would be a priority once all the mess with the carriage and its wheel was solved. They deserved some time alone in bed. Especially because they had put off their honeymoon.

He fell back asleep and did not awaken until the carriage pulled up in front of his home. As the carriage came to a stop, Sam became active, whistling and making odd noises under his cover.

The door opened and a footman lowered the steps. Arthur exited first and helped his wife down. All the while, he gave instructions to the footmen about taking Sam out of the carriage. Saying their thanks and goodbyes to Graham and Roxanne, Arthur followed Daphne up the stairs and into the grand hall.

"Did you tell them to put Sam in the small red drawing room?" she asked, giving her cloak to a waiting young man.

"Yes."

"After he settles in, I'll let him spend time in the conservatory. He likes it in there."

Arthur nodded. "Whatever you think best for him."

She drew closer to him and planted a light kiss on his lips. "I'm famished. I'll order tea to be sent to the drawing room."

"Already taken care of," Arthur replied with a grin.

"Thank you," she said, heading toward the drawing room. "Do join me."

"I shall."

He watched her walking away. The sway of her hips was more noticeable than usual, leaving him to believe she was doing it intentionally to tease him. Little did she know what sort of effect it had on him. In order to keep his control, he focused on a vase of freshly cut flowers sitting on a table in the hall. Bloody hell! What was wrong with him, lusting after his wife like a randy schoolboy.

Waiting a moment, he gathered his wits around him and walked towards the smaller drawing room. It was one his mother and father used frequently. As he'd grown up and became duke, he understood why. The room stayed warm in the colder months and led out onto its own private terrace, making the summer breezes easy to cool the room.

A footman opened the door upon seeing him. Stepping inside, the first thing he noticed was Daphne opening the door to the large, black iron cage. Arthur watched as Sam came out and climbed his way to the top. The parrot flapped his wings and immediately began demanding food.

"Sam hungry now! Feed me!

Daphne accepted a bowl a footman handed her. The young man had unofficially been assigned as Sam's caregiver when Daphne wasn't around.

She poured seed into a secured bowl on the side of his cage. Water was done in a similar way, though sometimes, Daphne preferred the food and water placed on a small table just far enough from the cage that it forced Sam to exercise his wings a little. But since he'd spent hours confined to his cage, she made it easier on the bird. Patting Sam on the back, she turned towards Arthur.

"He's happy now."

"I guess I would be too after spending all that time in the cold and in his cage."

Before she could answer, there was a knock on the door and a footman brought in a trolley with tea and food. Dainty sandwiches, biscuits, and scones prevailed. At that same moment, a streak of red came running into the room. Roddy. The setter set his sights on Arthur and jumped up on him, whining and crying the entire time. A man, his dog trainer and kennel master, followed.

"How's he doing?" Arthur asked, patting the dog.

"He's not, Your Grace. He belongs here with you. Every time, he wouldn't focus on hunting or the game. He was looking for you. So I'm returning him from the kennel to you."

"Well, you gave it your best try. I guess he'll stay here. We probably should have started earlier."

The man nodded. "I agree, Your Grace. He's a marvelous dog, though, and this will make him happy. He was quite unhappy in the kennel."

"Thank you," Arthur replied, and commanded Roddy, "You, sit."

The dog did as he was told but quickly noticed Sam. Sam noticed him as well and made sure to make everyone know he had.

"Alert! Bloody hell, there is a wild beast!"

"Sam, Roddy isn't a wild beast," Daphne scolded as she turned toward the tea cart to fix them both a hot cup of tea.

Arthur grabbed a plate and filled it with cake, sandwiches, and other sweets. He accepted the tea and found himself a place near the hearth to enjoy it all. Daphne chose a sandwich and a piece of marmalade cake before joining her husband.

"I'm glad it didn't work out for Roddy. I must confess I miss him," she said.

"I am too. I missed his silly antics and having him with me whenever I went out on the estate."

Looking down, Arthur spotted his faithful friend lying in wait of something to fall from his plate, his tail wagging all the while. He hadn't wanted to send him for training. He'd made Roddy into a pet and was glad he had.

"Do you think you deserve something?" Arthur asked him. Roddy's tail thumped harder.

"Are you going to give him something?" Daphne asked. She'd spotted him studying his plate for what to give his friend.

"Of course I am. I'm not sure what."

"Just give him this," she said, passing him a small sandwich made of eggs.

"Thank you," he replied.

Giving Roddy the egg sandwich, he watched as the setter gulped it down in one bite. "Geez, Roddy, at least chew it."

The setter's tail banged the floor, waiting for more.

CHAPTER SEVENTEEN

ONCE THEY FINISHED tea and Daphne was satisfied Sam would be fine on his own, she excused herself to check in with the housekeeper and cook, while Arthur went to his study to go through mail and make sure there was nothing needing his immediate attention.

He later peered up at the clock on the mantel. It had been almost two hours since he'd sat down. He'd forgotten everything except his work, as usual. Pushing back from the desk, he rose to his full height and left the room.

Not finding Daphne in all the usual places, he went upstairs in search of her. He came upon his bedchamber and entered. It was quiet; not even his valet was there. He opened the door between his and the duchess's suite and heard the distant sound of his wife humming and splashing about in a bathing tub. Immediately his trousers tented. He had no control when it came to her.

He stealthily moved across the room towards the splashing and giggling going on just the other side of the door in front of him. He wanted the element of surprise, so he took off his boots and slowly turned the knob. Standing there in silence, he could see the tub. Her back was to him, and so far, Arthur didn't think she'd heard him enter. He continued on one silent step at a time until he was so close he could touch her.

Stooping down, he put his hands on each of her shoulders

and kissed her damp neck. She tasted of orange and vanilla. She dropped her hand holding the sponge and moaned. Nothing was said as she turned her neck to look at him. He kissed her deeply on the mouth. The sight of her pink tongue darting in and out nearly ruined him.

"I followed the sound of laughter and humming. It seems you're enjoying your bath immensely, Your Grace."

"Mmmm, I am. I think it's going to become even better now that you're here," she replied.

"You have no idea," he said. His cock was painfully hard anticipating sliding into her slick passage.

She giggled. "The tub is large enough. You can join me."

"Right now, I'm going to move to the side," he replied. Once he was in position, he began to roll up his short sleeves, his muscular forearms showing his strength from time spent outside.

Planting a deep kiss on her mouth, their tongues met up to play a mating dance. His hand wandered down to her generous round breasts. He pinched the hard areolas between his fingers, which brought a deep moan not only from the depths of his throat, but hers as well. Bending over he sucked her while his hand slowly danced its way to the apex between her hips. Immediately she parted her legs, granting him full access.

Slowly, he inserted his middle finger inside her passage. She was ready for him, wet and sweet. He pushed on until he found her special spot. He began to work his magic, and it wasn't long until he added another digit. Daphne began squirming uncontrollably with his attention.

"Arthur, I need you…"

"And you shall have me soon, my dove. Soon. Relax and let yourself give in to your body's desires."

It wasn't but moments later when she burst into a million pieces. Water splashed over the edge and onto him and the floor. She'd thrown her arms around him and held on tight. Arthur stood, bent over, and picked her up out of the tub and carried her to their bed in the duke's suite.

Laying her damp body down in the middle of the mattress, he began tearing his clothes off in a hurry and mounted her. They shared a kiss before he broke it off to make a trail of kisses to her breasts. After making sure he'd satisfied his need, he moved south, and spreading her legs, he raised them to hang over his shoulders while he laved her cunny. He had her come once more in a matter of seconds. She bucked, wanting more. He raised himself and pushed his way into her passage. He was so ready for her, he wasn't sure how long he could last.

"Arthur," she moaned.

The sound of her throaty, lustful voice urged him to begin pumping harder into her. He grabbed her buttocks and in a matter of seconds, he was coming hard, dumping his seed into her. He shook as the last exited his cock. He had been so involved with the intensity of his release that he had only heard her coming to her peak as he did. He lowered himself over her, kissed her all over her face, before rolling off her and pulling her with him. They remained silent, in each other's arms for several minutes. Their breathing finally subsided.

"That was incredible," he said, kissing her on the forehead.

"Hmmm. I feel like jelly," she replied.

He pulled her closer. They were obviously both sated. It had been much needed, as the final day in London had been too busy and exhausting, leaving them too tired at night. Now they were home, and he would make sure they found the time, even if it were in some out of the way place. His body wanted more, and she obviously did as well.

"Are you cold?"

"A little cool, but being next to you keeps me toasty."

"There's a light blanket at the end of the bed. Let me pull it over us."

"Sounds nice."

He kicked the blanket up to his reach and covered them both. Looking over at her, he saw she had fallen asleep. Yes, she certainly was sated. He had no intention of this being their final encounter of the day. He would sleep with her, and later he could show her some new things. Things she would probably enjoy since she seemed so eager to learn.

MANY HOURS LATER, when Daphne finally awoke, she found the bed devoid of her husband. Sitting up, she brushed her pale blonde hair out of her eyes and looked around. Arthur was nowhere to be found. Rather than wait on him, she gathered the sheet around her and slid out of bed.

Walking into the sitting area, she found him sitting at a small writing desk, his head bent down as he was writing. He was as naked as the day he was born, but more glorious looking than ever. She walked across the room as quietly as possible, dragging the sheet behind her.

Putting her arms around his neck, she bent over and kissed his cheek. "Good morning. Have you been up long?"

He put the pen down and put his hand around her wrist. "I couldn't sleep, and I thought you needed some uninterrupted slumber, so I came out here."

"Thank you." She spotted the small square table where a tea service was set out, along with fruit, bread, and cheese. "This is nice."

"I thought you might be hungry—I know I was, so I ordered nothing that was hot and let you sleep."

She smiled. "I certainly needed the extra sleep."

"I wonder why," he teased.

"Seems some naughty gentleman wanted to keep me up all night."

"Why would he do that?"

"To show me naughty things he enjoyed and taught me naughtiness I've never known."

He swung her around and set her on his lap. The sheet fluttered to the floor. "Scandalous!"

"Indeed," she giggled.

Her intentions were obvious, but the sudden sound of a dog whining outside the door, followed with scratching, made her laugh. Daphne tried to hide her traitorous giggles in the corner of his neck and shoulder, but couldn't stop when Roddy insisted he needed to join them.

"He has the most impeccable timing," Arthur murmured.

"I suppose we should let him in."

Arthur nodded and helped her to her feet. He stood and motioned for her to return to the bedroom in case there might be someone with the setter. He grabbed the sheet off the floor and walked over to the door. As soon as the door cracked, Roddy pushed his way in. If there was someone close by, they were staying out of sight and had just come to keep an eye on the mischievous dog.

Closing the thick wooden door, he found his wife without a stitch of clothing on running across the room as quickly as possible to try and save the cheese and bread from Roddy, to no avail. The dog had the hunk of cheese in his mouth before either of them could get it out of his reach.

The dog was obviously happy with himself at his newfound snack, but it didn't last for long as Daphne bent over and snatched the cheese from him before he knew what was going on. She scolded him, which was all it took. There was a connection between the two and it seemed Roddy did not like displeasing his new mistress.

"Roddy, no!" she said in a scolding voice. "This is not yours."

"He's trying to figure out how far he can push you," Arthur said.

"You as well. He's testing us both."

Arthur nodded. "You're right. He's hoping you'll be a pushover."

"Just like you," she giggled. "While he's under control, I believe I'm going to take a bath. Afterwards, I'm going to have breakfast. A hot breakfast. Can you see to that while I'm bathing?" She fluttered her eyelashes at him with a seductive smile.

"I can, but you're making it awfully hard."

"Excuses, excuses," she replied, walking toward the bathing and dressing area of the suite. She dared not look at him for fear she'd either give in to carnal urges or laugh at his confusion as to how to handle the situation. "Oh yes, you best watch the bread before he grabs on to it." Daphne looked back for a second, seeing her husband going back after Roddy, who was indeed eyeing the crusty bread to snack on.

She checked out the dressing room to make sure her husband's valet wasn't hanging about somewhere out of sight. He certainly would be in for a shock at the sight of her naked. No one was around and noting a robe of hers, she grabbed it and put it on before heading into the bathing chamber.

There was a small stool next to the tub with what she assumed her husband would want while bathing. On another, just out of reach, was one set up for her. She didn't know who had done it, but most likely her maid and his valet had shared ideas on how to remedy new situations.

Cracking the taps, she watched as water flowed into the tub. When she was satisfied with the temperature, she brought the stool closer and added some of the orange vanilla scent she liked before climbing into the warm water. She lay against the back of the tub and closed her eyes for a few minutes until deciding she had enough water.

She didn't linger long, afraid if she did, Arthur would join her, and a repeat of the night before would begin. Not that she had disliked their night. Quite the contrary, but she knew there were things they both needed to be doing. Estate matters for him, and she needed to set up a time to meet with the housekeeper.

Unfortunately, she'd heard rain hitting against the windows, so she knew unless it ended soon, there would be no outdoor activities. Time for that would be less and less as the days got not only shorter, but colder.

Once she dressed, she would check on Sam and see how he was adapting to his new surroundings. Poor fellow had been moved around so much lately, she wanted to make sure he was comfortable. She would have him taken to the conservatory in a week, perhaps sooner. He loved it there, but she hated leaving him out there alone. She visited and spent hours with him, but it wasn't the same as being part of the household.

Not knowing where her maid was, she dried herself off and put the robe back on before going through the door leading to the duchess's suites. She smiled as she found a day dress and all her needs laid out on the bed.

CHAPTER EIGHTEEN

ARTHUR PAUSED AT the drawing room door. After spending several hours locked away in his study attending to correspondence and estate matters, he hesitated upon hearing Sam behind the door. He was calling out to Daphne, who must not be in the room at the moment.

He slowly opened the door and found Sam on the floor walking around the room, hollering as he usually did for his mistress. "Mama! Mama!"

"I'm sure she'll return in just a moment, Sam." Here he was, talking to a parrot again.

That didn't comfort the bird at all as he continued calling out for Daphne. Arthur was just about to go in search of his wife when the door opened and in she walked.

"Sam, are you being bad again?" she scolded.

"Mama! Sam happy!"

"I'm glad. Now up on top of your cage."

Arthur watched in amazement as the bird actually did as told. He noticed a pile of books a decorator from London had left weeks prior. "You've scheduled the decorator to come?"

"Oh, those? I'm returning them."

"You're not happy with him?"

"No," she replied. "I've decided I want to live here for a full year before I make any major changes."

He did a double take while looking at his wife. Not what he expected. He was sure that would be the first project she wanted to get started. "What brought this on?"

"I decided I needed to see the house through all four seasons before trying to undergo changes."

"Very well, but remember you're allowed to change your mind."

She arched a brow. "Thank you, but I won't," she replied.

"As you wish."

"I've penned a note to have the plates and books returned to London. They'll all change by the time I'm ready for them. There's no reason for me holding on to them."

"True."

She sat down in a crème-colored damask chair near the fire. "I gather you've gotten everything caught up?"

"I have. I'm going to meet with my estate manager tomorrow," he replied.

"Too bad it's such a horrid day. I would have suggested a ride."

He cocked his head as though in deep thought. "I could show you through the house. I know you haven't had the opportunity to see it all."

"No, no, I haven't, and I'd love to see more of it. I'm sure there are a lot of rooms rarely used."

"There are. A lot of guest rooms and a lot of family bed chambers are going unused. That's the case in every estate, I'm sure," he replied.

"I assume these unused rooms are not kept heated when not in use?"

"No, they're not."

"I'm ready if you are," she said.

"Let's go."

She arched a brow. "I would like to see the attics as well."

"Any particular reason why?" he asked.

"There could be something up there that could be used elsewhere in the house. My mother taught me that."

His curiosity was piqued. "How's that?"

"She said things go out of style and we shove them away only for them to come back into vogue later."

"I've never thought of it from that perspective."

He took her hand and led her out of the drawing room, much to Sam's disapproval. Ignoring the bird, the pair began to make their way to the grand staircase. They'd start on the main family level. He was sure she'd been to most of the rooms since her arrival. Arthur tried to make their walk interesting by pointing out the history of the house. She asked lots of questions, things most young ladies wouldn't dream of.

Finally, he led her up to a staircase which was narrower but still used by staff and himself. It led to the attics. Once at the top, they almost immediately found themselves in a hallway. On either side were two large rooms, locked away from intruders. At the far end of the hall was another door, locked.

"Where does that go?" she asked, gesturing to the end of the hall.

"Staff rooms are on the other side."

He found a key hidden out of sight and unlocked one of the two storage rooms. The first thing Arthur noticed was the amount of dust gathered on everything. In spite of this, Daphne entered and began to look around. Trunks, old portraits, and landscapes stood against walls. A broken chair, probably waiting to be repaired, lay on its side. Decades of things discarded were relegated to these rooms. Within these walls and the walls of the second set of storage rooms was family history. His family history.

A lot of what they were seeing, he didn't remember. Not something he would as a child unless it specifically had something to do with him. There was an old rocking horse he recognized as his. He'd broken it by being far too rough with the toy and his father reprimanded him by making him help the footmen carry it to the attic, never to be seen again.

It was funny, how of all his childhood memories of this house, that one incident was what he recalled.

"Have you found anything to your liking?" he asked his bride.

"Not really. Most all of what's here is broken and in need of some sort of repair."

"I think you'll have better luck in the room across the hall."

"I'm not done here," she replied. "Does anything here remind you of a time long ago?"

"Not really."

"What about the rocking horse? I saw you staring at it."

"A mere toy I grew out of."

Daphne drew closer. "One that holds meaning to you."

"Yes. I can't explain it. Sometimes I have this sense that there was more to situations when I was much younger. Like the rocking horse. Yes, I admit being rough with it, but I imagine most boys are. To me, there is more to that incident."

"You can't remember it?"

He shook his head. "No, I can't."

"Did you ever ask your father about it?"

"I did, but I was only told I had an active imagination."

She stood on tip toe and kissed his cheek. "He could be right."

"No, no. There was something more at play."

"It'll come to you. Trying to force memories sometimes triggers them to remain hidden."

Taking her hand in his, he lifted it to his mouth and kissed the back. "How did I get so lucky to find such a smart and beautiful wife?"

She giggled. "We have the gray to thank for that."

"Yes, we do," he replied. He led her out of the attic room, across the hall to the next. This one contained more furniture, but the majority didn't appear to be broken. In need of cleaning and polishing but nothing more.

Continuing to watch his wife inspect almost every piece of furniture, Arthur peered down at the floor to a small metal box that caught his attention. He leaned over and began to pick it up when dozens of metal toy soldiers fell out. Picking one up, he studied the small figure for several minutes. The hours he spent as a boy, especially on days like today, playing mock battles and never losing. Why did he feel as though he shared with someone? Shared his soldiers. He had two different armies, so it made sense he shared one of them to play the greatest battles of all time. But who? He carried the box with him for a few moments, setting it down on a nearby table as he tried to listen to Daphne as she inspected several tables.

"Find one you like?" he asked.

"Several, actually," she replied. "Do you have someone who redoes or repairs furniture?"

"Yes, there are several craftsmen on the estate." He noticed she was watching him curiously, then looked down and found himself holding one of the toy soldiers in his hand. "I found a box of them. I could spend hours playing with them on rainy days."

"I think it's a rite of passage for young boys. My brother had some as well. He was far too vocal when he got immersed in a make-believe battle. All sorts of yelling."

"Boys aren't meant to be quiet."

She sighed. "No, they're not. We girls were expected to be perfect little ladies and keep quiet."

"I can hardly believe that," he snorted. "Quiet and you don't mix."

"I'll have you know I can be most stealthy when needed. I can go in and out of a room and never be seen nor heard," she scoffed.

"Yes, you can."

Watching her pick up an old doll and inspect it, he had an idea. "That's probably one of Roxanne's. I wonder if I should invite her over to look and see if she wants them."

"What?"

"You know, she might want them for Mary."

"Arthur, sweetheart, when it comes time to introduce Mary to dolls, Roxanne can more than afford new ones."

"True, but it seems like a waste, them sitting up here," he said.

"She might be able to use them for decorating Mary's room at some point."

He nodded. "I'll let her know they're here next time I see her."

"We should have them over for dinner, especially after they gave us a ride home because of the broken wheel."

It was true. They would have had to spend the night at a coaching inn with Sam if Roxanne and Graham hadn't decided to take a meal at the inn. Overnight with Sam would have proved interesting and difficult because the parrot needed to be kept warm. He wasn't meant to survive in colder temperatures, and if anything ever happened to Sam, his wife would be inconsolable.

"I concur. We should have them over soon."

Daphne drew closer, intertwining her arm around his. The scent of her perfume was minimal, but it always reminded him of her. Every time he smelled vanilla with orange, his thoughts wandered to her. He leaned over and kissed the top of her blonde head.

"Is there anything else to look at here?" she asked quietly.

"Not unless there are specific pieces you want to move aside."

Daintily, she shook her head. "There are, but I doubt anyone will bother them. Once I know exactly where I want them, I'll accompany the men and show them what I want."

"Why don't I show you something else? Somewhere not a lot of people know about or have seen."

She smiled at him demurely. "You're sounding awfully mysterious, Your Grace."

Arthur threw back his head and his rich baritone laugh echoed around the room. "I have to keep some mystery about me."

"So tell me what this mystery is."

He shook his head this time. "I have to show you. It can't be described."

"Very well, lead the way," she replied.

Locking the storage room, Arthur led his wife down a flight of stairs and back into the main living section of the house. He took her past his study and continued down another corridor at the beginning of another wing. It was not as warm, meaning this area wasn't used all the time.

Finally, he stopped in front of a locked door. Pulling a key out of his pocket, he opened the door and stepped inside, taking Daphne by the hand and leading her in. Inside the room, time stood still. An easel with a half-finished landscape sat untouched. Canvases with finished and unfinished work lined both the floor and tables.

"What is this place?" Daphne asked lowly as she looked over a canvas lying on a table.

"This was my mother's studio. She used to come here to paint. After her and my father's deaths, I decided to keep it as she left it. She was quite good, don't you think?"

"Extraordinary talent. Is Roxanne aware of this room?"

He shook his head as he walked over to a table which held brushes and paints. "No, not to my knowledge. If she does know of it, she's never mentioned it. This would have been something the two of us would have shared since we shared most everything."

"Perhaps it's time to share it with your sister."

"You're right, of course. She might want some of the paintings."

"Don't you want some of her paintings?" Daphne asked as she looked through a stack of canvases stood in a pile against a wall.

"At some point, yes. For now, I'm content with preserving her workspace."

"The hurt is still too fresh in your mind."

"Yes."

He knew it was time to move on. Spending too much time in his mother's sanctuary made him melancholy and he didn't need to subject himself to the memories. Someday they wouldn't be so fresh and hurt so much. There had been nothing normal after learning of his parents' untimely deaths so far from home.

A thousand thoughts came whirling into his mind all at once. Things he'd gone over and over in his mind. He often wondered what went through their minds when they realized what was about to happen. Did they even know or were they caught off guard and never saw anything coming? Being surprised would have been the kinder of the two scenarios. Neither would have had time to think.

He realized Daphne was watching him closely. It was time to put on the mask and return to the present. He took her hand. "Come, why don't I show you the nursery. I'm sure we're going to fill it with beautiful babies soon, and I imagine you might like to freshen it up."

"You're full of surprises today, Arthur."

"Would you like to see it?"

She nodded with a sweet grin. "Of course I would." Daphne had found it on her own but wouldn't dare hurt Arthur's feelings by letting him think she'd already been to check the nursery out.

Walking arm and arm, Arthur would occasionally stop and comment on a painting or historical fact related to the home. He wondered as he repeated a story to his wife what generations before him would think of the world today and how the ancestral home had been maintained as close to original.

Before they came close to the stairs leading to the nursery, a red flash raced in front of them. Roddy was not slowing for anyone, not even the footman chasing him. Arthur wondered what the setter had done this time since it was obvious by his full mouth that he'd stolen something from the kitchens. Life was never dull with Roddy and Sam.

"He's stolen a roast chicken!" the young man said breathlessly as he ran past them.

"Get it from him! He'll be sick if he eats all of it," Arthur said in response.

"Yes, Your Grace."

Daphne looked up at him. "Maybe it's time to banish him from the kitchens."

"Almost impossible to do as that's where he stays when he comes in from being outside and is muddy and wet. This doesn't happen often with him."

"He's like a naughty child," she replied.

"As is Sam."

"Yes, and speaking of Sam, we should really go check on him."

"I'm sure he's fine."

She shook her head and smiled at him. "That's Sam we're talking about."

"You're right. Let's go see what sort of mischief he's gotten himself into," he replied. Taking her hand, he led her down a corridor. They walked until familiar things surrounded them.

Arthur opened the door to the small drawing room Sam was occupying. The macaw was nowhere in sight but was heard before he was seen. Cursing as usual.

"Bloody hell! Help Sam."

Daphne approached the bird first, lowering herself to his level. "What's the problem, Sam?"

"Sam here. Food there."

Somehow the ladder leading from Sam's cage and perch had fallen to the floor and he couldn't get to his food and water. Arthur, seeing the problem, walked over and picked up the wood ladder and placed it securely where it was meant to be.

"There you go, Sam."

"Sam happy," he replied.

"Sam, how did the ladder end up on the floor?" Daphne asked.

The parrot said nothing but sat halfway up on the ladder before stopping to preen himself. Making noises in his throat, Sam continued his journey up the ladder.

"Sam! How did the ladder fall to the floor? Did you push it?"

It took a few moments but finally Sam spoke. "Sam ladder fell when Sam walking down."

"That doesn't make sense," Arthur said.

"I think he tried to move it and it fell," Daphne replied.

Arthur approached and studied the ladder and cage. "Do you think he wanted on this table?"

"Getting the ladder to connect to the table would mean he could wander on the furniture more freely."

Sam finally started his journey up the ladder to his cage. He climbed onto the top where there were feeding bowls and a bowl of water and began eating.

Daphne and Arthur stared at each other for a moment. Finally, Arthur spoke. "Perhaps the ladder should be fixed to the cage so he can't do this again. Something we can move, but he can't."

"It would keep him out of some mischief. He could still climb down to the floor, but not the furniture."

"I'll see it's done," Arthur replied.

"Let's hope it helps."

Arthur chuckled. "With Sam? Who knows? He's smarter than most children."

"He is. I just wish he wouldn't curse so much."

"His vocabulary in that department could be a lot worse, you know."

She sighed. "I know." In a moment, Daphne began to uncontrollably laugh.

Arthur couldn't figure out what was so funny, but his wife had decidedly found something quite humorous. "Do you wish to share what is so funny?"

Saying nothing, Daphne continued to laugh. Finally, her laughter slowed enough to where she could answer his question or try to.

"We have a chicken thieving dog, a parrot that could make a sailor blush with his language. Can you imagine what it might be like with children? Chaos will ensue unless the children are kept in the nursery with a nanny."

"Our children will never be hidden away in the nursery," he

replied.

"No, they won't. If you'll excuse me, I'm going to write a missive to Roxanne inviting her and Graham to dinner tomorrow evening, if you agree with that."

"Most certainly."

"I'll go see about letting Cook know and see what we can come up with."

"I'm sure whatever you and Cook agree upon will be wonderful."

She smiled at him and walked out the door. Making sure Roxanne received her invitation was priority. She didn't expect anything outside of a positive reply.

After Daphne left, Arthur went in search of Roddy to see if the footman was able to catch the setter and the chicken he stole from the kitchen. No, life would never be dull, that was for sure. The peal of children's laughter would resonate through the halls in a few years. Though he and Daphne hadn't sat down and had much of a talk about a family, it was assumed by him she wanted children as much as he did. It wasn't like they had been preventing it from happening. For him, an heir would be most important, but they would fill the house with babies. And it wouldn't matter where each child was in the birth order; they'd all be loved equally.

For months, since his parents had died, Arthur felt there was something missing in his life. He couldn't put a finger on it, but somehow, he knew there was a missing link. Roxanne and he had had numerous discussions lately about it. Whatever it was, and that gnawed at him quite frequently.

He had been thinking of writing their aunt and uncle in Scotland and see if they knew something or could lead him and Roxanne in the right direction to whatever this was. Or if there was nothing to his gut feelings, they could reassure both of them they were chasing something that didn't exist. Right now, it wasn't clear to him, but he would have his answer, no matter what it led to.

It occurred to him as he found both Roddy and the footman in the grand hall, that perhaps his father's journals might hold a key to whatever was eating him. Arthur had looked through one or two and it might happen the late duke wrote about it along with other personal thoughts. His father had been meticulously detailed in his lifetime and Arthur meant to find out by reading them in full.

CHAPTER NINETEEN

ARTHUR WAS SITTING at the table, enjoying his breakfast and a newspaper when Daphne joined him. He looked up as she entered. She was as beautiful as always. Her face seemed to have a glow to it, but their night of what seemed to be endless lovemaking might have something to do with that.

She walked over to the sideboard where breakfast items awaited and made her choices. Turning, she joined her husband at the table.

"Good morning," he said quietly.

"Good morning," she replied, holding up a folded paper. "Roxanne and Graham will be joining us for dinner tonight."

He picked up his half-empty cup of coffee and took a sip of the hot, black beverage. "Excellent."

"Yes. I always enjoy their company." Picking up a piece of toast, she slathered it with marmalade before taking a bite. "I asked Cook to serve something special."

"Cook does well at adapting. Her meals are all lovely regardless of how many people are here."

"Yes, she's good at what she does," she replied.

"I've got to take care of some things as soon as I finish here. Do you have any plans for the day?"

"You mean, do I have any plans while you're working?" She smiled briefly.

He nodded. "Something like that."

"I was thinking of having my mare saddled and going for a ride. It's a beautiful day and it would be a shame to waste it by sitting indoors."

"Take Roddy with you. He can always use the exercise. I'll join you if I finish in a timely manner."

She smiled. "That would be nice. I'll look forward to seeing you later. I thought I'd go through the meadow and up the hill. It has to be beautiful on a day like this to look down, and I imagine it's even more breathtaking when it snows."

Putting his newspaper aside, Arthur contemplated his reply. "It's the highest point on the estate, and yes, it's beautiful when it snows."

She didn't answer right away, and he noticed she was moving the eggs around on the plate and not eating them. "Are the eggs not to your liking?"

Daphne stopped and looked up at him. "No, they're fine. I guess I'm not as hungry as I thought." He watched her eat a forkful. She made a face. "Could I get them a little more done?"

A footman came right away and took her plate. "Of course, Your Grace."

"All you have to do is ask," Arthur replied.

"I know. I'm not fond of runny eggs. Not that runny anyway."

"Remind Cook in case a kitchen maid helped her. She can inform her staff so that it won't happen again."

"I'm sure she'll know when she sees my plate of eggs being returned."

Moments later, a fresh plate of eggs were placed in front of her. This time, they were fluffy and firm like she preferred them. Biting into a forkful, Daphne sighed in pleasure, closing her eyes as she enjoyed the eggs.

Hearing her sigh like that made Arthur's cock come to attention. He had no control when it came to his wife and knew he needed to excuse himself.

"I'm going to leave you to enjoy your breakfast. The sooner I start with my day, the faster I can join you."

"I'm going to check in on Sam before I go upstairs and change into more appropriate riding apparel."

Pushing his chair away from the table, Arthur unfolded his tall frame. "Hopefully, Sam is beginning to settle in."

"Yes, that would be nice."

He bent over to kiss her on the cheek. "Enjoy your ride."

"I shall, but it'll be made more enjoyable when you join us."

He walked to the door which a footman opened. Breathing a sigh of relief, Arthur continued on to his study.

A short while later, Daphne walked through the front door and down the stairs to her mare who had been saddled and brought to her. Roddy ran around in huge circles in pure excitement as he waited for his mistress to begin their trek. Moments later, she was walking the mare towards the meadow. Without looking back, Daphne knew there was a groom riding with her a safe distance behind her. Arthur insisted she not ride the estate alone. As a compromise, Daphne agreed, but only if a groom followed her a discreet distance behind her. Far enough back that she could lose him with little effort.

As the meadow came into view, she urged the gray to pick up speed. Clucking to the mare, she set off in a gallop, Roddy leading the way. Though the day was sunny and clear, the temperature reminded everyone winter was upon them. Moments later, she turned her mare into a large circle as she contemplated how to enter the tree line and lose her chaperone.

Nearing the trees, Daphne slowed the gray down to a walk as she followed one path leading to the small lake. Moments later, she was able to pick up a new lane which would take her to the top of the hill. Roddy ran about, sometimes veering off the path if he picked up the scent of a rabbit or other small game. Small branches snapped under her mare's hooves as they continued. It wasn't long before she came upon a clearing and the path leading to the highest point on the estate.

She marveled at the view when she finally stopped. She could see why Arthur loved to come here. It had to have been used as a lookout point at some time in the past. A way to alert residents of intruders. The spot would have been perfect to build a manor home on, but Arthur's ancestors probably didn't want them to be that exposed.

Regardless of what happened in the past, Daphne felt this was a special place to visit and she would continue to do so, especially when she needed to reflect on her life or something taking place.

Smiling, she wondered if the groom had figured out he'd been tricked. If he didn't find her, he'd never let anyone know he'd been duped by a woman. She didn't want him to get reprimanded, so if need be, she would just say they got split up and she hadn't realized it for some time.

She called out to the setter who came running from out of the tree line. Evidently, as always, there were a million things for him to discover. She enjoyed having him keep her company. Not only was he funny, should anything bad happen, she knew she could depend on him to guard her or go find help, hopefully in the form of Arthur.

"Come on, let's go back to the house. It's cold out here and I'm beginning to feel it. I'm sure you'd like to lie by a fire and warm up yourself."

Roddy barked as though he understood, wagging his feathery red tail. He jumped up to let her know he was ready. Daphne clucked to the mare and followed the setter to the trail leading down to the meadow. The grade was a gentle slope, making it quite easy to make the downward journey.

Arthur must have had more needing his attention than he originally thought. That was not unusual, and with him getting ready to take his position in Parliament, she knew things would only get busier. She was proud how he took things in stride and never seemed to let anything get him out of sorts. The only thing that even came close was the trial of the man responsible for murdering his parents. With the man being found guilty, Arthur had washed his hands of the matter. He wanted nothing further to do with it.

Their relationship had blossomed. Still getting to know each other, she had no doubt the bond they were forming now would be with them for a lifetime. What she got when she married him was exactly what she expected. He was kind and patient with her, which was amusing considering how much of a pain in the arse she'd been when they first met. She had certainly tested his patience.

As she neared the bottom of the trail, she heard Roddy barking playfully. To one side at the entrance of the meadow stood the young groom assigned to accompany her. From first glance, he didn't appear to be too put out with her. He simply nodded.

"Your Grace."

"I didn't know where you'd gone so Roddy and I made the rest of the trek up to the clearing. It's lovely up there," she said. "It seems to be getting colder so I believe we should return to the house."

"As you wish, Your Grace."

Making her way towards the stables, her groom rode a comfortable distance behind her. Daphne knew he was upset with her for deliberately ditching him. She was the duchess, and he was to cater to her. The only time she deemed him necessary was if she were injured from a fall or something similar. Not that she'd fallen that much in her lifetime. She valued the time she did have alone and didn't need others crowding her.

After dismounting at the stables, she headed towards the house, with Roddy circling her before running ahead. She was almost to the garden gate when she spotted her husband looking quite handsome on this sunny but cold day.

"I was just headed to the stables to see if you were still out," he said. Roddy greeted his master, and Arthur patted him before turning his attention back on to Daphne.

"It was getting a little chilly, so I thought it best if I return. I did get to the top of the hill. Beautiful view."

"I told you," he replied. "Did you ride through the meadow on your way?"

"Of course." She smiled. "Didn't you see a gray running across the meadow?"

He watched in disbelief as his wife began running in the direction of the veranda steps, giggling all the way. Knowing he could easily catch her, he allowed her to keep up her pace before pursuing her. Her peals of laughter were music to his ears.

CHAPTER TWENTY

Having finished one of the best meals, Daphne and Roxanne retired to the drawing room for tea while the men stayed in the dining room to enjoy a glass or two of port and smoke cigars. Daphne considered the tradition silly and out of date with the times. Men, however, thought otherwise and continued the ritual because they wanted time away from their wives in order to be able to discuss politics and other things a woman wouldn't be interested in. Or so they thought.

Daphne began to pour a cup of tea for each of them. Sam sat atop his cage eating a piece of apple.

"He certainly has calmed down," Roxanne said, eyeing the parrot.

"He has, but apples are one of his favorite treats."

She handed the cup of steaming tea to her sister-in-law and picked up her own and sat back. "I abhor that men still think they have to continue with this silly ritual."

Roxanne put her tea on a table in front of her. "I know, but they're never going to change."

"It makes them feel important, so why let them think any different?"

"Exactly," Roxanne replied.

Daphne watched as Roxanne fiddled with her teacup. She finally took a sip and put it back down. "I have some news to share, but you must promise not to tell Arthur or mention it to Graham. I haven't told him yet."

She arched a brow. "What have you bought?"

"Nothing."

"Then what is it?"

"I believe I'm with child," she said lowly.

"What? That's wonderful news."

"I haven't told anyone but you because I want to be sure before I tell Graham. I'm planning to see a midwife I know and see if she can tell. If not, I'll wait to see if I miss my courses again."

"Then you'll go to a doctor?"

"Yes, and then I'll tell Graham."

Picking up her teacup, Daphne took a sip. "You've had a child, so I'm sure you're probably with child."

"Yes, but that was a long time ago. I'm older now."

"You'll be fine."

"I know, but I just want to be certain."

"I promise, I won't tell a soul until you tell me."

"Thank you," she replied. "Are you and Arthur planning to start a family any time soon?"

Daphne grinned. "Let's just say we're not doing anything to prevent it."

"Newlyweds," Roxanne said.

"You and Graham are much the same."

"True. I hope that part of our marriage never changes."

"Me too. I would miss it if it did."

Daphne had learned a lot from her husband on ways for him to please her, for her to pleasure him, and ways for them to do it together. Never had she imagined how good it would be. Arthur, knowing she was a virgin, had been very patient the first day or so. From there he moved on to showing her things she'd only read about in the secret stash of books her mother kept in her chamber. Some of her books were naughty romance novels and others were nonfiction, making Daphne wonder how her mother even got the books into the house, let alone how she purchased them without her father being the wiser. Or perhaps he did know.

"You know how a man approaches sex can change over time. Some never do change, others turn into copies of their fathers, and not in a good way," Roxanne said.

"How would they know that about their fathers?" Daphne asked.

"Probably seeing how their father treated their mothers. How he treats women in general."

"I see."

"Enough about me," Roxanne said. "How are you adjusting to your new role?"

"Well enough. I'm thankful Arthur has such a devoted staff. They've been quite patient with me."

"I can't imagine there's much that needs to change."

"No, and I'm perfectly fine with leaving things as they are. I even told Arthur I wanted to postpone redecorating. I decided I want to live here a year before I do anything."

"That's a brilliant idea, Daphne. It makes sense to live in the house a full year and to see it in all seasons."

"Do you really think so? Arthur thought it made perfect sense but told me I was more than welcome to change my mind if there was something I wanted to change."

"It makes perfect sense. I mean, what if you redid this room and two months after you'd redone it, you hated it. Then you'd be stuck with it."

"I see your point, and I'm glad I've put it off. I'll have time to decide what room should be redone first and what order the rest fall."

Roxanne sighed and finished her tea. Putting her teacup down, she glanced over at Sam who was still being quiet, eating his food. "He certainly makes for a conversation piece."

"Doesn't he? I plan to have him present next time I invite ladies over. It's hilarious to see their reactions, especially when he curses."

"He certainly has a colorful vocabulary," Roxanne replied.

Pointing at the windows, Daphne grinned. "Look. It's snowing."

"It appears winter is here. It's cold enough for snow, but I thought rain might be all we'd get."

"I love snow!" Daphne said, walking towards the windows.

"It's nice to look at from in here. It's too cold."

As they were watching the snow come down, Arthur and Graham walked in. Neither Roxanne nor Daphne turned around to greet them. They simply continued to watch the white precipitation continue to come down.

"When did it start snowing?" Graham inquired.

Roxanne turned towards her husband's voice. "Just now."

"It looks like it's coming down at a steady pace," Arthur added.

"I certainly hope so," Daphne squealed.

"We should probably return home before the road becomes impassible," Roxanne said.

Graham shook his head but grinned in his wife's direction. "My wife isn't a winter person."

Arthur snorted. "Yes, I remember having to force her outside to make snow angels. She complained the entire time, even though she loved doing it."

"I only did it to appease you. I was miserable lying on the ground flopping around like that," Roxanne replied.

"Arthur, do you have a sleigh? It would be so much fun to go out for a drive if the snow continues," Daphne asked.

"Yes, there's a sleigh. I had the stablemaster see that it was cleaned and polished for this winter."

"Graham, please see to the carriage. I know we don't live far, but I don't care to get stuck on the road between here and there," Roxanne said.

Graham bowed deeply towards his wife. "Your wish is my command, countess." He walked from the room to have the carriage readied.

"I hate to end such a lovely evening so early, but we'll do it again soon." Roxanne smiled at her brother's wife. They seemed to be a perfect match. Daphne was not set in her ways yet and loved things she had never imagined. Daphne's upbringing had been unusual with her parents allowing her to do more than simply learning to dance, play pianoforte, or embroider. While Arthur learned things necessary to become duke, Roxanne was expected to learn the typical things a young lady should know in order to find a good marriage, even though that hadn't been the case for her.

"Come," Arthur said, "let's go to the entrance hall so you can put your cape and gloves on. I imagine by the time we reach there, the carriage will be around front."

The trio walked through the house, downstairs to the grand hall. Graham walked in as Roxanne was preparing herself for what she thought was frigid cold.

Arthur and Daphne donned their coats and followed them out to their waiting carriage. Saying their good-byes to their guests, they watched as the carriage disappeared into the night. There was no moon this night, and ordinarily it would make for a very dark time, but the snow made everything brighter.

Daphne grabbed her husband by the hand and pulled him along to a grassy area just off the drive now covered in a blanket of snow. She sat down in the fresh snow and lay on her back and began to make a snow angel.

"I bet my snow angel will be far better than yours," she taunted.

"I rather doubt it. I have a few more years practice making them than you do," he replied as he began to make his.

Here it was late in the evening and the two of them were lying on the ground making snow angels like they did when they were children. His wife was giggling madly, enjoying herself tremendously. He couldn't ask for more.

"Oh look, Arthur. There's the gray! How did she get out?"

He sat up with a jerk. Sure enough, the beast was once again loose and running through the open lawn. "She seems to be enjoying herself."

"Shouldn't we go after her?"

"No," he replied. He stood and helped her to her feet. "I'm sure she'll return to the stables when she's had enough. In the meantime, you and I have better things to do." He pulled her in close and kissed her as though he couldn't get enough.

The End

About the Author

J R Salisbury writes Victorian era English and Scottish historical romance with perfectly imperfect heroes and strong, sassy heroines.

Writing has always written. It was the continuous encouragement of a high school creative writing teacher to further her craft. Bit with the self-publishing bug in 2011 she started out her on-line eBooks as contemporary romance before switching to her preferred and loved genre, historical romance. Her books can be found at the majority of on-line bookstores.

Raised outside Seattle with three years in the South American country of Chile, traveling is in her blood. Dividing her time between Atlanta, GA in the United States and the UK gives her a unique perspective on history.

Author Links
Website: www.jamiesalisbury.com
Facebook (historical): JRSalisburyHistoricalRomance
Facebook Profile: JamieRSalisburyAuthor
X (aka Twitter): @JamieRSalisbury
Book Bub: jr-salisbury
Instagram: authorjamiesalisbury
Email: jamiesalisburyauthor@gmail.com